PRAISE FOR *ROMANTIC TIMES* READERS CHOICE AWARD NOMINEE KIMBERLY RAYE!

"If you're lamenting the lack of sexy, funny, character-driven romances on the bookshelves these days, you absolutely will not want to miss reading . . . *Midnight Kisses*."

—*All About Romance*

"Kimberly Raye has a unique and special talent that will no doubt be heard and remembered for years to come!"

—*Affaire de Coeur*

"[*A Little Bit of Magic*] is magical and charming, not to mention steamy!"

—*Under the Covers Book Reviews*

"Ms. Raye's creative plotting and vivid characterization herald a strong new voice in romantic fiction."

—*Romantic Times*

"Hot! Hot! Hot!"

—Vicki Lewis Thompson, bestselling author of *That's My Baby*

A THRILLING PROPOSAL

"You want me to give *sex* lessons?" The minute the question was out of her mouth, she regretted it. She had to have misunderstood what he'd said only a moment before. But she hadn't.

"You all right?" he asked.

"F—fine," Elizabeth stammered. More was becoming clear. The garter *was* magic, just like that strange witch-woman had claimed. Somehow, she had imbued the satin strip with a magical sex appeal, perhaps Sinful Sinclair's own. The stripper had been sexy, vibrant, and irresistible to men—and somehow her essence had been captured by the fabric of the garter.

And that essence had somehow been retained—so much so that by slipping on the strip of satin, Elizabeth had somehow assumed the woman's identity. Taken her place. Right now, she *was* Sinful Sinclair, and as long as she kept the garter in place, she was living in the past. Staid, reserved Elizabeth Joanna Carlton was living in the moment.

Her gaze met Colt's.

He smiled, a sly twist of his lips that sent a thrill racing through her. "Everything you know, sugar. *Everything.*"

The word burned in her mind, stirring all sorts of wonderful ideas. Crazy ideas, she reminded herself. She didn't even know this guy. Worse, she didn't know much about sex. Certainly nothing she could teach the handsome cowboy who stood before her.

MIDNIGHT FANTASIES

KIMBERLY RAYE

LOVE SPELL BOOKS   NEW YORK CITY

A LOVE SPELL BOOK®

September 2000

Published by

Dorchester Publishing Co., Inc.
276 Fifth Avenue
New York, NY 10001

ISBN 0-505-52392-2

For Curt—
For all of your love and support,
and even the occasional kick in the butt to keep me on track.
What did I ever do without you?

And an extra special thank-you to Natasha and Laura,
For your understanding and friendship,
And most of all, for not giving up on me.

MIDNIGHT FANTASIES

Prologue

Louisiana Bayou Country, 1882

"I want to be *every* man's fantasy."

Sadie Sinclair sat in the old cabin on the banks of Bayou Blue in the heart of Louisiana swamp country and listened to her twin sister's desperate plea. Twin, as in flesh and blood. Linked. Connected. On the inside, that is.

On the outside, Sadie and her sister, Sinful, were as different as a mud bug and a lobster.

At sixteen, Sinful was already every man's fantasy. She'd been to barn raisings and cotillions and even a fancy party at the Beaumonde plantation just outside of New Orleans with Jake Beaumonde himself—heir and the most handsome boy in the territory. Sinful had turned his head with her voluptuous figure and her sparkling laugh and full lips that any man, Jake included, would sell his soul to kiss.

Meanwhile, Sadie had kissed only Deak Guidry, eighteen and long-legged and about as ugly as a lizard's butt. He lived just on the other side of the bayou with his mama and his eight brothers and a mess of pigs that squealed day and night and had caused Sadie more than one sleepless night.

But he'd wanted a kiss. A *kiss*, and as ugly and undesirable as he'd been, no boy had ever wanted to kiss her before. She'd spent too many nights tossing and turning, listening to pig squeals and dreaming about Prince Charming and his kisses to pass up the chance to experience what she'd only heard Sinful ooh and ahhh over.

It had been wet and sloppy and she would have been better off kissing one of his pigs. Still, she'd cherished the moment until she discovered that he'd only done it as a bet. She'd been hurt and mad—crazy because she hadn't even liked him. But it had been the principle of the thing.

That had been last year, when she was at the tender age of fifteen. Her first and last kiss. Since then, she'd given up on love and beauty and concentrated on the magic flowing through her veins, a magic that didn't exist without Sinful to urge her on. Encourage her. Believe in her.

While men wanted to kiss Sinful, however,

not one of them wanted to court her. Instead, she was stuck in the run-down cabin where their mother had been born and raised, with little food and even less hope.

But Sinful wanted more. She wanted to live. To travel. To turn every man's head from here to Texas and beyond.

"We can't stay here, Sadie. We're rotting away the best years of our lives. We have to do something now. *You* have to do something now. I know I can make my way in New Orleans. I'll own the stage."

Sadie watched as her sister attempted a pivot and fell flat on her face.

Sinful gathered her composure and stood. "*If* you help me," she pleaded. "Make me sexy and attractive and graceful, just like mama."

"You're already sexy and attractive."

"Yes, but not like mama. I want men to want me so badly it hurts. *Every* man. I want them to look at me the way they did mama when she was alive. I want them to give me gifts and money and any and everything I want, and I want it without risking bodily injury, because I can't walk in a pair of high-heeled boots. I want to go to New Orleans and walk down the sidewalk and turn *every* man's head. I ain't wasting my life rotting away on the banks of this old bayou, and you aren't either. We're going to do this together. You and me." She dropped to her knees and stared up at Sadie. "I need something more than looks. Something inside. Mama had it. You could see it in her eyes. An intensity that drew men, that made them give her anything she wanted. Don't you want more than this old run-down shack? Don't you want to have fine things and live in a fine place and have more?"

"This ain't so bad." It was safe. Familiar.

A squeal filled her ears and her gaze went to the window and beyond, to the litter of pigs running around the bank on the opposite side of the bayou.

Make that safe and familiar and smelly.

Sinful looked out the window. "It's awful, what with Deak and his nasty brothers just on the other side. I want fine things. I want to waltz out onto a stage and not break my neck."

"But I've never cast a spell on anyone."

"It won't be on me. It'll be on this." Sinful held up the garter that had once belonged to their mother. "Just cast the spell on this. I'll wear it and we'll climb up out of this hole together." Sinful took her hand. "You can do it. I know you can. You're a powerful witch. Just like mama. No matter what everybody else thinks. We're her daughters. We're just as good. Together, we're just as good. And you can do this. You *can*."

With Sinful looking at her with such confidence, Sadie actually felt as if she *could* do it. That she could wiggle her finger and do something better than give a frog spots or cure a bad case of hives or ease old Mr. Dupree's dog's ailing stomach when he ate one too many sausage links. She could cast a real spell the way her mother had so many times in the past. For love and luck and beauty.

Her mother had had all three, which was why she'd been the most famous stripper ever to walk out onto a stage—until she drowned in the Mississippi two years earlier when she'd fallen overboard the *Natchez Queen*. She'd lived for the adoration and attention, so much so that she'd forsaken her girls and left them with her aging father on the banks of the bayou.

Sadie fought back a wave of tears. She wasn't crying over her mother anymore. She was making her proud. She'd given up on the love and beauty parts a long time ago—those two usually went hand-in-hand. But since she'd inherited her mother's powers while her sister had inherited her looks, she'd yet to forsake the luck part. Not yet.

She *could* work magic. The question was, how much and how?

Her gaze went to the garter.

"You can do it," Sinful said again. "I know you can. *We* can do it. Together."

"Together," Sadie repeated, picking up the garter and stroking it with her fingertip. *"Together."*

Chapter One

"I've always wanted to do it wearing nothing but a bad attitude and a pair of spurs."

"Yes, yes," giggled the forty-something woman, who sat up excitedly and placed her hand on the leg of the imposing man beside her. "It's been a fantasy of ours for a *very* long time."

"Then you've come to the right place." Elizabeth Joanna Carlton smiled across the marble desktop at her newest clients, the fifty-year-old vice president for Laramie Oil and his attractive wife. "Fantasies are my business."

"That's why we came to you. Esther and Roger had such fun with their sheikh–harem girl fantasy. Why, she told me you even had a trio of *real* eunuchs standing guard outside the tent so they wouldn't be disturbed."

"I do work hard at authenticity." It was true, she did pride herself on her dedication to reproducing everything accurately in her work, and that couldn't have been done if she hadn't also had some great connections. Tom, Dom and Melvin were a trio of part-time sumo wrestlers-cum-wannabe actors who performed at a Japanese dinner theater in downtown Houston. While she seriously doubted they were eunuchs in reality—Dom had triplet boys—they put on one hell of a show. Her clients had been more than satisfied.

That was the key. Satisfying the people who came to It's Only Make Believe by bringing their ultimate fantasies to life.

As the owner and operator of Houston's only "romantic catering" company, Elizabeth had coordinated everything from quaint candlelit dinners to much more challenging fantasies, such as that of the lawyer who fancied herself Dorothy from *The Wizard of Oz* and her husband a sexy, flirty Tin Man.

She'd had to have his suit custom-made by a costume company that specialized in body armor. The man had been covered in metal from his neck to his feet. Elizabeth still hadn't figured out how he'd . . . How they'd . . . *How*. They'd asked for no special attachments or trap doors. The suit had been fashioned to copy the original, with no room for any surprises popping up or out.

She fought down a wave of heat and forced the thought aside. She didn't worry herself with those *hows*. Her job was simply to scout out the appropriate locations and set up the scenarios down to the smallest detail—from costumes to props to food. It was up to her clients and their significant others to worry about the rest.

"Big spurs," the man drawled. "I want the biggest pair you can find."

"Now, now, honey. They don't have to be that big." His wife patted his arm. "You know by now that size isn't important to me. I don't care if you've got the teeniest, tiniest spur in the saloon. I still love you. Not that yours would be *the* tiniest. It's just a little smaller—"

"Next week," Elizabeth cut in, eager to steer the conversation onto safer ground. The last thing, the very *last* thing she wanted was to discuss a man's "spur." Especially since it had been so long since she'd actually seen one, she wasn't sure she even remembered what it looked like.

There has to be more to life. The thought filled her along with a sense of restlessness. Of need.

She drew in a deep breath and got to her feet. "I'll have my assistant call you with all the details first thing Monday."

"We know you'll do a wonderful job." The man extended his hand as he stood. "We've heard so much about you, and all of it good. Now we see why." He handed her a book then. "I've been looking at this. Maybe it'll give you an idea of what we're hoping for. And as for being discreet, thank you."

"Thank *you*," Elizabeth said.

A few minutes later, after they had gone, she sat at her desk and stared at the large advance check Mr. Laramie had left.

"That good, huh?" Jenna Walters, Elizabeth's personal assistant and Spice Girl wannabe, walked into the room wearing blue-jean cut-off shorts, a halter top and black glitter platform shoes. She had blond shoulder-length hair and enough powder-blue eye shadow to make-up an entire Vegas chorus line for a month.

Elizabeth handed Jenna the check. "This is the reason I gave up traditional weddings and Bar-mitzvahs." She made more off one fantasy than from ten weddings combined. Also, the competition was practically nonexistent, and she didn't have to advertise or offer specials. Her business came from word-of-mouth among a small but elite group of people who could afford her services.

It was all about money. This job was all about business.

That's what she told herself, but deep down she actually *liked* what she did for a living. When she was honest with herself, she knew that by setting up someone else's fantasy she could experience, vicariously, a few of her own.

"What are we doing this time?"

"Saloon girl and gunslinger."

"Mmm . . . a cowboy. My personal favorite."

An image rushed through Elizabeth's mind, that of her own private fantasy man. A cowboy. A wild and wicked and dangerous cowboy.

"*I want you . . .*" his deep voice whispered in her head and sent a shiver through her. It was a voice she'd heard too many times to count since she was a teenager, and it was always the same. Ever since she'd had her first cowboy fantasy, thanks to Michael Landon and all those *Bonanza* reruns her brothers had watched. Of course, her fantasy cowboy was better looking than Michael Landon. Hotter. Sexier.

". . . cowboy once. But he wasn't a real cowboy. Just one of those weekend, suburban bozos with the designer jeans and the oversized belt buckle from *Midnight Cowboy*." Jenna's voice pushed past Elizabeth's thoughts and drew her back to the present. "I always wanted to try the real thing."

"You and at least forty percent of women everywhere, according to Isabella X." Isabella X was the leading guru on fantasies and widely known for her first book, *The Naughty Nine*. The book described the nine core scenarios that fuel the sexual fantasies of women and men alike, and it had quickly become Elizabeth's bible. While she didn't participate directly in the action, the more she knew about what motivated her clients' desires, the better job she could do setting them up. "She gave a listing at the back of her last book of women's favorite fantasy types. Cowboys have the top honor."

"And where does this gunslinger–saloon girl fantasy fit into the Naughty Nine?"

"I think what the Laramies are really after is number eight—sex for pay."

"They might also be interested in number four—being seduced by a faceless stranger. That is, if Mr. Laramie keeps his hat on and wears a bandanna tied around his face." The third-year psych major was quick, and she kept up with her reading, which was why Elizabeth had hired her in the first place. That and the fact that the girl brought a breath of fresh air into the office. Elizabeth's own ultra-conservative and appearance-oriented taste felt somehow wrong considering her profession.

Jenna's eyes twinkled. "So who's playing the saloon girl? The mister or the missus?"

"You're a riot. Did I see you on Leno last night?"

"It was Def Comedy Jam, and I'm totally serious. Which one?"

"The mister."

"That's what they all say. But behind closed doors . . ."

A quick visual of Mr. Laramie in a corset pushed into her thoughts before she shoved it back out and reached for her notes. "Get a listing of old houses in the area and let's get some costume samples today—"

"It's the day before Thanksgiving."

"I want to narrow down some sites before I

21

leave. That way after I get back from Cherryville on Friday, I can scout out a few—"

"Actually," Jenna cut in, "I forgot to tell you. Your father called and said there'll be a lot of press at the dinner. He said it would be too crowded for anyone to really have a good time and it would be better if you stayed in Houston until things calmed down. Then the two of you can sit down and have a quiet, peaceful, traditional Thanksgiving later. Without all the hoopla to unsettle the digestive system."

Elizabeth eyed her young assistant. "Those were his exact words?"

"Of course." Another penetrating look from Elizabeth, and Jenna folded. "Okay, he might have said something like 'tell her to stay home.'" She mimicked Walter Carlton's short-clipped monotone. "'The last thing I need right now is the press being reminded of what you two do for a living. She can come for Christmas. Maybe. I'll call.'"

The words sank in and Elizabeth blinked against the sudden burning at the backs of her eyes. Which was crazy. It wasn't as if she'd actually counted on having a traditional holiday at home. She never counted on any holidays because they were major publicity opportunities. They were a chance for the voters of Texas to peek into the life of conservative Walt Carlton, his lovely wife of thirty-eight years and their five lovely children.

Well, four lovely children these days. It seemed she no longer counted.

"I can't believe I told you. I'm too honest for my own good."

"That's okay."

"And I really can't believe he's doing this to you the day before Thanksgiving," Jenna said. "What a creep." Count on Jenna, whose heart was as big as her teased blond hair, to be outraged on Elizabeth's behalf.

"He's not a creep. He's just careful." And distant, but then she'd grown accustomed to that a long time ago. "It's no big deal. I'm used to it." Ten years and she could count on her hand the number of times she'd been back to Cherryville, to her home and family. "These things fall through all the time. I wasn't even really planning on going. I haven't even packed." She forced aside the disappointment and reached for the large tome the Laramies had left her. It was a history book: *Famous Gunslingers of the Wild, Wild West*. She'd have to look it over.

"It's still a rotten thing to do. Nobody should have to spend Thanksgiving alone."

"A few people have to make sacrifices for the good of the many." She repeated the phrase she'd heard so many times during her childhood, like when she'd asked to get her ears pierced. Or when she'd begged her mother for a hot pink mini-skirt. Or when she'd asked to go on her first date. The answer had always been the same.

"It isn't always about what we want, dear. This family has an image to uphold."

An image. That was what her parents had wanted her to be. A perfect, pretty little picture. And living life—really *living* it—wasn't part of the equation.

"Maybe so, but you're not the one running for governor. *You* shouldn't have to sacrifice so much."

"I might as well be the one running. For my father, I'm just a reflection on his 'family values' and tomorrow's just another press opportunity."

"Turkey day, a press opportunity? That man has his priorities messed up. Why, my tastebuds have been watering for weeks. I've got my day all planned out. We're eating at noon. Then I'm going to watch *Pretty Woman* and let everything digest. By the time Richard climbs to the top of the fire escape, I'll be ready for pie and *Shakespeare in Love*. By the time that's done, I'll be ready for another round with the turkey and *Message in a Bottle*. You could join me. It'll just be me and Butch and Harold."

Butch was Jenna's father and at seventy-two, probably the oldest living Harley rider. Harold was her pride and joy, a pit bull. "Come on," she said. "It'll be fun."

"I would, but I shouldn't take the time off. We're busy, right? It's really for the best that I won't be going anywhere."

"You're just afraid my dad will want to take

24

you for another ride like on Easter. I swear, I'll hide his starter plug."

"It's not that."

"You don't want to sit through *Easy Rider* three times like we did on the Fourth of July. Don't worry. I'll hide the videotape."

"It's not that."

"I swear, no listening to Springsteen's *Born to Run* CD five times like we did on Labor Day."

"No, it's not that, either. I really need to get a jumpstart on the Watsons' Anthony and Cleopatra fantasy."

"That takes two hours to plan and I've already booked the resort."

"And then there's the Carrs' Tarzan and Jane fantasy," Elizabeth pointed out. "I still haven't found costumes."

"You sew together a few fig leaves. That's a no-brainer."

"Tarzan wears a loincloth. It's Adam and Eve who were in fig leaves. And I really appreciate the offer, but I'd rather work."

Jenna gave her a knowing look. "You'd rather hide. Because then you don't have to see how alone and miserable you are."

"I'm not alone and miserable." At Jenna's knowing look, she added, "Okay, so I'm alone. But I'm not miserable. I just haven't found the right guy."

"You're not going to find any guy if all you do is work. You need to *socialize*."

"By sitting around your house smelling turkey all day?"

"There aren't any hot men there," Jenna conceded. "But turkey is almost as good. And pie definitely gives the same rush as a really great kiss. And don't even get me started on chocolate mousse. I'll give you one word—ecstasy." At Elizabeth's look, Jenna shrugged. "All right. What can I say? I haven't exactly been burning the midnight oil with any hotties myself." She blew out a breath. "Why am I badgering you? I need to get my own social life."

"And I really need to work." Her job was distracting, consuming, and *fun*—the only fun Elizabeth could allow herself.

"Maybe I'll take some hot, sexy pictures and get myself a web page." Her assistant contemplated the thought for another moment. "We could even do it together. I could wear my zebra-skin thong and we could get a leopard print for you and—"

"Don't even think it. I like to keep a low profile, remember? Leopard definitely screams 'over the top.' "

"So you say. I bet you're just a wild woman waiting to be set free."

Amen. "I'm a busy woman waiting to get home, and just the thought of a thong makes me uncomfortable. Give me a pair of nice, conservative granny panties any day."

Jenna eyed her for a long moment. "Okay,"

she finally said, but you know where I live if you change your mind."

"Thanks. Now, for work; what do we have for the Laramies?"

Jenna slid on her eyeglasses and leafed through a file. "For a gunfighter and saloon-girl routine? Five prospects. An old farm near Corpus Christi that once doubled as a house of ill-repute. A brownstone in downtown Houston that used to be the Black Dog saloon way back when—lots of ill repute going on there, or so the books say. Two old saloon sites between here and Galveston. And *this*." She waved a prospect sheet as if she held a winning lottery ticket.

Elizabeth grabbed the paper and stared at the property name. "The Red Parlour Room? What is that?"

"Only the most notorious bordello ever to grace the Galveston watcrfront. The place is legendary."

She studied the property listing. "It's still standing?"

"For the time being. The owner wants to tear it down, but the city wants to preserve it. It's collecting dust right now, and available for lease at the right price. And if we got it, we could use it for all the gunslinger fantasies we do. After it's been fixed up a bit, of course."

"I'll go there first thing in the morning."

Jenna paused in the doorway. "I'm really sorry about your father."

"So am I."

She was sorry, but not surprised. Since she'd moved her company from Cherryville to Houston eight years ago and invented the unique It's Only Make Believe, she'd become a liability to her family. An embarrassment. And on the few occasions she saw her father, he never failed to remind her of the ten-percent plunge he'd taken in the polls when the press had done a story on it.

The uproar over the staunchly conservative Mayor Carlton's daughter catering for other people's fantasies had only recently died down, thanks to Elizabeth's professionalism and the fact that personally, she was still every bit as prim and proper as ever.

She sighed. Her innocent nature was a truth she'd accepted would never change; she'd had her chance the night of her senior prom when she'd been voted Cherryville High's Most Likely to Die a Virgin, and at the party that had followed. She'd had her chance to prove everyone wrong, and she'd blown it.

For her father, she reminded herself.

She'd finally come to terms with the fact that there would be no hot and hunky men in her future. No acting on impulses or giving in to the lust burning in her veins. She rarely dated, and when she did, she leaned toward the men of whom her father would have approved. Men who were smart. Conservative. Clean-cut. Appropriate.

Boring.

The men she dated would never stir her to a grand passion, true, but her father was in the big leagues now, making a play for governor. The last thing Elizabeth wanted was to hurt his chances by taking up with a wild man, even though that was what she secretly longed for—a man like the one who starred in her own most private fantasies.

She grabbed the real estate listings and her briefcase. After a quick stop for dinner, she was headed home to unpack her suitcase and do a little research.

Everything about him screamed SEX.

From the way he looked—his tight-fitting black pants were tucked into black cowboy boots, and his upper body was bare and broad and muscular beneath a black fringed vest—to the way he looked. His gaze was dark and piercing and wild beneath the low brim of a black cowboy hat.

Her heart pounded and the blood rushed through her veins in anticipation of what would come next. What always came next.

He filled her line of vision as he stepped closer. His piercing stare caught and held hers. His nostrils flared as he seemed to catch her scent and drink it in. His sensuous lips tilted into a grin. A few steps and he reached her. The aroma of warm male and leather stole through her senses. Her nipples pebbled, her thighs itched, and desire rushed through her, hot and molten and greedy.

29

She wanted him.

And more important, he wanted her. He always wanted her.

He leaned toward her and she knew he was about to whisper the same sexy words that always melted her faster than a scoop of ice cream on hot Texas pavement. His lips parted—

"Say, lady, you want chili on your fries, or just cheese?"

The voice, impatient with a nasal twang, shattered her fantasy and drew her back to the present, to the busy interior of Buffalo Bill's Burger Barn and the pseudo-cowboy waiter leaning over her. She'd incorporated him into her lustful musings.

He was every bit as handsome up close, and her left eye gave a quick twitch—an annoying trait that happened whenever she found herself faced with a good-looking man—but the voice, not to mention the Born to Boff tattoo that peeked past his vest when he reached into his back pocket for his order pad, totally blew the effect. This was not her dark and exciting cowboy. This was no fantasy. Her eye stopped twitching.

"Which'll it be, lady?"

Tall, Dark and Twangy spoke again, and she found herself staring into his eyes. They were watery blue, not nearly the intense color she'd imagined a few moments ago. She sent up another silent prayer of thanks. The farther away he was from her real fantasy man, from the blue-eyed cowboy who haunted her most private erotic thoughts, the easier it was to calm her beating heart and ignore the urge to rip off her clothes and beg for him to show her a good time. All she'd want would be a few exciting memories.

That was what Elizabeth secretly thirsted for: excitement. She was so tired of her boring life, of always living up to everyone's expectations, of always, *always* doing the right thing. Just once, she'd love to say to hell with everything. To cut loose. To really live.

Just once.

"So what'll it be, lady? What do you want?"

A cowboy. A wild, wicked, hunky cowboy.

"The chili and cheese, please." Oh, well. Old habits were hard to break, and Elizabeth had been walking the straight and narrow for much too long to detour now. And she didn't think she could order a cowboy, anyhow.

Besides, she loved her father, even if he didn't seem to return her affection, and this guy wasn't anywhere near worth disappointing him for. He wasn't her fantasy man.

No, her dream man only came out at night. When the lights were low and the doors were locked and the world was shut out, and Elizabeth could actually be herself.

A few people have to make sacrifices. . . .

Her father's words echoed through her head, shattering her thoughts and drawing her back to the present, to the nearly empty restaurant and the sign hanging in the window.

WE WILL BE CLOSED ON THANKSGIVING.

She sniffled and blinked against sudden tears. She wouldn't cry over this. She was working, darn it, and tomorrow was just another day.

It was the worst day of her life.

A flat tire. Three missed turns. An undercooked burger at Sloppy's Slab of Beef off Highway 45—the only place she'd found open on Thanksgiving—and now this. The Red Parlour Room.

She stared at the boarded-up building through her windshield. She'd wanted old, but old and restored. This place looked as if it hadn't been touched in a hundred years. Now, if Mr. and Mrs. Laramie had wanted a handyman fixer-upper fantasy, this would have been their dream. As it was, it would never do.

At the same time, she hadn't driven an hour and a half just to turn around and head back. She was here, and so was the realtor, an impatient man who was pacing back and forth in front of the building. She might as well take a look. She got out of her car.

"Miss Carlton." The heavy-set man greeted her with a smile as she walked to the front door.

"It's Elizabeth, and I can't thank you enough for meeting me this morning. I hate to inconvenience you like this—"

"No problem. I'm here to serve." He unlocked the door and practically pushed her inside. "You just take your time." Seconds ticked by as

32

her eyes adjusted to the dim interior, and she took in the cobweb-covered chandelier, the rotting red drapes spanning from wall to wall.

"So? What do you think?" he asked.

Old. Decrepit. It would take far too much to set up Mr. and Mrs. Laramie's fantasy in a place like—

The thought stalled as her attention shifted to the large stage at the head of the room. It was T-shaped, its flat top spanning from corner to corner, and its main body pushing out into the room, extending into what had once been a sea of tables. The floor was bare with the exception of a thick layer of silver dust that caught the shafts of light filtering in through partially boarded-up windows.

"So?" he prodded. "Do we have a deal?"

Hardly. The word was there on the tip of her tongue, but instead, she heard herself saying, "I'd like to look around first. Maybe go upstairs. Can I walk upstairs?"

"It's old, but solid." The realtor stomped his foot for emphasis. Boards creaked and cracked beneath his weight and he gave her a sheepish smile. "For the most part. Just step softly and follow me." He led her in a brisk walk toward the staircase and a large, fading portrait of a woman wearing nothing but bright red feathers, a red-jeweled garter and a smile.

"Sinful Sinclair," the man told her. "A stripper who used to dance here way back around the turn of the century."

But Elizabeth already knew who the woman was. There'd been numerous passages about her in the Laramies' book. Miss Sinful had had many, many male friends, including two legendary gunslingers who'd actually gotten into a shootout over her.

She stopped and eyed the portrait. The woman wasn't a knockout by any means, but there *was* something about her. Her challenging eyes, her knowing smile, the high thrust of her breasts and her I-am-woman-and-damned-proud-of-it pose. A pang of longing shot through Elizabeth.

Here was a woman who'd really *lived* life.

". . . still the original furnishings upstairs." The realtor's voice reminded her where she was. "Nobody's touched much of anything here. For awhile, the Galveston Historical Society wanted to preserve it, but the owners wanted to sell the lot. Then the owner died and the kids started fighting over it. There's been lots of legal mumbo jumbo that has tied up everything in court, so the place looks pretty much the same as it did way back then. With the exception of some dust and aging."

"Lots of aging."

"Nothing a good cleaning couldn't fix. This way." The man tapped an impatient rhythm on the banister.

"If you're in a hurry, I can look around by myself."

"Hurry?" He looked perplexed for a moment,

then he seemed to notice his hand. His fingers clamped tight. He gave an apologetic smile. "I'm sorry. It's the whole turkey thing," he went on. "I've spent the entire morning smelling it, thinking about it, and wanting it."

"I'll look around and lock up myself, then."

He seemed to consider the option before shaking his head. "I can't. I'm a realtor, you're a buyer. I'm here for you."

"But it's Thanksgiving."

"It's just another day."

The words made her think of her father's work ethic. His fierce push to put business before everything else. Had it rubbed off? Guilt welled inside her. It was just another day for her, but this man probably had a family waiting for him. "I'm really fine on my own."

"I can't—"

"White meat," she blurted. "Juicy, tender, succulent white meat." He licked his lips and she knew she had him. "And stuffing."

"Cornbread stuffing," he added.

"*Cornbread* stuffing," she agreed. "And cranberry sauce and homemade sweet potatoes with marshmallows and pecans and—"

"Call me on Monday if you have any questions." A minute later, she heard tires squeal as he pulled away from the curb. Silence settled in after that, disrupted only by the break of waves against the pier outside and the occasional grumble of a passing car engine.

"I guess it's just you and me," she said to the

woman depicted in the fringe-framed portrait. With that, Elizabeth set to work.

She spent the next half-hour going through the upstairs, trailing her hands over the iron bed frames, sitting on the edge of the ancient mattresses, and doing her best to ignore the image of a dark, delicious cowboy that kept pushing into her thoughts.

This wasn't about her fantasies, about her erotic dreams involving a hunky cowboy and a seductive striptease. This was about the Laramies. It was strictly business, and from a purely professional standpoint, this place would hardly suffice as a posh Wild West bordello.

Once upon a time, she told herself as she walked the bedroom-lined hallway, but not now. No matter how big the bedroom was at the far end. Or that she could actually picture a king-sized bed draped in red velvet, and a ceiling covered with a giant mirror, and a velvet settee draped with a forgotten gun belt.

She pushed her imaginings aside as she walked back downstairs. From there, she climbed the stairs behind the stage and found a small dressing room. The chamber had a cracked oval mirror hanging on the wall, a scarred armoire and a large dust-covered trunk with the initials SS carved into the top.

SS, as in Sinful Sinclair? That couldn't be. The thing would then have to be an antique, and people didn't leave valuable antiques sitting around. Unless the antique in question was tied up in a court battle.

"Sinful, you were definitely a bad girl," she said when the lid's rusty hinges finally allowed it to be opened with a loud creak. She stared at the contents—everything from feather boas and silky stockings to a jewel-encrusted garter.

The garter from the picture!

She fingered the satin band as her mind rushed back to the portrait. The garter was so gaudy and bold and outrageous.

It was everything she wasn't.

Everything she'd ever wanted to be.

A smile tugged at her lips, and before she could think better of it, she peeled off her clothes. Opening the armoire, she tugged on one of the costumes she knew would be inside. Just to see what it felt like to trade in her old, stuffy, conservative suit for something naughty and wicked and exciting.

Okay, so she felt more itchy and smelly and uncomfortable, she admitted when she stood wearing nothing but a short red dancing dress. But while she felt ready to jump out of her skin, she looked good. The tight-fitting, low-cut bodice did more for her not-so-voluptuous chest than any Wonderbra she'd ever tried, and the flared skirt camouflaged her not-so-perfect hips.

She reached for the stockings next, followed by a pair of outlandishly high lace-up shoes that were at least two sizes too large—Sinful had obviously had some mighty big feet. Then she hooked her foot through the garter, slid it up over her calf, her knee . . .

Her hands trembled, an odd tingling sensation spreading up her arms and into her body as she pulled the satin into place and turned toward the stage. For a split-second, a memory rushed at her, overwhelming all of her senses. The after-prom party. The cheering and chanting of the crowd. And her one shot to prove she wasn't as prim and proper as everyone had thought.

She'd blown it. Well, there was nothing stopping her now. She was alone, and she could do whatever she cared to do. . . .

She stepped forward into a gleam of blinding sunlight, and for a split-second, it was as if she stood in a spotlight, surrounded by music and smoke and men. Lots of men.

Cheering and shouting and grabbing—

She blinked and glanced down, away from the stream of light to see a hand around her ankle. It was a hand attached to an arm, attached to a scraggly face, attached to a beefy body, surrounded by a throng of more bodies.

People. The room was full of people when five seconds before it had been empty and dusty and—

"Come here, woman." The order derailed her frantic train of thought and sent panic racing through her. What was going on?

"Forget it. She's coming over here first!"

"Out of the way and give a feller a chance!"

"Give a little kiss, darlin'."

She tugged and pulled at her ankle, but the fingers clamped tighter . . . then suddenly they let go. She pitched forward, straight over the edge of the stage into a hard, warm body.

A hard warm body? Reality intruded as strong, equally warm hands closed around her. It was a body, all right. A man's body, with a man's hands. And she stared into a man's intense blue eyes.

Intense and piercing and wild.

The thought struck just as the man's mouth spread into a lazy, dazzling grin. He adjusted her so that she was sitting, then murmured for her ears only. "As much as I'd like a little dance on my lap, sugar, I don't think the fellas around here would be too obliging."

His voice which was somehow familiar, was also deep and stirring. It rumbled through her head, sending her already frazzled nerves into a tizzy. Her mouth opened and closed as she tried to comprehend what had just happened. What *was* happening. She was half-naked in front of a room full of cheering cowboys. More important, she was sitting on one of their laps. And the man she was straddling was *the* cowboy.

Mr. Fantasy, himself.

Chapter Two

She was losing her mind.

That was the only explanation for what was happening. Correction, for what she was *imagining* to be happening. Another holiday alone had sent her smack dab over the edge, straight into Looney Toons land. No way was any of this real. She was hallucinating it all, including the clapping and clamoring that echoed so loudly her ears rang, the smoke-filled room that made her eyes water, and the cowboy who held her in his arms. Her heart pounded faster.

Every nerve in her body zeroed in on his close proximity, and her gaze shifted to his.

Eyes of the bluest color she'd ever seen stared back at her. Strong, warm hands burned into her waist and warmed her skin. His sweet breath feathered across her lips and made them tingle. And his smile—his lips were full and sensuous and tilted at one corner—made her palms itch and her right eye twitch.

Oh, God, this is real.

The thought hit her as she sat there, her eye twitching in tempo to the piano music, that was playing raucously in the background.

This was a *real* cowboy. And she was really sitting on his lap. Somehow, someway, the world had turned upside-down in those few moments when she'd closed her eyes and tried to imagine Sinful's life.

"You'd better get back on stage." The cowboy's deep voice cut through the questions racing through her mind and grounded her in the moment. He was so close she could see the fringe of his dark eyelashes. "I don't think this bunch is long on patience."

"I . . ." The words faded as she searched for something to say, and before she could gather her wits, she found herself hoisted back up onto the stage. The cowboy's hands lingered a moment and her heart shifted into overdrive. Then he let go and she was standing on the edge of the stage, the lights fixed on her along with every eye in the place.

"Go for it, girlie." The voices rang out one after the other.

"Take it all off."

The phrase rang in her ears, stirring a memory of that long-ago prom night when she'd finally accepted her destiny. She couldn't do this. She was prim. Proper. Boring.

"Give us what we been hearing about."

"Yeah, Sinful. Show us what you got!"

Sinful? They thought that's who she was? A burst of denial shot through her, then she admitted the truth. She was in a room full of chanting men who thought she was Sinful Sinclair—the *stripper*.

She became keenly aware of her scantily clad state and the fact that these men were waiting for her to strip naked. They wanted her to take it all off, to let loose and be as wild as she'd always dreamt of being.

"Come on, Sinful!"

Sinful.

The name had a wonderful ring to it, and it stirred a heat deep inside her. The thirst for excitement she'd always fought to supress. She wasn't sure what had happened, or how. She only knew that she was here, in this moment, and she was no longer the prim and proper Elizabeth Joanna Carlton. She was the wild and wicked Sinful Sinclair.

The realization sent a rush of boldness through her and before she knew what she was doing, she pulled her shoulders back and took a tentative step toward the center of the stage.

The men cheered. The clapping faded as the music started up again; apparently the pianist had been waiting on her. Elizabeth drew in a deep breath. She took one step, and then another, her hips swaying with each movement in what had looked seductive when she'd seen Demi Moore do it in *Striptease*.

It was definitely seductive, she noted as she looked out at face after face in the audience and saw the men's bright eyes, their mesmerized expressions. A sense of empowerment coursed through her, much more intense than anything she'd ever dreamed. This was real.

But that meant *he* was real.

The thought rooted in her mind as her gaze collided with that of the blue-eyed cowboy. A wave of self-consciousness swept through her. Before she could stop to think that no self-respecting wild woman would turn tail and run, she spun on her heel and fled from the mesmerized crowd, from him. She darted past a huge man who stood in the back, and ducked behind the curtains, her heart pounding like a jackhammer.

The music rose and the clapping grew louder. The men had come to their senses and they wanted more. They wanted Sin—

"There she is." The voice sounded to her left a moment before a hand closed around her arm. "Hold up there, sweet stuff. We've got a little business to discuss."

"I—" She found herself staring up at a burly-looking man with red hair and a full beard. Next to him stood another man with the same color hair and beard, but who was several inches shorter. Beside him stood yet another, ditto the hair and beard, but who was young and very skinny. They were practically the three little red-headed pigs.

Only these pigs had guns strapped around their waists.

Guns? Wait a sec—

"Come on." The biggest pig tugged on her arm, his fingers digging into her skin. His ring, a small silver pinkie number, cut into her and she winced.

She wanted to pull away, to kick and scream and do some of the moves she'd learned in that self-defense class she'd taken last year. But she was still in shock from the past few minutes. The cheering. The chanting. The stripping.

Or the lack of.

She hadn't stripped. Little Miss I-long-to-be-free Elizabeth Joanna Carlton had been given a chance to actually get wild and crazy for the second time in her life—to be truly wicked like she wanted—and she'd blown it. Again. She'd chickened out.

"You got something we want." The burly man tugged her backwards a few feet when suddenly the huge bruiser she'd seen in her dash from the stage—obviously the old-fashioned equivalent of a bouncer—intervened.

"Back up, Slick." The bruiser, a gun in hand, wedged himself between Elizabeth and the red-headed trio. "Any business you got with Sinful, you got with me and old Charlie here." He motioned to the Colt in his hand. "And I'm tellin' you right now, there ain't no 'business' until after the show."

"We say there is." Another Colt appeared, this one in the hand of one of her assailants. "She's got something we want and we aim to get it."

"You and every other cowboy in this place." The bruiser motioned behind him to the noise from the stage. "Hear that? They ain't all riled up over Ima Jean's apple fritters, I can tell you that. Now back on up, boys."

"We say you back up." The slow cocking sound of a gun followed, penetrating the shock beating at Elizabeth's brain. In a heartbeat, the situation crystalized—these were large, intimidating men. With guns. And enough testosterone to supply King Kong.

This was not good.

"She's got something we want." The burly man repeated as he hauled her up against him. She slammed into his barrel-like chest. "She's got—Ouch!"

Her survival instincts had taken over in the form of a well-aimed kick dubbed the "nutcracker."

A gasp and a groan sounded just before she kicked again. The large hand restraining her fell away and she found herself again on her feet. She darted past the men, fleeing farther backstage, away from the clapping and the chanting and the Three Redheaded Pigs.

"Dammit, woman!"

"Stop her!"

"Hold up, Sinful!"

The called name drove home what was going on, the bizarre situation she was in. She ducked behind another curtain and found herself in a small alcove complete with a small table loaded with miniature bottles of paint, a row of hats and a mirror. The mirror was the same one she'd spotted when she'd first entered The Red Parlour Room, but there were no cracks, now, no dust, just a polished gold edge framing her reflection.

With a sigh of relief she saw that the image reflected back was her own, not that of the woman she'd spotted in the picture downstairs. Regardless of the weird twist things had taken, at least she hadn't actually morphed into Sinful Sinclair. She still looked every bit like her old self—minus her clothes, of course, and the conservative air that she wore like body armor.

Her usually smooth, simple hair was mussed and wild, as if she'd just rolled out of bed. Her cheeks were rosy, and her bosom heaved in the tight confines of the corset. She looked every bit as sexy as Sinful, and by that Elizabeth was startled.

"Where is she?" The question, accusatory and angry, came from directly behind her. She whirled and came face-to-face with a young woman.

There was something oddly familiar about her, but Elizabeth had no clue why.

She had lifeless blond hair, and huge eyes as

dark as coal in her small, round face. She was shapeless, despite the crimson dance-hall dress she wore that was supposed to mold to her curves and accent them, and make her look like a voluptuous rose ready to be plucked. Instead, it made her look thin and pale. Totally unpluckable.

The frown on her face and the glare in her eyes just added to her hands-off aura.

". . . got business!" She heard the angry voices, those of the men, and Elizabeth knew the Three Pigs hadn't given up their pursuit, either. Her arm throbbed where the one man's ring had cut into her, and panic overwhelmed her. Maybe this other woman could help.

"I have to get out of here," she told the young woman. "Will you help me?"

"Help you?" The woman gave her a what-planet-did-you-come-from look before shaking her head and tossing a velvet robe in her direction. "Oh, I'll help you, all right. Come on." She pulled her down a skinny hallway toward a door at the far end. It opened into another dressing room, Elizabeth realized when she walked inside and found the place lined with costumes.

The woman turned on her as soon as she'd shut the door. "Now. First off, who in jumpin' Jehoshaphat's name are you? 'Cause you ain't who all those cowboys think you are."

"You know?"

" 'Course I know. So who are you?"

"Elizabeth Joanna Carlton." She searched for

47

some sign of recognition. The name had always sparked recognition before. Her father had been in politics since she was knee-high, and everyone in Texas knew him. Her rescuer just stared at her blankly, and the truth solidified even more.

This was real. She really had made some strange trip to another—

"What'd you do with her?"

"Who?"

"Sinful. You tell me where she is right this very second or you'll be sorry." She waved her finger at Elizabeth. "I'll zap you for sure."

Elizabeth fought for a calming breath. "Zap me?"

"Hex you." The woman did more finger wiggling. "Put a spell on you. I've been castin' spells since I was four years old. I'm a witch, from a long line of witches. My mother was Jade Sinclair," she declared proudly.

"I'm sorry, but I've never heard of her."

The young woman gave her another look of disbelief. "Jade Sinclair was only the most powerful witch in the Louisiana territory."

"So this is Louisiana?"

"It's Texas, girl. But I'm from Louisiana. Bayou country near New Orleans. Everybody knows my mama. They loved her. She could do anything, she was beautiful and she could tear up a dance floor quicker than you can eat a plate of grits."

"That's nice."

"Nice?" The young woman shook her head and glared. "You're a witch like me, aren't you? You cast spells. That's what you did to my sister Sinful, ain't it?"

Okay, so maybe this whole time-travel thing wasn't real. Maybe the Looney Toons theory was more on the money. This was obviously some horrible dream. Maybe she'd fallen and hit her head. . . .

"Well?" the woman demanded when Elizabeth didn't respond. She waggled her finger again and declared, "That's it. I'm hexing you." Her dark eyes glittered fiercely. Her fingers twitched. "Toads and snakes, spiders and bats, tell the truth or turn into a cat!"

Before Elizabeth could stop herself, she reached up and felt for whiskers. Relief washed through her when she felt only her hot cheeks. "I must be going crazy."

The woman stared at her finger and shook it. "Oh, no." Her face fell. "It didn't work."

"Lucky for me. I'm allergic to cats."

The wannabe witch shook her head. "But it should have worked. It *always* works."

"So you turn lots of people into cats?" Oh, no, she *was* going crazy. She was talking to this woman, practically encouraging her. What was she thinking? She should be trying to figure out what was going on. She'd definitely taken a dive straight off the deep end.

"Just that man that tried to get fresh with Sinful one time. And then Doobey Guillet. He was the meanest eight-year-old to ever go craw-fishin' along Darjean Bayou. He used to call me so many names, so one day me and Sinful paid him back. . . ." Her words trailed off as her gaze narrowed. "You better tell me what you did to her." She waved the finger menacingly, but Elizabeth wasn't scared this time.

Okay, so maybe she was a little scared. The woman looked so serious, and lots of weird things had been happening. This woman could have accidentally misfired the first time. Next time, Elizabeth was liable to be rolling on her back and purring.

"I don't know where she is." She held up her hands. "I swear."

"And I'm s'posed to believe that? She walked out onto that stage and you walked back. You sure as shootin' know what happened to her. You did somethin' with her." Another finger wag and Elizabeth held up her hands again.

"I *swear* I don't know what you're talking about. One minute I was walking around in this dusty old dress and the next I'm here and everybody thinks I'm Sinful Sinclair. I don't even look like her."

The young woman seemed to look her over for the first time. Dark, suspicious eyes swept her from head to toe. "You got that right. You're too skinny and puny to be Sinful. She's got meat on her bones."

Skinny? Elizabeth wore a size ten and this woman thought she was skinny? Okay, forget

Looney Toons land. This might just qualify as Heaven.

"Not that it matters none," the woman was saying. "We just got off the boat this mornin' from N'Awlins. Her and me. Not a one of these boys ever seen her up close, so it's no wonder they all thought you were her. What with you wearing the garter and all."

"What are you talking about?" She stared down at the jewel-encrusted piece of satin on her thigh.

"That garter's got some powerful magic thanks to these." She wiggled her fingers. "The garter is blessed. It enhances Sinful's sex appeal. Makes every man within seein' and smellin' distance want her. Makes them want to do anything and everything just to get close to her. I gave her that power and she gave me my . . ." A sudden brightness filled her eyes and she blinked, narrowing her gaze into a scowl. "I want her back right now, or you're in for a heap of trouble."

"Believe me, if I could, I'd give her back to you. I'm already in a heap of trouble. One minute I was somewhere else and now I'm here." *In another time and place.*

She didn't want to believe it. It was impossible. Logically she knew that. Still, here she was, caught in the moment, trapped with a raving lunatic who wanted to give her the finger.

"And I s'pose she was here and now she's there."

Had they switched places? Was Sinful prancing around in that dusty old dress right now, minus her magical garter?

The question, added to those already swirling in her brain, made her head hurt even more than her feet stuffed into their awful lace-up boots. But the witch woman didn't give her any more time to bemoan her fate. She was getting truly nasty.

"Where *is* she? Better tell me now, or there's going to be trouble."

Before Elizabeth knew what was happening, she found herself staring at a deadly-looking blade the woman had pulled from her cleavage.

"Big trouble," the woman added. She touched the weapon's tip to a spot just below Elizabeth's nose. "Now where is she?"

"I don't know. Cross my heart and hope to . . ." She clamped her lips shut before the word could make it past. Not a good thing to be saying. She didn't want to give the woman any more ideas.

Elizabeth drew in a deep breath and tried to calm her pounding heart. "Look, I'm having a hard enough time dealing with where I am and—"

"I'll cut out your lyin' tongue!"

The statement was meant to send a rush of fear through her, but Elizabeth was several steps past that. She'd been mauled, cut and fingered, and all in the course of five minutes. Enough was enough. "I don't think so." Her target wasn't exactly the same, but the "nut-cracker" worked just fine anyway.

The young woman howled and doubled over long enough for Elizabeth to haul open the door and flee into the dark hallway. She rushed down the corridor and around a corner, but as she did, her heel caught. One too-large shoe slipped off as she tumbled forward, straight into a solid mass of muscle.

Oh, no, who now?

She must have caught him off-guard because her weight pushed him backwards and they both fell to the ground. Elizabeth landed on top of him, the side of her hip pressed into his groin.

"I'm so sorry. I didn't see—"

"You're determined to sit on my lap, aren't you, Peaches?" The deep, sexy drawl slid into her ears and she knew it was *him* even before her head jerked up and her frantic gaze found his. His eyes were still that intense blue that took her breath away.

It was her cowboy.

Her cowboy? No, no. He wasn't *her* anything, even if he did have eyes as compelling as any she'd ever imagined, and the same strong hands she'd felt in her dreams, and the same hard body that had slid against her in all of her—

"Are you all right, Peaches?"

All right? Was he kidding? She'd traveled back to a time where everyone thought she was a stripper—everyone but a crazy woman with a malfunctioning "magic finger" and a sharp knife. And to top it all off, the only thing that separated her from the hunkiest guy she'd ever glimpsed was a stripper's outfit and a dressing gown.

"I—I'm fine." She fought for a deep breath and inhaled leather and male and the faint scent of tobacco. "I mean, I'm not fine. There's this woman after me, and these men, too, and—"

From the stage, the piano music grew louder and the audience cheered appreciatively. They must have found a replacement dancer. Suddenly, a voice rose above it all. "Check and see if she's back there." The husky redhead, he was close! She had to escape. She didn't want to be caught by them *or* the woman she had kicked.

"I have to get out of here." She struggled to her knees. "They're after me and—"

"Calm down, sugar." Her cowboy got to his feet. A strong hand closed over hers and he lifted her up next to him.

"Calm down? There are crazy people chasing after me with knives. This whole place is insane. It's like a big, bad, crazy dream and—"

"Easy." One warm finger pressed against her lips and silenced her. "I'm not gonna let anybody hurt you. I need you."

Elizabeth came up short. His words swirled into her ears and for a fast, furious second, she forgot all about the danger that lurked around the corner; she focused only on him. His close proximity. His warmth. His smell.

I need you?

"W-what did you say?" she finally managed.

"I need you. Rumor has it that you're one finely schooled woman in the bedroom—and that's exactly what I need."

Elizabeth hadn't thought anything could shock her after a time travel, an impromptu striptease, and two near-death experiences. She had been wrong. "You think I'm an expert in the bedroom?" Yes, this was definitely Looney Toons central and this guy had to be their king.

"One thousand men." He gave her a knowing look, his lips hinting at a smile that she knew would make her faint. "I know all about you, Peaches, and you're exactly what I'm looking for." His drawl, slow and sexy, poured over her like hot caramel over cheesecake. Her heartbeat slowed and her breathing grew shallow. For a few breathless moments, she forgot all about her situation and saw, heard, and *felt* only him.

"It's gotta get tough having a bunch of rowdy cowboys grope you night after night. Probably damned hard for an expert such as yourself to enjoy this much, anymore. You must be bored doing the same old thing."

She struggled to find her voice. "You don't know the half of it." What was she *saying*? This was ridiculous. Crazy.

No, this was *real*.

"A little one-on-one would probably be a welcome relief, then. For the next three weeks, say? I know that seems like a long time for a woman of your background to stay in one place, but I'm sure you can figure out a way to keep things interesting."

"Three weeks?" She hated to keep repeating what he said, but she couldn't help herself. This was too unbelievable.

"It's not very long to teach someone everything you know, really, but I figure with an eager pupil, the lessons should fly by."

She tried to picture Mr. Tall, Dark and Delicious sitting in a school desk, eager and attentive as she explained her experience—her very limited experience—when it came to sex. She couldn't do it.

But was that really what he wanted?

"I'm Colt Durango." He took her hand in his. His eyes gleamed with a knowledgeable light that took her breath away. This handsome man obviously knew what he was doing; Elizabeth had the sneaking suspicion that he would end up being the teacher and she the pupil. An eager one, too.

If she were even considering such a thing, which she wasn't. Sex for hire? Of all the nerve . . . Just what kind of woman did he think she was?

"Sin-ful."

The name was being chanted in the other room, the audience of rowdy men apparently all anxious for another glimpse of The Red Parlour Room's star attraction.

"This is crazy." Elizabeth leaned over and grabbed her lost shoe. Throwing it onto the ground, she wobbled as she slid her toes into the oversized footwear. "It's not really happening. Not you or these people or *this*. I'm not caught in some time warp or anything like that. Maybe it was those chili cheese fries I had last night. That's what I get for indulging. Weird, twisted, crazy dreams.

A dream. That was it. This was a dream. Just another fantasy. A doozy, but a fantasy nonetheless.

"Why is your eye twitching?"

She became keenly aware of the spasm and slapped a hand over it. Oh, God, her eye *was* twitching. She'd never twitched in her fantasies. Nor had she run away when faced with a prime striptease opportunity.

But she had run this time. And now she was twitching. And sweating. And her heart was racing ninety to nothing.

This was real. She had to admit it.

No! "This is not happening. It's those chili cheese fries. I knew I shouldn't have eaten a double order. And then there was the milkshake. And the extra chocolate sauce, and . . ."

The words faded as she twisted away from him. Was she dreaming? This had all begun when she had tried on the garter—maybe that was somehow linked to what was happening.

57

She reached down, furious, and slid the satin band she'd taken from Sinful's trunk down to her knee. A roaring sound filled her ears. She shook her head as if to clear the sound and kicked off her shoe. She skimmed the garter over her knee and toward her ankle. The cowboy's image blurred and the present descended over her like a thin shimmering veil. She saw the decayed building, the fading velvet, the cracked floor. The farther down the garter slipped, the more the scene sharpened and the man seemed to fade into the background.

He was an illusion, not a real man. She could lose *him*.

The thought sent a burst of panic through her and she snatched up the garter and slid it firmly back into place on her upper thigh. The veil lifted. His features returned to focus—his deep blue eyes, the firm set of his jaw, his sensual mouth. The tantalizing smell of leather and warm male filled her nostrils. The deep, even sounds of his breathing filled her ears.

This was all because of the garter.

Magic.

"You all right?" he asked.

"F-fine," Elizabeth stammered. More was becoming clear. The garter *was* magic, just like that strange witch-woman had claimed. Somehow, she had imbued the satin strip with a magical sex appeal, perhaps Sinful Sinclair's own. The stripper had been sexy, vibrant, and irresistible to men—and somehow her essence had been captured by the fabric of the garter.

And that essence had somehow been retained—so much so that by slipping on the strip of satin, Elizabeth had somehow assumed the woman's identity. Taken her place. Right now, she *was* Sinful Sinclair, and as long as she kept the garter in place, she was living in the past.

She was living in the moment.

Her gaze met Colt's.

"You want me to give *sex* lessons?" The minute the question was out of her mouth, she regretted it. She had to have misunderstood him.

He smiled, a sly twist of her lips that sent a thrill racing through her. "Everything you know, sugar. *Everything.*"

The word burned in her mind, stirring all sorts of wonderful ideas. Crazy ideas, she reminded herself. She didn't even know this guy. He was a stranger. He could be a serial killer, for all she knew. I mean, what did she really know about him?

She knew that his hands were strong but gentle, that he'd held her as if she were made of precious glass when she'd fallen off the stage, and that he was offering her a way out right now.

But was it only so that he could rape her in private?

No. That didn't make sense. Rape equaled force. This guy was offering to pay her for lessons. He wasn't shoving her into the back corner and forcing some fast moves on her.

The thought of him doing just that suddenly appealed to her.

"Three weeks, you say?"

He nodded. "For this." He thrust a small pouch filled with gold coins at her. "I know your time is money."

She fought to play at righteous indignation, to muster the courage to slap his face and turn on her heel and tell him to go to hell. That was exactly what prim and proper Elizabeth Joanna Carlton would have done. After all, she would have an image to uphold.

But then again, escaping to his dwelling might not be a bad idea. Here, she had a crazy woman with a knife currently searching the upstairs for her, and three large cowboys somewhere backstage eager to talk about a certain "something" they wanted to get from her. The decision was quick.

"You've got yourself a deal, but we have to leave now."

Elizabeth was impressed by her snap decision. This cowboy was offering her a quick escape and an armed escort. But more than that, he was offering her the chance of a lifetime. She could have whisked the garter off right then and escaped if she'd wanted. But, she wanted something more. Here, finally, was the chance to play the bold and daring woman she'd always dreamt of being, to be wicked and sexy and *sinful*, with no worry over disappointing her family or tarnishing her good-girl image.

She could live out her ultimate fantasy, then take off the garter and return to the real world when it was all over. No worries. No consequences.

Just three weeks of sex lessons with the hottest student she'd ever imagined.

"I think she went back here." The voice came from closer now and fear made Elizabeth question her decision for only a moment. Then, she glanced up into her handsome new employer's smiling face.

"We'd better get out of here," he said.

"Lead the way."

His smile widened and her heart sped up. "Honey, that's what I'm paying you for."

Chapter Three

Colt needed to get her to the hotel. Quick. Before he gave in to the lust that had gripped him the first moment he'd felt her curvaceous bottom pressed into his lap. Before he backed her into the nearest alley, pressed her up against a wall, peeled off her bloomers, and plunged himself as deep as he could go into her hot little body.

That was not part of his plan.

"Where are we going?"

"The Galveston Inn. We'll stay there tonight and leave at first light. The Triple-C is about a two-day ride northwest from here."

Colt stopped around the corner from the hotel and shrugged out of his duster. He held it out to her. "Here."

"I'm not cold."

"You could have fooled me, Peaches." His gaze slid over her, drinking in the swell of her luscious breasts spilling over the top of her corset. Two mouth-watering impressions appeared where her erect nipples pressed against the satin garment.

Her attention followed his and he'd be damned if a rosy blush didn't color her pale skin and creep up her neck. It was sight that floored him, because none of the women Colt had ever known—and there had been plenty—had ever turned such an enticing shade of pink. Not unless he was actually touching them, stroking them, or loving them. But never at just a glance.

And he would never expect it from a woman like this.

"It's not just to ward off a chill," he told her, forcing his gaze away and his mind back to business. "You need to cover up if we're going to walk into that hotel and up those stairs without causing a stir."

At that explanation she accepted it, but even wrapped in his coat she still drew attention—from the desk clerk's hungry eyes to the eager looks of several male guests smoking in the parlour. Every man paused to drink in the picture she made wearing his duster, even though nothing, was visible but a minimal amount of cleavage where the top button parted, her slender neck and her face framed with the prettiest mess of red hair he'd ever seen.

"They're looking at me."

"They're only human, sugar."

"I can't believe they're looking at *me*." A smile curved her full lips. "They're *staring*." He was surprised that she seemed to enjoy the attention. Something twisted in his gut.

He frowned at her. "You're not helping matters any by staring back."

"I'm not staring back."

He ushered her toward the staircase. "Sure looks like it to me."

"I am not. I'm simply observing them observing me."

"*Observe* that first step, sugar, or you're liable to fall flat on that pretty face of yours." He should have let her arm go, but he didn't. He kept a firm hold on it, steering her up the stairs and down first one hallway then the next.

He had to keep a low profile, he told himself. That was the only reason he was in a hurry to get her inside her room; so he could get back to his own. It certainly had nothing to do with the fact that he was touching her. The thought of someone else touching her made him want to draw his Colt and shoot something.

She wobbled and leaned against him to steady herself. His body throbbed in response. Eager. Desperate.

"We're here." He unlocked the door and urged her inside. A few seconds later, he lit an oil lamp, and its glow pushed back the shadows.

He watched as her gaze swept over the small but clean room, from the feather mattress made up with fresh cotton sheets to the washbasin. A strange expression crossed her face.

"I know it's not what you're used to," he started.

"You've got that right."

"Not a scrap of red velvet in sight."

Her gaze snapped to his. "Red velvet? Oh yeah," she said. "Not a scrap."

"But it's clean and quiet. Respectable." And that's why he had checked in here rather than taking a room over at Miss Emma's down the street. Because he'd traded in his wild, carousing ways nearly six months ago for respectability.

For his step-brothers.

Her gaze traveled from his hat to the tips of his boots and back up. Bright green eyes met his. "Funny, but you don't strike me as the respectable type."

"Looks can be deceiving."

His comment seemed to strike a nerve. She shrugged and held his duster tighter around her body. "You can say that again." She drew in a deep breath. Her breasts heaved against his coat and his mouth went bone dry.

Easy, he told himself, willing his gaze to shift anywhere, everywhere, but on her. But damned if he could manage. Her cheeks were rosy, her skin pale, her eyes bright in the lamplight. She looked as ripe as a summer peach—and he was as hungry as a bear who'd been hibernating all winter.

65

"So," she breathed, as if desperate to fill the sudden silence between them. "It's really cold out."

"Yeah." He licked his lips and told his feet to move. To turn. To hit the doorway and get while the getting was good. They didn't listen.

"For November, I mean. It is still November?"

The strangeness of her question struck him, but then she pulled in a deep breath and her breasts heaved again. The coat parted a few delicious inches and gave him a mouthwatering view of her cleavage. He forgot everything else for a few frantic heartbeats.

"It is, right? November?" He nodded and relief seemed to sweep her features. Then unease appeared as her gaze locked with his and she seemed to note his expression.

"Now you're the one staring at me."

"With a face like that, a man can't help himself." *What are you saying? What happened to respectability?*

"I think my face is a good twelve inches higher." His gaze snapped to hers and if he hadn't known better, if he hadn't known dozens of women like her in the past, all experienced and comfortable with their sexuality, he would have sworn he saw apprehension.

But that was crazy. This woman oozed sexuality, heat and a physical magnetism that were damn near impossible to resist.

"With a face *and* a body like that, a man can't help himself," he found himself saying. But it was just staring, he thought with a sigh. No touching. No peeling away the coat and the corset and stroking the satiny skin beneath. No licking her nipples until they were ripe and swollen from his touch. And certainly no kissing her until—

"Kiss me."

"What?"

"Kiss me." When he didn't move save for the furious pounding of his heart, she stepped toward him. "What am I thinking?" She moved closer. "I'm supposed to kiss you."

Before he could react to the statement—before he could so much as breathe—she pressed herself close. The soft smell of perfume and warm woman filled his nostrils and stole his hard-won control.

Her lips touched his, softly, sweetly, innocently.

Innocently?

He forced aside the crazy notion before it could take root. This woman was about as innocent as a cattle rustler caught with a steer in hand.

Seasoned. Experienced. That's what she was. That was why he'd come for her and offered such a hefty amount of gold; he needed a woman who knew how to give a man pleasure. And not just any woman, but the best.

A woman who knew how to part her lips just so, how to slide her tongue into a man's mouth and stroke and tease him just enough to get his blood pumping, to make him want more.

"Wow," she breathed when she pulled away, her eyes bright with desire, the color high in her cheeks. "I, um . . ." She licked her lips. "It's um, your turn. I kissed you, now you kiss me."

He wanted to with an urgency that made his pulse pound. He wanted her more than he'd wanted any woman in a long, long time, and so he did the only thing he could do when faced with such temptation. It was what he he'd learned to do in the past six months since he'd traded in his wild ways and settled down all right and proper-like.

He turned on his heel and strode from the room.

As much as Colt wanted to kiss her again, to press himself against her lush curves, to touch the heat between her legs and see if she felt as warm and flushed down *there* as she looked up above, he'd made a promise to his family. And if there was one vow that he intended to keep, it was that one; the very *last* thing he intended to do was bed Sinful Sinclair.

He wasn't here to sate his own lust, no matter how fiercely it raged. He was here for his step-brother. Cameron—already seventeen, yet every bit as wet-behind-the-ears as Colt had been at thirteen—needed the experienced woman on the other side of the door far more than Colt did. And he wasn't the type to share.

No. This woman was for his step-brother, and Colt didn't need her. At least that's what he told himself. But damned if the iron-hard spike throbbing in his pants didn't argue just the opposite.

"Frog's breath and tongue of yak, hear my plea and bring Sinful back!"

Sadie Sinclair opened her eyes and stared at the empty chair sitting in the corner of the dressing room. Her sister's dressing room. Her *missing* sister's dressing room.

She blinked rapidly against a sudden burst of blinding tears. She was not going to cry. Crying had never solved her problems before and it wasn't going to solve anything now. She had to think. To act. To *do*.

Staring down at her trembling hands, she damned herself for turning her back on Sinful for those few moments. But she'd needed to get her sister's robe—she hadn't wanted her to walk off the stage half-naked. Not that it would have bothered Sinful. She'd always liked showing her body, drawing looks, being the center of attention, Sadie, on the other hand, had always been content to let Sinful take center stage. Somewhat content. It wasn't as if she'd had a choice. She'd inherited their mother's powers while Sinful had inherited the woman's good looks. The problem was, they were still twins, though not identical.

Sinful had a glorious mane of golden-blonde hair, while Sadie's leaned more toward a dirty blond that was dull and lifeless and straight.

Sinful had skin like fresh milk, while Sadie tended to look too pale, even sickly when the lighting was too bright. Sinful had a curvaceous figure while Sadie was flat as an ironing board. And the eyes . . . Sinful's were a vivid blue while Sadie had been cursed with dark brown.

Still, they *were* twins in every other sense. Inside, where it really counted. They thought the same. Shared the same facial expressions. Their voices even sounded similar.

Born just seconds apart, Sinful and Sadie Sinclair were forever linked. They were two halves of the same whole. And they needed each other.

Sadie's powers just didn't seem to work right unless Sinful was there to reassure her, just as Sinful's sex appeal wasn't at its peak, despite the garter, unless Sadie was nearby. Sure, the scrap of satin *was* magical, but it wasn't nearly as powerful as it could be without Sadie to fuel its force.

Yes, they needed each other. That had always been the way of things, much to their mother's dismay. Jade Sinclair had been beautiful and powerful and she'd wanted a daughter to continue the family tradition.

Unfortunately, she'd gotten two daughters. Together, they were the spitting image of their beautiful, irresistible mother, but apart, they fell far short of Jade's expectations. She'd wanted one child. One beautiful, powerful child.

Sadie and Sinful had spent their entire lives working together, complementing one another, trying to make their mother proud, to follow in her footsteps and be everything she'd wanted them to be.

They'd been succeeding. Together. Thanks to Sadie's magic, Sinful had gained her own reputation with the men, while Sadie, thanks to her sister's strong belief in her, had made hers among her mother's people. Sadie was Jade's plain but powerful daughter. A witch.

But now . . .

She eyed her precious finger that had worked so many wonderful spells, and dread welled up inside her. She couldn't feel the tingling in her fingertip. The power. *Nothing*.

She fought back another wave of tears. This couldn't be happening to her.

It wasn't. She wouldn't let it.

Taking a deep breath, she wiggled her finger and closed her eyes. Maybe she was wrong. Maybe her gut feeling—that Sinful was far, far away—was wrong. Maybe their twin connection wasn't as strong as it used to be.

Eyes closed, she drew in another deep breath. "Lizard gizzards and eye of deer, please, please, *please,* I need Sinful here!"

Her eyes opened to the empty chair. She sniffled. Not a fishnet stocking in sight, or even a whiff of Sinful's perfume. Her sister was long gone. Far away. *Unharmed*.

The notion struck her and she embraced it.

She felt it. Sinful was, indeed, unharmed. Sadie would have known it otherwise, just the way she'd known the time her sister had fallen and broken her arm when they'd been five. She'd felt the same pain in her own arm then. And when Sinful had lost her virginity, Sadie had felt the pain as well. She knew when her sister was angry or sad, hurting or lonely.

The only thing she sensed now was confusion, and distance.

She couldn't do anything about the confusion part, except send good thoughts her sister's way. But the distance . . . She could damn well do something about that. She could find her.

She *would* find her.

But first she had to find her sister's impersonator. The woman knew the truth about Sinful's whereabouts. She'd undoubtedly had something to do with her sister's abduction. All Sadie had to do was catch up to her.

She walked over to the window and stared at the street below. The lively play of a piano drifted from upstairs, along with the sound of laughter and chaos. A wagon rumbled by. Her gaze swept the buildings lining the opposite side, before pausing on one in particular. The hotel.

A dozen other possibilities raced through her mind. Perhaps the woman a had place in town, clothes stashed, a wagon waiting to carry her away. . . . The scenarios were endless, but she had to start somewhere.

She retrieved the knife and slid it underneath her skirt. Her finger wasn't going to do the job, so Sadie had to be prepared.

The woman would either talk and spill her guts, or Sadie would just have to spill them for her.

The thought sent a wave of revulsion through her. She'd never been the bloodthirsty sort. Then again, this was her livelihood at stake. Her power. Her pride. Her sister. And a girl had to do what a girl had to do. But maybe she could find her sister before she had to do it.

She'd kissed him. Elizabeth had actually taken the lead and kissed *him*.

Of course she had, she told herself. This was the chance she'd been waiting for. And she would have kissed him again if he hadn't turned and run.

Elizabeth touched a hand to her trembling lips and tried to slow her pounding heart. If Colt had spoken truly about his experience, and this is what he did to her as an untried novice, she didn't even want to think about what would happen once he'd practiced his technique a few more times. She would faint for sure.

She paused. That would be a dead giveaway that she wasn't nearly the cool, experienced woman he thought her to be.

The woman she was, she reminded herself. Deep, down inside she *was* a wild person. She was simply cutting her teeth. She shouldn't be too hard on herself. This was the first time she had been able to cut loose. The shock would eventually pass and she would relax and be herself. Her true self: *sexy, sophisticated, experienced*.

She blushed again as she recalled her reaction. No experienced woman would say something as naive as *wow*. Ugh. She had to get over this initial nervousness, to really open up and crawl out of her shell. And she wasn't going to do it by sitting on the bed and reliving the past few moments. The only way she was going to really cut loose was to get on with things. To find this cowboy and make a few more exciting moments.

Or at least find out a few more details about where she was.

It was still November, but she had no clue as to the exact date, or the exact year. Not to mention she had no clue where they were ultimately going. His ranch, but where was that?

She got to her feet and crossed the hardwood floor to the washbasin in the far corner. She ran her hands along the porcelain, felt its coolness against her hand. It was white and simple, and looked like something she might pick up at an antique shop for a production for one of her clients.

But it was *real*. The thought made her shiver with a mixture of apprehension and delight.

Her gaze swept the room again. So this was what an old-fashioned hotel looked like. It in no way compared with the saloon gambler–dancing girl fantasy she'd produced a few years back. The hotel room she'd obtained had been posh, with lots of velvet and brocade and a functional toilet—her clients wanted fantasy, after all, not hardship.

But this was *her* own fantasy. Her chance to be a woman who was bold and brave and daring. A woman who went after what she wanted. A woman who would haul open the closed door to her room and face her destiny. . . .

Okay, she thought as she did so, maybe she was facing the three men from The Red Parlour Room rather than her destiny. Three scowling men carrying three very lethal-looking pistols.

Uh-oh.

"You didn't think we was just gonna let you git away, now didya, sweetness?"

Before she could answer, she found herself backed into the room. The door slammed shut and the men closed in.

"Don't—" The protest faded into a grunt as the biggest man caught her in the stomach with his shoulder and folded her over his beefy body.

The bed creaked under her weight and she found herself sprawled on her back before she could breathe, much less scream.

Scream. Now there was an idea—

"Don't even think it." The cold press of a gun barrel near her temple stifled the sound in her throat. "You raise your voice and it'll be the last time you raise anything. I guaran-damn-tee it."

Beefy hands locked around her ankles and she realized what was about to happen. What *was* happening. Oh, God, they couldn't mean to . . .

"You can't do this," she blurted out, struggling against the strong hands.

"We shore as shootin' can, honey."

"You *shouldn't* do this."

"I got three hundred dollars says we should. 'Course, that's not nearly what you got. Is it, Sinful?"

The name echoed through her head and sent a burst of hope through her. "It's not me," she rushed on, an hysterical laugh bubbling on her lips. "I'm not Sinful. I'm *not*."

"Yeah, yeah."

"Really. My name is Elizabeth Joanna Carlton. You can check my driver's license." That garnered her three strange looks. "I mean, you could check my driver's license if I had it with me, which I don't. I left my purse back in the dressing room and—"

"—my name is Buffalo Bill. And this here's Billy the Kid. Now loosen up them legs, woman."

"You're making a mistake. I'm not her."

"There's a room full of men back there says you are."

"It's the garter making them think that. Making them think I'm sexy and wild, but I'm not. I'm anything but sexy and wild, and I haven't been with a thousand men and—"

"She's telling the truth," the smallest man cut in. "Heard tell it was a thousand and fifty."

"It's a thousand and fifty-one," said the medium one.

"Says who?" Skinny countered.

"Says me," Medium said.

"And that's s'posed to mean somethin'?"

"Sure enough—"

"Would you boys just shut the hell up?" Burly scowled at the other two men. "I don't care if she's bedded down with two thousand fellas. It ain't none of our concern."

"It was just one," Elizabeth heard herself saying. *When one was this close to having her legs pried apart by three redheaded thugs, one should stall.* "And it wasn't a bed. It was the sofa in my father's study, and it wasn't even great, much less legendary. Not that I thought it would be. I mean, I did think it might be a little fun, but not great. I never would have expected great from Greg. He was sort of cute, but not *cute*-cute."

She knew she was rambling, but better to ramble and have them stare at her as if she'd grown an eye in the middle of her forehead than have them touch her or kiss her or . . .

"Geeky," she blurted. "He was one-hundred-percent geek and as inexperienced as me, which was probably why things were so awkward and he couldn't even figure out where to put his—"

"Hush up now." Burly glared at her, grabbing at her legs as she tried to kick free of his grip. "Jes' hush up and let us get on with this."

"That's right," Medium piped in. "It'll be over and done with real quick-like if you just keep your knees to yourself."

"And those teeth." Skinny drew back and looked at his hand as Elizabeth tried to take a bite. "You damn near broke the skin!"

"I'm not going to let you do this," she told them, summoning her courage. "If you think it's going to be easy, just forget it."

"There isn't much you can do to stop us. You got somethin' we want," Burly said.

"No, I don't. I know you think you want me, but it's just because I'm wearing this garter." She shook her leg and felt the brush of satin against skin. "Without it, you wouldn't feel near the urge, believe me. I know. Men *never* feel the urge around me. Please," she gasped as he pulled her legs wider. "Please, don't."

"You can either cooperate or fight," Burly told her as he hauled her legs open with two meaty hands that clamped down tighter than vises. "Either way we're getting Mr. Ripley's ring back."

Chapter Four

A *ring?*

The word echoed through her head and stopped her cold for a long moment.

"Wait a second." She stopped struggling long enough to draw air into her lungs and eye the men. "You're looking for a *ring?*"

"Sure enough."

"And what is this? A little fun on the side?"

Burly glared at her. "There ain't nothin' fun about a woman who won't open her legs."

"Except Mabel Kennedy," Skinny said. "She couldn't open her legs on account of that bad arthritis, but she was still fun. Played a mean game of poker."

"And sang as purty as a bird," Medium added.

"And cooked like an angel," Skinny continued.

"And—"

"Enough!" Burly glared at his two partners. "Mabel was eighty-three years old. I'm talking young and strong and *fun*, and fun you ain't, lady. This is business. You've got Ripley's ring and we aim to get it back."

"But I don't—" she started, only to be cut off again by Skinny.

"It ain't really Ripley's. It's his wife's. He bought it for her and was wearin' it when he met up with you."

"Yep," Medium added. "And he sort of left it behind when he—"

"Enough!" the largest man bellowed. "In the ever-lovin' name of God, would you two put a plug in it and stop yappin'?"

"Just keepin' things straight," Skinny said with a hurt look.

"Yeah," Medium agreed. "We ain't the ones that said it was Ripley's. You did. But it ain't. Not really. It's hers," he said when his gaze fell on Elizabeth.

"It's not mine. I don't know anything about a ring. I swear."

"Maybe she's tellin' the truth," Skinny said.

"And maybe I'm gonna sprout wings and fly right out of here."

"She could be tellin' the truth," Medium said, scratching his head. "I mean, it ain't likely, but there's always a chance."

"Hell's bells, the man ain't payin' us to speculate. He's payin' us to find his ring, which is what I aim to do." He pulled at her legs.

"W-what are you doing?" Elizabeth wiggled and kicked.

"Lookin' in the last place he left it. So just cooperate and this'll be over and done with real soon."

The last place . . .

Her gaze riveted on her open legs. "You mean—"

"He didn't leave it," Skinny corrected. "He lost it."

"And I aim to find it."

"Not there you won't." Elizabeth fought against the man's grip. "I can promise you there's nothing down there. Nothing at all."

"I'll just see for—" He yelped as she kicked out at him. It landed an inch shy of her intended target and Burly let her go. *The nut cracker strikes again.*

"Reflex," she said when Medium drew a gun and shoved it into her temple. "Honest."

Burly gripped her legs and pulled them apart. "Okay, Billy," he said to Skinny. "Go on and take a look."

For all his bravado, the guy actually blushed. "Uh, not me. Let Bobby do it." He pointed to Medium. "He's much better at hide and seek than me."

"I ain't doin' it."

"I'll do it."

"No. You—" Elizabeth's words stumbled to a halt as she realized that none of the three men surrounding her had said a word. She peered past them to the shadows. Colt Durango leaned against the far wall looking calm, cool and poised as if he'd just volunteered to clean the coffee pot. Only his eyes gave away any emotion—they were dark and deadly.

"You boys better back off."

"Look, mister. We don't want no trouble. This ain't none of your worry. Our business is with the lady, here."

"Then you've got business with me," Colt told them. "The lady works for me."

"Yeah," Elizabeth said as she scrambled from the bed, outrage overtaking her. "You boys are in serious trouble. You're not going to get away with this. If I talked to the law, they'd—"

"You've got three seconds to get gone before I pull the trigger," Colt cut in, effectively killing her useless threats. Useless because in the past justice didn't lie in a courtroom. A man carried it strapped to his hip. "And don't think I can't get all three of you before you get to your guns."

"One." He began counting, his deep voice sending a ripple of fear down her spine. She couldn't help herself; she clamped her eyes shut. She was brave when it came to the nutcracker, but watching Colt shoot someone was another matter entirely. And looking into his eyes, she was sure he would.

"Two."

Boots scraped as the three men scrambled for

the exit. A door slammed and Elizabeth's heart pounded with relief.

"They're gone," she breathed, relief flooding through her as she cracked open an eye and stared at the now-empty room.

"Not for long. Come on," he told her as he took her arm. His skin burned on hers, sending a warmth through her that chased away the cold of fear. Or maybe it was the way his thumb stroked her cheek and smoothed a tear when she hadn't even realized she'd been crying.

He was sexy and handsome *and* nice.

Forget fantasy. This guy was nothing short of a full-blown dream. And he was all hers.

For the next three weeks, that was.

Fourth door on the left.

The desk clerk's instructions echoed in Sadie's head as she topped the stairs and started down the hallway of one of Galveston's busiest hotels. She couldn't believe her luck. Her first stop and she'd found Sinful. One mention of her sister's name and the desk clerk's face had lit with recognition. He'd seen a beautiful, attractive woman, all right. The most beautiful, attractive woman to ever walk through the doorway of the Galveston Inn.

Yep, it was her sister, all right, and she was here with a man.

Sadie fought down a wave of panic. Not because her sister was with a man. That was the only thing about tonight that seemed normal.

No, the problem was that Sinful, despite her weakness for a handsome man and a pocketful of gold, would never just up and disappear without telling Sadie something. No matter how powerful or how rich the man in question was.

Even Jackson Ripley, back in New Orleans, hadn't been enough to lure her sister away without an explanation.

The man had hired Sinful for a night with an obscene sum of money and then whisked her right off the stage and into a waiting carriage. Even then, despite the haste of their departure and the gold dancing in her pockets, Sinful had slipped a note to Sadie regarding her whereabouts.

Sadie had checked with the doorman several times before leaving The Red Parlour Room. No notes. No words of explanation. Nothing. Just her missing sister and an impostor.

No, something strange was going on, and Sadie intended to get to the bottom of it and find her sis—

Bam! A door slammed open just ahead of her, cutting off her train of thought and sending another wave of panic skittering through her. She ducked back into the nearest doorway, her heart racing faster than a stampede of longhorn cattle.

It wasn't just any door that had opened. It was *the* door. Fourth one on the left.

Her mind raced as three redheaded men barreled out into the hallway. *Three*. The desk clerk hadn't mentioned three men. Three angry men. Three angry men with guns.

Her heart jumped into her throat as she grappled for the doorknob behind her. A few frantic breaths later, she retreated into a pitch-black room. The door closed with rusty groan and a soft thud.

She didn't know what was going on, but she had a feeling it wasn't good. And Sadie always trusted her feelings. It was the one thing that had come with her power that was hers and hers alone. Her instinct. Her gut feeling.

These men were bad news, and they wanted to harm her sister. She wasn't likely to do Sinful any good by charging forward before she knew exactly what she was up against.

She dropped to her knees and peered through the keyhole.

In a slap of boots and a rumble of heated curses, the men scrambled down the hallway, headed toward her. She crouched even lower, straining her ears to hear what they were saying as they went by.

". . . catch up to Sinful later," one of the men was saying.

"We need her now," grumbled another.

"I ain't messin' with that cowboy."

"I ain't messin' with him either," came a third voice.

"Let 'em have Sinful if'n he wants her."

"Yep, let him have her."

"Like hell. She's got somethin' we want. The boss ain't payin' us to go givin' up."

"He ain't payin' us nearly enough to face down the barrel of a shotgun."

"Damn straight."

"It was just a bluff and you're both just a couple of full-blooded chickens. Why, there's three of us with three Colts between us. What's that cowboy got?"

"His own gun."

"One against three," one of the men pointed out.

"And plenty of bad attitude."

"Yep, bad all the way."

"Dammit, we're the Redd brothers."

"And I aim to stay a livin', breathin' Redd brother."

"Yep, me, too."

"Chickens . . ." The voices faded as the men descended the stairs and left Sadie to her pounding heart and her frenzied thoughts.

Sinful. The name echoed in her head.

Yes, her sister was here, all right. Relief rushed through her and she reached for the knob. Just as she started to pull, another door opened. She let go and dropped to her knees again. A few frantic heartbeats later, a man and woman passed through her line of vision. It was *the* woman who'd waltzed off the stage in place of her twin.

"You really think they'll come back?"

"You really think they won't?" The cowboy

steered the woman past the closed door where Sadie crouched. "They want you, Sinful. They aren't going away that easy. They'll be after us, and we'll be long gone."

Sinful? Wait a second. That woman wasn't her sister.

"Come on, Sinful. Get a move on."

Sinful. The cowboy actually thought that woman was her sister.

The knowledge sank in as the sound of footsteps faded. *Faded*, as in going away, as in she had to catch up to them. While the woman wasn't her sister, she was the only connection Sadie had left to Sinful. The woman might now what had happened. She *had* to know. She'd switched places with Sinful on stage in front of dozens of men in a trick that would have done any magician proud. Yes, she knew.

Sadie gripped the doorknob and pulled. And pulled. And pulled.

It was locked.

She forced the notion away. It couldn't be locked. It had to be stuck. She pulled harder, fighting with the stupid knob until she heard voices below. She turned and rushed toward the window in time to see the man and woman emerge and head for the stables down the street.

They were getting away!

She turned back and flew to the door. Retrieving the knife from her bodice, she went to work on the stubborn knob, scraping and twisting and prying. If she could just get the blade into the crevice . . . there!

Yanking open the door, she started for the stairs, only to turn on her heel and rush back to the room. Just to be sure. While they'd called the woman Sinful, there was nothing to say that the man wasn't in on the charade. Her sister could be bound and gagged and sitting in the hotel room right now waiting for help.

Her slim hopes plummeted when she found the room empty, the bed a mess of tangled quilts and sheets. There was no sign of anyone, let alone her sister.

Gone.

She closed her eyes and sent out a mental cry to Sinful. She would know if her twin needed her. She would sense it. Wouldn't she?

She forced the doubts away. She had enough of those without entertaining more. But she could trust her gut. Now her powers . . . those were a different matter altogether. She needed her sister in order to use her powers. Sinful fed her courage. She was the other half of the perfect whole, and Sadie needed her.

She took off back down the stairs and hit the street in time to see two figures disappear on horseback. She was too late. Tears burned her eyes, but she fought them back. She had to stay strong. Calm. She had to think!

First things first, she needed to find a horse. The thought sent her toward the stables where she came up short just outside. A familiar voice carried from inside.

"Are too gonna follow them."

"Are not."

"Are too."

She peeked into the stables and spied the three redheaded men.

"We ain't," said the smallest one. He was puny in her opinion, although he did have a nice face. And really pretty dark eyes that caught the flare of his match as he finished rolling his cigarette and lit the tip while the other two men loaded their horses, obviously intent on going somewhere.

"We're following them. I ain't stuck with the job this long, following that gal all the way from New Orleans just to give up now. I want that money."

"There's more to life than money," the puny man said.

"Says who?" The question came from the third man, medium-sized compared to the two on either side of him. "Money's reliable. Money ain't gonna go flirtin' around with Earl Grayberry."

"Cain't you just forget that woman?"

"She's forgotten." The medium-sized man jerked at the cinch on the saddle. "History. And history ain't repeatin' itself. Money," he quipped. "That's what it's all about."

"Well you two might be of a mind to get your

heads blown off on account of some money, but I ain't."

"Chicken." The largest man made a few cackling noises, drawing a frown on the puny man's face. "You're chicken, boy. Shoulda known. The runt of the litter is always chicken."

"I ain't chicken."

"Are too."

"Are not."

"I'm saddlin' up, ain't I?"

"Looks more like you're talkin' than saddlin'."

The puny man took a last drag on his cigarette and tossed it aside before reaching for his saddle. "There," he announced as he draped the leather over the animal's back. "I'm saddlin'."

The next few minutes passed in a flurry of bickering and teasing, while Sadie stood outside the doorway and came up with a plan.

It was really good plan, as long as she could keep her wits and her confidence and pull it off. Butterflies danced in her stomach as the men started to walk out. She could do this. She would do this. She *had* to do this. There was no way she could follow the woman on her own. She didn't know the first thing about tracking. The men were her best bet. Now to convince them of that.

She drew in a deep breath and started forward.

The largest man was the first to catch sight of her as she walked into the stables in a rustle of hay and straight up to the smallest one. She eyed his horse. "This should be just about right," she announced.

"What are you talking about?"

"For riding. I'm small and you're small." She eyed the puny one. "The two of us should fit just about right, unless you gentlemen have an extra horse hiding around here somewhere."

"Two of us?"

"Gentlemen?"

"Extra horse?"

The three comments sounded simultaneously.

"Yes, yes and yes," she told them. "I'm riding along with you all."

"You're *what*?"

"I'm going after the same people you are, so there's no reason for us to ride separately. We might as well join forces and help each other."

"Listen, lady," the big man started, "I don't know who the hell you are, but—"

"Sadie. My name is Sadie, not lady."

"You ain't comin' with us." The man shook his head and stared at her as if she had three of them. "You sure as hell ain't."

"Yes, I am."

"No, you're not."

"Yes."

"No."

"Yes."

"*No.*"

"Are you sure about that?"

"You're damn straight."

91

"That's a shame. I didn't want to have to do this, but you're not giving me much choice." She pointed her finger at them and put on her most intimidating glare. "Say good-bye to Mr. Willie."

"Mister who?"

"Your . . ." She let her gaze drop to the body part in question. "Like I said, I didn't want to have to do this. Not that it's painful or anything. At least the last man didn't complain. He just cried. But I think that was more because he was envisioning a lonely, vast future all by his lonesome."

"You're crazy, lady."

"I'm not crazy."

"Are too."

"Are not."

"Are too."

"Are not."

"I'm a witch," she admitted.

"Damn straight on that," the big man said. "You're acting like a full-blown bi—"

"That's *witch*," she cut in. "And I can zap you in the blink of an eye." She waggled her finger south. "So you'd better watch it."

"—Witch?"

"—Zap?"

"—Watch out?"

The comments came simultaneously again.

"That's right." She pointed her finger at the three men, waving it from left to right. "And this is my zapper."

"That's a finger," one man pointed out.

"That's right."

"So it's a *finger*."

She glared. "And your point is?"

"That it's a finger and you're obviously a few straws of hay shy of a bale," the puny one with the nice eyes said. They were very nice eyes. "No disrespect intended." He had manners, too.

"Dammit, Billy." The big man cuffed the little one on the shoulder. "We can disrespect her if we want. She's plumb loco." The large man glared. "Look, unless you want us to get rough, I'd suggest you just mosey on back where you come from."

She tilted her head back and stared up at the man, fighting down a wave of fear. Ordinarily, she wouldn't have been the least bit afraid. But this was different. This wasn't flaunting her talents, this was bluffing.

She needed to get her powers back. In order to do that, she needed to find her sister, which meant she needed to find the woman, which meant she needed to make these men afraid.

Or at least a little doubtful.

"I'm a witch," she stated again.

A roar of laughter erupted around them. "You expect us to believe that?"

"Believe what you want. It's the truth."

"Ain't no such thing."

"There is," she insisted.

"Ain't."

"Is."

"Ain't."

"Look, the way I see it, you boys got two choices here. You act real smart-like, take me along and everything will be fine. "Or"—she let her gaze drop for effect—"you can refuse and find out for yourself that I'm telling the truth." She let her gaze sweep across each man at belt-level. "But I'm warning you right now, I ain't got no handkerchief, so no crying."

A moment of silence ticked by and she braced herself. They were going to refuse her and she was going to have to resort to a little crying of her own. It wouldn't be a pretty sight. Sadie had never been a beauty, and, crying, she was down-right frightening. But a girl had to do what a girl—

"Come on," the big man grumbled.

Yessssssssss!

"I'm stuck in the middle of a nightmare," Elizabeth muttered. It was late the next day—much later, after an entire night and nearly a full day spent on horseback. The sun was just starting to sink below the horizon. She straightened from where she'd been kneeling by the river. Pain jolted through her, pulsing from her sore bottom to every nerve. She straightened the oversized shirt she wore—she'd borrowed clothing of Colt's—and tugged up the too-large pants. They weren't exactly the slacks and blouses she was used to, but the new attire was better than prancing around the countryside wearing a corset, and little else.

The clothing would do, at least until they got to where they were going and she could purchase something more suitable.

She stepped toward her winded horse and winced. "Where's a nice, comfortable cab when I need one?"

"A cab?" Colt's deep voice drew her around to see him standing by the creek bed, his shirt hanging open, water glistening like diamonds in the dark hair covering his chest.

He shook the cup he'd been washing out and the muscles in his torso rippled. Her mouth went dry and she licked her lips. "A cab?" she repeated his question, her mind barely registering the remark, while her body registered the heat that he stirred. This guy definitely rang a ten on her lust-o-meter.

"You said you need a cab." He stepped closer to her. "What's that?"

"A cab?" She swallowed again and followed a drop of water as it dripped down his rippled abdomen to where it disappeared into the waistband of his pants.

"That's right," he said. The sound of his voice, cool but amused, drew her gaze up. "What are you talking about?"

"I meant—That is, I said—A *cat*," she finally blurted. "I—I really need my cat. I never go anywhere without her."

He gave her another odd look before his gaze

went to her flushed face. "Are you okay?"

"I'm not used to riding." He looked startled and she quickly realized her mistake. Horses were the primary means of transportation, and there likely weren't too many people who hadn't done a good amount of riding. "I'm allergic to horse hair," she amended. She rubbed her nose for good measure. "I break out just watching Mr. Ed."

"Mister who?"

"Never mind." She pretended to have another itch. "Horses make me flush."

He reached out and caught a drop of perspiration that slid down her temple. His callused fingertip sent a shiver through her. "Don't forget the sweating. Horses must make you sweat."

She swallowed, eager to ignore the way his eyes caught the waning sunlight and sparkled. "Uh, yeah. They, um, definitely make me sweat."

"I had a buckboard all ready for us to rent this morning," Colt said, "but those three cowboys changed our plans." They'd ridden out of Galveston the night before, fleeing on horseback like a couple of thieves. Elizabeth hadn't wanted to stick around to see if the Three Red-headed Pigs would come back. Colt gave her an appraising look. "Were those guys friends of yours?"

"Did they look like friends?"

"They did look like they were about to get awful friendly, darlin'." He glanced at the darkening horizon. "Still might if we don't stay ahead of them. But we've got enough of a head start to camp out for the night. I can't imagine that they'd ride as hard as we have, and I covered our trail as best I could."

"You really think they'll follow us?"

He arched a brow at her. "You really think they won't?" When she didn't answer, he added, "Seems to me a ring is all they wanted. You could always give it back."

"If I had it, I would." When he didn't say anything, she pinned him with a stare. "You don't believe me, do you?"

He shrugged, turning back toward his horse. He started untying his saddlebags. "Doesn't really matter if I do, sugar."

But it did. It was crazy, but she wanted him to believe her. To believe *in* her.

She shook away the notion. How could she expect him to trust her? She was supposed to be Sinful Sinclair. To be wild and wanton, exactly the sort of woman a man might lose a ring to. *In*to. She shuddered.

"You don't believe me," she stated as she followed him to a nearby clearing where he dropped his saddlebags.

He turned toward her and tipped his hat back on his head. "All that concerns me is keeping you safe for the next three weeks until our business is over and done with."

Business. The word echoed through her mind, reminding her of the "business" of last night, of the way his mouth had felt moving against hers. She couldn't help herself. She licked her lips.

His gaze followed the movement and the air stalled in her lungs. He was giving her the same look she'd seen those few moments before she'd found her nerve and kissed him.

The want. The lust. The need.

There was something about him that drew her, that stirred her. Her heart pounded. Her body ached. Her hands trembled.

These were going to be the best three weeks of her life.

"We'd better get started," he told her.

"My thoughts exactly." Her fingers went to the top button of her shirt. The best three weeks starting now.

"On the fire," he said as she slid the first button free.

"That's already blazing." The moment she'd seen him dripping with water and grinning at her, the first flame had flared to life.

"The *camp*fire," he clarified just as she slid the second button free.

"Campfire?" Her fingers stalled, trembling as her gaze met his. He grinned, but there was nothing teasing in his eyes. Just heat. And regret.

Regret?

Before she could dwell on the strangeness of that, he turned away. So much for getting a start on his lessons.

"It'll be dark soon," he told her. "And cold."

A girl could only hope. She drew in a shaky breath and slid the second button back into place. Her cheeks burned, but not half as much as her body, a heat that followed her for the next hour as she helped Colt collect wood and set up camp. She needed the evening cold in the worst way.

Unfortunately, the falling temperature wasn't nearly enough to calm her down. By the time she collapsed next to the blazing campfire and accepted the canteen he handed her, she was still on fire, and her stomach was jumpy. She was anxious. Hungry.

He grinned as a gurgling sound vibrated the air. "Here." He handed her a piece of the squirrel he'd roasted.

"I'll pass." Another grumble and she grinned. "Maybe just a bite. A *little* bite." She was living a fantasy, but in her fantasies she was much thinner.

Unfortunately the meat was much tastier than it looked and she soon finished off the morsel. Her stomach grumbled for another.

"You've got a healthy appetite," he said, handing her another piece.

"Thanks a lot."

"That's a good thing."

"Not for my hips." At his questioning look, she added, "They're already too big."

"Says who?"

"Calvin Klein and his size-ten jeans hanging in my closet. So when do we get to where we're

99

going?" she rushed on, eager to move onto a safer, and smaller, subject.

"Tomorrow. The Triple-C is still about a half-day's ride northwest from here."

"Let me guess. The C stands for Colt?"

"Actually, it stands for Cameron, Cain and Colt; the other two are my step-brothers. It was my pa's place up until six months ago. His dream. He bought it when the boys were just babies and built it up into one of the biggest horse ranches in Texas."

"And where were you?"

"Everywhere but where I should have been." At her raised eyebrows, he added, "I wasn't much for staying in one place. There isn't a saloon I haven't been inside of, a street I haven't walked, or a card game I haven't played." A strange glimmer lit his eyes as he spoke, and Elizabeth had the feeling that Colt Durango missed those things a lot more than he wanted to admit. "But I'm through moving around. The Triple-C is my home now."

"I've never been to a real ranch, unless you count those ten acres up near Kingsville, but that was a used-to-be ranch that hadn't seen a cow in at least twenty years." She'd leased the place for a banker and his wife who'd wanted to play the poor ranch widow, her husband the outlaw bandit who takes her hostage for a night. It was classic anonymity fantasy, the one Elizabeth's assistant Jenna called "taken by a faceless stranger." It was the number four fantasy of Isabella X's Naughty Nine.

Elizabeth had to agree. Eight years in the business and she'd been asked to set up the faceless stranger scenario, in various forms, more times than she could count. Almost as often as she'd had requested "the audience," which was number six.

Her gaze strayed around her to the shimmering creek, the moon full and bright overhead. Crickets buzzed and a coyote howled somewhere in the distance. The fire crackled, drawing her gaze to the flames, to the man visible on the other side of them. His dark eyes stared back at her over the rim of his coffee cup.

She was smack dab in the middle of an audience fantasy right now, in its most simplistic form: Mother Nature was the onlooker, surrounding them, watching and listening and encouraging.

The wind whipped softly, slipping into her partly unbuttoned shirt and blowing across her nipples. Heat sizzled along her nerve endings.

"I don't think I've ever heard of Kingsville," he said, his deep voice sliding into her ears and sending a bolt of electricity down her spine.

"It's just a few miles up Highway—" She caught her bottom lip as the absurdity of what she was saying hit her. "I—It's not a very big town," she finally finished. "Only a few thou— thoughtless," she amended. "Only a few thoughtless people." *Thoughtless?*

Okay, so she'd never been good at quick saves. She liked to think and plan. That's why she'd been so good at her job; she was great at thinking, at fantasizing. Much better at that than at living. And it had never been a problem.

No more. She was living the fantasy now. Colt Durango was right here, staring at her from across a flickering campfire, the moon shining high in the sky above them. She couldn't have envisioned a more perfect scenario.

Or a more perfect man.

He didn't move. He simply eyed her from the other side of the fire. Watching. Waiting.

Okay, so maybe he could have been a little more perfect. He could have said something suggestive, or better yet, he could have made a move instead of just sitting there.

He wanted to kiss her. She could see it in his intense expression, feel it in the expectancy stretching between them.

"Better turn in," he said, tossing the last of his coffee onto the fire. It broke the strange connection that had forged between them for those few seconds. Flames hissed, shooting sparks as he turned away. He threw her a blanket, then settled onto his own bedroll.

After a while, she realized he wasn't going to kiss her.

Duh. Of course he wasn't. He was paying her, not the other way around. Obviously he wasn't comfortable making the first move. Last night proved that. She'd had to kiss him. And when he'd been asked to kiss her back, he'd run off.

Intimacy obviously wasn't Colt Durango's friend. Apparently he liked to play hard-to-get. But with any luck, Elizabeth—as Sinful—was going to change all that.

She was going to earn every bit of Colt's gold. Starting now.

The fire crackled and her covers rustled as she threw them off. She crept around to his side of the fire.

Elizabeth leaned over and paused, her heart in her throat. He was so handsome, so warm and masculine and real. And she was going to kiss him and touch him, despite the doubts rushing through her. She *was*—

A strange snorting noise shattered her intention and stopped her cold.

Panic bolted through her as she leaned over him. Maybe he was choking. Asphyxiating. *Dying*. But from what?

Soft breath rushed against her lips as he exhaled. Then his chest rose, his nostrils flaring, and the sound echoed in her ears again, even louder since she leaned so close.

She chided herself for being silly. Snoring. The man was *snoring*.

She leaned back and stared down at him, at his handsome face and the dark sweep of lashes on his tanned cheeks. He was so handsome. So masculine.

So clueless.

The man was *snoring!*

No wonder he had to hire a woman to teach him about sex. He was certainly up to speed in the kissing department, but he obviously fell asleep before he got to the really good stuff.

She nudged him once. Twice. The only thing that stirred was another great big snore. Her gaze shifted to his canteen and she reached for it and unscrewed the lid. Twisting it, she was very close to dribbling a few drops onto his sleeping face when her conscience hit her.

As she eyed his peaceful features, a strange warmth spread through her, and for a moment she thought she might actually like watching Colt Durango sleep even more than she liked watching him sip his coffee.

A day's growth of beard darkened his jaw. A dark lock of hair fell across his forehead and she couldn't help herself—she reached out and brushed the soft-as-silk strands aside, her fingertips gliding across his forehead.

A sharp intake of breath echoed in her eardrums, but when her gaze snapped to his chest, she saw that it rose and fell rhythmically, giving no indication that the sound had been anything more than her own wishful thinking, her own fanciful imagining that he'd actually felt her touch.

She sighed, lifted the canteen to her own mouth and took a long slug, praying with all her heart that the contents would be enough to quench the fire that burned inside her—because that was all she was getting tonight.

No kissing or touching and . . . *No*.

They'd had a long day and he was obviously exhausted. She knew the feeling. Her own muscles ached at even the tiniest movement. She needed some rest herself.

"Besides, I'm more of a morning person," she said, trying to talk herself out of the state of ultra-awareness she was in. If she was turned on tonight, despite the cold and the exhaustion, she'd be even better come morning, and she wanted to be at her best. She needed to be in top form if she had any hope of doing Sinful's reputation proud.

Not right now, certainly. She would do best to let him rest for now. He had to open his eyes sooner or later, and when he did, she would be right there. Ready, willing and eager with lesson number one.

"Go away." Elizabeth swatted the hand tickling her cheek.

"Time to get up."

She cracked an eye open to the surrounding darkness. "The sun's not even up yet."

"Sure it is, darlin'. If you crane your neck and peer over them treetops, you can just see it coming up."

"I don't want to see it coming up. I want to sleep." She snuggled deeper into the horsehair blanket.

"We've got to get a move on."

"You move on and I'll stay right here." She

tugged her cover up over her face, only to have it pulled back down. A split-second later, it disappeared entirely. Her eyes snapped open to see Colt Durango's tall shadow looming over her, blanket in hand.

"Give that back."

"Get up and I'll give it back."

"If I get up, I don't need you to give it back."

His grin split the surrounding darkness and a strange tickling sensation spread through her. "That's the idea."

She scowled. "If I had a gun right now, I'd shoot you dead."

"I thought you were a morning person."

"I am. It's not morning. It's still dark out . . ." The words trailed off as she stared up into Colt's face, his dancing green eyes. "You were supposed to be sleeping."

"Surprise. I wasn't."

"But you were snoring."

"I don't snore."

"Yes, you do."

"Not half as loud as you."

"*I* don't snore." She snatched the blanket from his hands.

"Sure sounded like snoring to me."

"Well, it wasn't."

"Sure it was."

"No it wasn't." She wasn't sure why she was arguing with him. Maybe she did snore. But it was the principle of the thing. No woman wanted to think that she snored, especially with her fantasy man only a few feet away. "I don't snore in my sleep. I've never snored in my sleep."

"Is that what they tell you?"

The only *they* in her life amounted to two cats and a St. Bernard, but she wasn't about to tell him that. She was supposed to be Sinful Sinclair. One-hundred-percent femme fatale and not the sort of woman who got around to much *sleeping* in a bed, let alone snoring in one.

What was she worrying about? She *was* Sinful deep down inside. Wasn't that what she'd been telling herself for years? She was wild. Wicked. Daring.

"I can't say that I've ever had a complaint." If she hadn't known better, she would have sworn she saw his shoulders stiffen, as if the notion of her bed partners bothered him. Which was crazy, of course. He'd sought her out precisely because she was experienced.

"A man ain't inclined to complain when he's floated clear to Heaven," Colt said, perhaps a bit too quickly.

A smile tugged at her lips as she snatched up her blanket and settled back down. All at once, his hand made contact with her rump and she jumped, scrambling upright and glaring. "What the hell did you do that for?"

"We have to get moving, unless you're up for another mattress tumble with those three men from the hotel."

"There are no mattresses out here."

107

Kimberly Raye

"That would make things more interesting, certainly."

A few nasty possibilities rushed through her head and she found herself climbing to her feet. "If that man was so concerned with what his wife thought, he should have kept his pants on and his ring to himself," she grumbled.

"You make it awful hard when you turn that delicious shade of pink, Peaches. Awful hard."

And Colt Durango had the aching body part to prove it. Despite the fact that Sinful Sinclair had a mess of hair, her eyes rimmed with black stuff and a blanket crease across her flushed cheek.

Was she really flushed?

Yes. He noted the pink of her skin, the way her eyes darted away when he stared just a little too long.

She really was something. If Colt hadn't known better, he might have thought she was actually embarrassed.

But he knew better. Even if he hadn't known this woman's reputation, the quick way she'd reached for her buttons last night would have told him she'd done it many, many times before. That and the lust in her eyes. An innocent didn't stare with such hunger, such need. But her blush was truly convincing. . . .

Yep, she was something all right. Experienced and practiced and—completely off-limits.

His head knew that. Now if his body would just get the dadblamed message. With a head shake of annoyance, he lifted himself onto his saddle.

It was the longest, most miserable ride of Elizabeth's life. Every inch of her body ached by the time they rode up to the sprawling ranch. The afternoon sun had warmed the air considerably.

"This is your place?"

"Our place. Mine and my stepbrothers'. It was my pa's, but he's gone now. It's just me and the boys."

"I'm sorry."

"Yeah, me too. Giddyup!" Colt kicked his horse into a gallop, riding past the house and heading for a cabin just a little off the main house.

"You'll be staying here. This place used to be Horseshoe's. He's my ranch foreman, but he moved into the house to help with Cain. He's the youngest." He dismounted and pulled off his gloves. A few seconds later, he stared up at her. "Come on down."

"I don't think I can move. My butt is permanently attached to the saddle."

He grinned and reached up a hand. "You have to move."

"I'll just sit here."

"Saddle sores."

"What?"

"You keep sitting there and you're going to get saddle sores—if you don't already have them."

Ugh. This fantasy was getting better and better by the minute.

She let him help her down, her pain quickly forgotten for those few seconds as she felt Colt Durango's strong fingers press into her waist and his hard body brush the length of hers.

Hard. The word conjured up other images in her head for as he held her, stared down at her. Did he want her to . . .

Colt let go and turned away, and Elizabeth was left to wonder if she'd only imagined the past few moments. A curiosity that quickly faded as the first jolt of pain went through her.

She managed by sheer will to follow him into the small cabin, her muscles aching. A bed had never looked so good. She sank down onto the edge and vowed never, ever to take another ride for as long as she lived. Her thighs hurt. Her bottom ached.

"I'll give you a little time to settle in," he told her as he turned toward the doorway. "Then we'll get started."

"On what?"

He cast a glance over his shoulder and gave her a smile. "The lessons, Peaches."

Her heart pounded and heat flowered low in her belly. Anticipation. Excitement. Need.

Okay, so maybe she could talk herself into one more ride.

Chapter Five

Yesssssss!

The pain in Elizabeth's body faded into a rush of excitement as she sat up. She'd fallen asleep, briefly. Resting on the bed had been too much of a temptation for her sore muscles. But now she was awake and ready for Colt. Ready to get on with her new self . . . until she turned and glimpsed her reflection in the small oval mirror hanging near the bed. Next to it was a wash-bowl.

Forget fantasy—she was stuck in a nightmare. Only in a bad dream could she look so hideous. Her hair, windblown and two days shy of a good conditioner, went this way and that. Sweat dotted her brow. Trail dust caked her face and neck. Leftover mascara rimmed her eyes. Her lips were chapped and her nose was red and Colt Durango was coming back in who knew how long.

That last thought spurred her into action. She poured water from a nearby pitcher into the washbowl and rushed around the room searching for something—anything—with which to wash.

She'd waited too long, wanted for too long. She wasn't going to blow this, no matter how awful she looked. She gathered her control and her composure and spent the next several minutes cleaning up. Her hands and a bar of soap she'd found managed to clean away much of the grime. When she finally stared into the mirror again, she looked somewhat better. Not playboy quality, but then Colt Durango had surely never seen a centerfold or a hot, buxom babe from a music video. Heck, he'd never even seen a black-and-white Victoria's Secret advertisement.

She definitely had an advantage.

Her thoughts went to the garter. She felt the press of its elastic on her thigh beneath her oversized pants, felt the caress of its lace as she walked across the room. The sensation was highly erotic, and by the time she reached the bed, her entire body thrummed.

A knock on the door sounded, followed by Colt's deep, rumbling, "We're back," and her heart shifted into overdrive.

We?

The oddness of his words struck her just as

the door opened and he walked inside. The man looked as tall and dark and delicious as ever. But it wasn't the sight of him that struck her speechless. It was the second person, the *boy*, that followed him who did.

Okay, she'd had her share of audience fantasies, but this was not really it. When she was imagining dangerous exhibitionist scenarios, she envisioned things more like hot, heated sex in an elevator, with an audience nearby but not actually watching. Or participating.

"This is my brother, Cameron. Cameron, this is Sinful."

"Pleased to meet you, ma'am," the boy said, his gaze fixed upon her. His eyes were intense, determined, but his ears were fired a bright red.

"Likewise." She turned to Colt. "I don't know if I'm really ready for this. I thought we could start with something a little more traditional—"

"Start with whatever you like. You're the teacher." And with that, Colt turned and left.

It took a few frantic seconds for his words to register. When they did, Elizabeth hit the door and flew after him. It was now night outside; she must have slept longer than she'd thought.

"But I'm supposed to be *your* teacher," she told him when she caught up to him. He was headed back to the house.

"Me?" He turned on her. Moonlight sculpted his features, playing across the fine angles and planes, making him seem darker and more dangerous, and sexy enough to take her breath away.

But he did that anyway. Whenever he looked at her a few seconds too long, or smiled or simply breathed. *He* was the one she was supposed to be training.

"Peaches, there isn't a thing you could teach me that I don't already know."

"But *you* hired me."

"Damn straight I did. For Cameron."

"You hired me to teach your stepbrother?" she breathed. The truth cemented inside her. "Not for you, but him."

"He's got his eye on this gal in town, but he's too shy to approach her. He needs some experience to boost his confidence."

"But what about you?" Elizabeth stepped closer, until she could feel the warm rush of his breath against her lips. Her skin tingled and her heart thudded. "What do you need?"

You. The answer was there in his eyes, in the way he stared down at her, hands clenched at his sides as if he fought to keep from reaching out and taking her.

At least that's what she imagined, but then his expression faded into a teasing grin as he murmured, "A good night's sleep. The crack of dawn comes awful early around these parts. Speaking of which"—he nodded toward the cabin—"don't keep him up too late. He's got chores first thing tomorrow."

"You're serious about this, aren't you? You

really want me to waltz back in there and teach your stepbrother about sex?"

"Everything you know."

"He'll definitely get to bed early then." The words slipped out before she could stop them, and while she'd meant them as a personal reference to her own meager experience, to Colt the words conveyed an altogether different meaning.

"Just go easy on him. He's seventeen, but never been with a woman before."

"Well, he's not starting now. Not with me. He's underage, for heaven's sake—and while I know that most seventeen-year-olds consider themselves old enough for sex, they usually do it with someone closer to their own age. Why, I'm old enough to be his moth—um, older sister," she blurted. She shook her head. "I can't do this."

"There's a thousand satisfied men out there who'd say otherwise."

Ha! As if. "That's just it. They were *men*. Your brother isn't."

His gaze narrowed. "A deal's a deal."

"I thought the deal was with you."

"It is with me. It's my money that's paying you."

"Then you should be the one getting the lessons."

"I don't want any lessons."

"That's not how it seemed last night. You kissed me," she reminded him.

"If I recall correctly, that was *you* kissing *me*."

"At first, but then you joined in."

A frown tugged his lips into a thin line. "Force of habit."

"That's not how it seemed to me."

"What are you trying to say?"

"That you liked kissing me. That you'd like to kiss me again." She drew in a deep breath and searched for her courage. If she was going to stay in this time, in this fantasy, then she was going to get the man she wanted. "I know I'd like for you to kiss me. Right here. Right now."

Colt leaned forward as she spoke but then, "Cameron's waiting," he murmured, jerking away just a fraction from actually pressing his lips against hers. He turned and walked away without so much as a backwards glance.

Elizabeth felt her heart sink. While Colt Durango starred in her most erotic thoughts, she obviously hadn't found her way into his.

Sure, he wanted her. She wasn't *that* naive, despite her limited experience. She knew when a man was interested. But for some insane reason, he didn't want to be interested, to give in to the lust so evident in his gaze—but he would. She hadn't studied each of Isabella's Naughty Nine for nothing. All she had to do was uncover Colt's most private fantasy and become it—then he wouldn't even think of resisting her.

In the meantime . . .

She walked to the cabin and stepped up onto the porch. Through the window, she saw Cameron seated at the sawbuck table. Tall and gangly with white blond hair and a round, babyish face that lent him an angelic air, he was nothing like his tall, dark and delicious stepbrother. Colt looked much too wicked to be heavenly. The only resemblance was the vivid blue eyes.

But where lust had filled Colt's gaze, fear filled Cameron's.

As she watched him drum a nervous tempo against the tabletop, she mentally reviewed her options. One, she could refuse to tutor Cameron Durango, and Colt would most certainly send her packing. Two, she could actually tutor Cameron—as in verbally instructing him—and Colt might possibly send her packing when he found out the truth. Three, she could do what Sinful would have done and give innocent Cameron the time of his life.

One was out. She had no intention of leaving the Triple-C and returning to her drab, ho-hum life—not until she'd garnered a few spicy memories to warm her on the cold nights to come, not until she'd let the wild woman inside her loose. Surely this would be her last and best chance.

Three was *definitely* out. Cameron was underage . . . and she didn't do minors . . . but most importantly, she wanted his brother. Which left only option number two.

She *could* give Cameron some verbal instruction. She could claim that he should start out slow and memorize all the basics before actually applying them. That would buy her a little time before he expected any hands-on guidance. That would afford her enough time to seduce Colt and force him to admit that he wanted her for himself and not for his younger stepbrother.

"You can do this," she told herself as she reached for the door latch.

She'd done some student teaching in college, actually. She'd even assisted the infamous Jane Marie Gorman, one part high school English teacher and the other part ball-buster. She'd been strict and professional and had made an hour-long English session seem like eight.

Hauling open the door, Elizabeth pulled back her shoulders, put on her best pinched expression and slid into her best Miss Gorman imitation. "School's in session."

A good night's sleep.

Now that was the best idea Colt had had in a very long time.

That's what he told himself as he headed toward the bunkhouse where he'd been camping out for the past six months since coming home to the Triple-C.

Home. The word echoed through his head, stirring the all-too-familiar restlessness in his gut. A feeling he quickly stifled. The Triple-C *was* his home, and it would be just a matter of time before it started to feel like home.

His gaze strayed to the large ranch house sitting several yards ahead. The windows were ablaze and he knew Horseshoe McAllister was probably sitting on the sofa reading bedtime stories to Cain.

Horseshoe was the best foreman ever to ride the Triple-C, and the meanest old coot ever to spit a wad of tobacco. Mean, as in tough and strict and the only reason Colt had come home in the first place. It was Horseshoe who'd had the guts to brave Hell's Mouth—a hole-in-the-wall town reserved strictly for horse thieves and cattle rustlers—just to find Colt's drunken ass and tell him about his father.

"He's gone, boy. He's gone."

The words had sobered him the way no amount of cold water ever could, and he'd been dry as parched corn ever since. And serious. And committed. *Home.* There was no turning back. No giving in to the restlessness that ate at his soul.

He was back and he was staying, and it was only a matter of time before he started to fit in with his younger stepbrothers. Right now he was little more than a stranger.

Time. That's what he told himself. His brothers needed time to adjust to him, to trust him before he claimed a permanent place in their lives. Then everything would fall into place and Colt Durango would fit in.

He would belong.

Until then . . .

The bunkhouse was already dark, every hand

having already turned in with anticipation of an early day. Colt slipped inside through the darkness and searched out a small semi-private area in the back. There was a simple cot, a small chest and a wash bowl. All the necessities as far as he was concerned. Enough to tide him over until things settled down and he started to fit in with his stepbrothers and their way of life. He didn't want to impose.

He peeled off his shirt and pants and stretched out on top of his bunk. Immediately, his thoughts went to her. To last night and the soft sound of her voice so close to his ear, the sweet rush of her breath near his face as she leaned over him.

She'd been right. He had been playing possum, in the interest of self-preservation, of course. She'd been too close, too tempting for a man who'd always been a slave to his hunger for beautiful women.

But he'd turned over a new leaf, as the preacher in town was fond of saying; he'd given up his wild and wicked vices. They had nearly gotten him killed more times than he could count.

He rolled over and punched his pillow to find a comfortable position.

Yep, sleeping was a fine idea, indeed.

Certainly a damned sight better than any of the fool notions that had been running through his head since the moment he'd seen Sinful Sinclair step out onto that stage. He could still see her skimpy red costume with the barely-there corset, the fishnet stockings and shimmering garter.

How he'd wanted to unlace that corset and pull those skimpy stockings down her long, long legs. He'd have left the garter, because he liked the way it hugged her creamy thigh, but the rest was history. She would stand before him wearing nothing but a come-hither smile, her flame-red hair streaming down around her pale shoulders, her luscious pink nipples drawn tight, her body trembling with need.

The image haunted him for several fast, furious moments, before he tossed over to his opposite side and found himself staring through one of the bunkhouse's open windows at the small cabin in the distance. A light burned in its window, revealing two shapes.

He clamped his eyes shut, but even that didn't block out the sudden vision that hit him, of Sinful's smile. Of her naked and panting and riding his brother. . . .

He rolled onto his back and forced his eyes closed.

Sleep, he told himself. *This is what you brought her for. Sleep.*

Then he wouldn't have to think about how she looked or felt or tasted. And what's more, he wouldn't have to worry over what sinful, wild, wicked, wonderful thing she was doing at this very moment.

To someone else.

*   *   *

"Come on, Cameron. Open your mouth wide. Really wide." Elizabeth demonstrated. "Now close it. Now open, then close." She watched as the boy mimicked her. "This loosens your lips and keeps them flexible," she explained, fully expecting the boy to question the exercise. He didn't. He'd seemed almost relieved when she'd walked into the room, taken one look at him slouched over the table and ordered him to sit up straight for some breathing exercises.

He'd done everything she'd asked, pausing of course to scribble notes on each specific thing before moving on to the next. She'd known after the first five minutes that he was a dedicated student, committed to beefing up his education, yet at the same time so shy that he blushed bright red whenever she even looked at him.

Elizabeth sent up a silent thanks for her good fortune, and they'd moved on to a few shoulder rolls, some neck stretches and everything else she'd picked up in that aerobics class to which she'd once dragged herself.

A stress reliever, Jenna had called that class. A solid hour standing in the back of a room full of buff women wearing leotards? Gimme a break. She'd been so upset afterward, not to mention exhausted, that she'd had to make herself a chocolate shake just to calm her frazzled nerves. From then on out, she'd stuck to her usual exercise regime—walking to the bagel stand on the corner rather than hailing a cab.

They did a few more lip exercises before Elizabeth tried to mask a fake yawn. "Sorry. I'm usually in bed by this time." The minute the words were out, the tips of Cameron's ears flushed scarlet. "Asleep," she clarified. "I'm usually asleep by this time. Alone."

"Me, too."

She patted his hand, felt him tremble and thanked the Powers That Be that Cameron Durango was as shy as Colt was sexy. "Then let's call it quits and pick up where we left off tomorrow night."

"Yes, ma'am." He rushed to collect his things.

"And Cameron," she added as he reached for his slate. "Remember, the first rule that any man should know when it comes to women is discretion. What we do here is private. You don't discuss any of it with anyone. Understand?" He nodded vigorously and her fear level fell another notch. "Self-confident men don't talk about their private exchanges with women. Now, run along."

"Yes, ma'am."

"I'll see you tomorrow," she said just as he closed the door. But it wasn't the anticipation of seeing Cameron that made her heart beat faster as she turned down the cabin's lamp and crawled between the covers of her bed.

Tomorrow night, after she'd finished her lesson with Cameron, she intended to crawl into Colt Durango's innermost thoughts. She would find out what he spent his nights fantasizing about, no matter what.

And if he spends his nights dreaming about doing something as mundane as sleeping, just as he said?

Nonsense. Colt had fantasies—just like everybody else. He was her fantasy, of course, which was why she was so turned on. So all she had to do was uncover his most secret wish, bring it to life, and he'd feel just as revved up as she did.

But there was only one way to do that. She would start at the top of Isabella X's Naughty Nine and work her way down. Eventually, she would find out exactly what Colt Durango desired. Then she would move in for the kill.

The notion brought a smile to her face as she lay down. She closed her eyes and let herself give back in to the exhaustion that an entire day on the trail had fostered.

But it wasn't a dreamless sleep that waited for her as she had anticipated. It was him.

C'mere, Peaches.

"Don't wag that finger at me." The largest Redd brother—Barney, as Sadie had quickly learned—glared at her and moved around the campfire and out of her line of fire.

"I'm not wagging. I'm swatting a mosquito."

"Tell it to the posse." The second comment came from Bobby, the medium-sized Redd brother. He rounded the campfire, coffeepot in hand. He kept one eye trained on her as he poured himself a cup, as if he were waiting for the Devil himself to jump out.

She swatted and he jumped. Coffee sloshed and he cursed, and Sadie barely contained a smile.

Where the Redd brothers had been skeptical in the beginning, they were all now genuinely spooked thanks to a little slight-of-hand trick she'd learned from her card-playing grandfather back in Louisiana.

She'd had a larger object, of course. A canteen. But the size had made it even more believable. One minute it had been in her hand and the next, it had been gone. She'd recited one of her numerous rhymes that never failed to set the mood, and bam, she'd slipped the thing out of sight with such a now-you-see-it-now-you-don't expertise that had left no doubt in their minds that she could make other things disappear. She could still picture the men in her head. Their eyes had widened and they'd all stared down at themselves and prayed. And fallen headfirst for her bluff.

"Ouch!"

Another mosquito slap and Barney let out a curse. "Dammit, woman. We're lettin' you tag along . . . with us, the best in the West!"

"I didn't do anything," she said.

Barney ignored her and said thoughtfully, "Though, Jack Bartlett is the best shot to ever ride these hills."

"Jack Bartlett?" She raised an eyebrow at Billy, the youngest of the Redd brothers.

"He's one of the baddest bounty hunters around these parts," Billy said. "Him and his brothers. All crack shots."

"They ain't that good," Barney said. "We're better and Bartlett knows it. That's why our boss hired us."

"He hired us 'cause you all but got down on your knees and begged him."

"Did not." Barney puffed out his chest. "He knows a good deal when he sees it."

"Barney, here, rode with Jack for a little while 'til his brothers come into business with him. Then Jack told Barney to take a hike. My brother didn't liken to that none, so's he got with us and now we're giving Jack a run for his money, goin' after the same bounties. Barney's out to prove a point and get himself a little revenge."

"I damn well ain't. I know the point. It's that I'm a better shot. Why, Jack wouldn't be anythin' if it weren't for me. I made him and he never once said thank you. Why, the no-good, ungrateful, sorry sonofa—"

"Revenge," Billy cut in, a grin tilting his lips. "Here. Have something to eat." He handed her a plate of beans and some cured bacon. "It ain't fancy, but it's all we've got."

"Actually, it doesn't have to be fancy. I'd settle for sweet." From the very beginning, Sinful had been receiving gifts from men, namely imported chocolates and sweets, and Sadie had long ago become addicted, particularly when she was nervous.

What she would have given for a bonbon right now.

Billy arched an eyebrow at her. "Got a sweet tooth, do you?"

"The worst."

"Would you stop associatin' with the enemy," Bobby snapped.

"She ain't the enemy, and I was just being hospitable."

"This ain't no tea party, and she ain't our guest."

"Here." He handed her a spoon. Their hands brushed. The young man's clear gold eyes twinkled back at her and her heart stalled for a frantic second.

Stalled?

She shook away the ridiculous notion and concentrated on the plate in her hands. She'd been around men her entire life, particularly the latter half since she'd worked her spell on the garter and enhanced Sinful's sex appeal. She'd been around handsome men, sexy men, men with great eyes and nice hands and pockets full of gold, and not once had her heart stalled.

Then again, no man had ever looked at her with such a sweet smile. As if he liked what he was looking at. Those looks were always reserved for Sinful because Sadie always faded in her sister's shadow—"Ouch!"

"God*dammit*!" Barney exploded.

Sadie shrugged. "Calm down. It's just a mosquito. I didn't *do* anything."

"You sure as hell better hope not, 'cause I got plans for this thing"—he indicated his lap—"when I collect that gold and get into town."

"Me, too," Bobby added, "and I want everything fully functional."

"What about you?" Her gaze went to Billy. Even as the words passed her lips, she couldn't actually believe she was saying them. What did she care what his plans were? She didn't care. She only cared about catching up to the woman who knew her sister's location and getting her powers back.

"I ain't much for socializing. I get around, but the only thing I plan on doin' is hittin' the nearest saloon and gettin' myself a great big piece of apple pie. I like sweets myself."

It wasn't a bonbon, but it was close enough. Here was a man a girl could fall in love with. If she'd been looking to fall in love, which she wasn't.

"Apple pie is for babies." Bobby tossed his coffee onto the fire. "I got bigger and better plans."

"You ain't got a woman waitin' for you," Billy pointed out. "Your woman dumped you."

"I dumped her," Bobby said, shooting Billy a glare. "And I don't got one woman waitin' for me. I got lots of women. That's what it's all about. About havin' a lot of 'em, for a little while. Who needs just one?" He didn't wait for a reply before shooting Sadie a narrow-eyed gaze. "So don't you go making anything disappear."

If only. If she could use her powers she wouldn't be on this ridiculous trip. She would be back home, back with her people, doing her mother proud while Sinful did whatever made her happy.

As it was, when the good lord had deemed them twins, he'd meant it. Two halves of the same whole. Forever connected.

Where are you, Sinful? She sent out the mental plea, and heard nothing back. Now, there was a good side and a bad side to that. The good was that she didn't get any bad feelings. No cries for help. No terror-filled screams. The bad side was that she didn't get *anything.* No clue as to her sister's whereabouts, or the fact that she had to be moving closer. They'd been on the woman's trail all day. Surely she had to be moving closer?

"We'll leave at sunup. From the looks of those tracks, they cain't be too far ahead of us." Barney eyed her. "And the sooner we catch 'em, the sooner we get rid of you."

"Now that ain't a nice thing to be sayin'," Billy cut in. "She probably ain't any more thrilled with your company than you are with hers. Are you, little lady?" Twinkling gold eyes turned on her again, and for a long moment, Sadie forgot all about Sinful and her whereabouts, and most of all she forgot the unhappiness at losing her powers.

She forgot everything except for Billy Redd and his pretty eyes and the fact that he made her heart pound because she was going to be spending the night only a few feet away from him.

Suddenly the food didn't seem so distasteful or the ground so hard or the mosquitos quite so bad—"Ouch!"

"Dadblame it!"

"Sonofabitch!"

She watched the men scramble again as she rubbed her swollen skin. On second thought . . .

"I'm here," Sinful panted, her nipple pressing against his palm as she arched and lifted her hips. "I can't wait any longer. Touch me now. There. Please!*"*

She was warm and wet and soft and his fingers slid easily into her dampness. Her body bowed towards him. Her legs fell open, drawing him deeper. He slid another finger inside, stirring her, making her moan. She was so close to finding release, and he wanted to give it to her.

He wanted to watch her.

He found the small button of flesh that he knew would bring her pleasure, and he touched it. Her lips parted and she gasped, crying out his name—

"Colt!"

Boy, her voice sounded just like his brother's. . . .

Colt's eyes snapped open to find his youngest stepbrother, Cain, standing beside his bunk. The six-year-old stood a few cautious feet away and peered at him.

"Are you okay?" the young boy asked.

"Ugh. Yeah."

" 'Cause you're all red."

Colt didn't answer.

"And sweaty," Cain added. He was wide-eyed.

Colt gave him a stern look.

"And you was growlin'," the kid went on, apparently unfazed by his brother's scowl. "You were breathin' awful hard, too. And cry—"

"Bad dream," Colt cut in, gathering his control and slowing his pounding heart. Crying? Nah, more like crying out. He hadn't been crying, but he damn sure felt like it now. He'd been so close. She'd been so close. They'd been so—

"Are you sure you're okay?" Cain eyed him suspiciously, twirling a strand of blond hair around his finger. "Although, I guess you're talkin', aintcha." His voice seemed very small. "I suppose that means you're fine. I was worried that you was sick . . . like Pa."

Something twisted in Colt's chest. The boy's father was dead—*their* father was dead. And he was here to make amends for that. It was a strange feeling that stirred memories of his past, of the boy he'd been long ago—and of being left by his mother.

He swallowed against the lump in his throat and gathered his resolve. That was then, and this was now. There was nothing to worry about.

"You wouldn't wake up," the little boy continued, his eyes a little tearful.

"I was just tired," Colt said, his tone short and clipped. He needed to kill this subject, and fast. "What are you doing out here, anyway? Shouldn't you be eating breakfast? Doesn't Horseshoe have pancakes waiting up for you—I know he takes a lot of pride in the stacks he makes for you. . . . He'll tan your hide if you don't get in there and eat."

"I was out here trying to catch that old fox that keeps eating Cameron's chickens' eggs." At the mention, the little boy teared up again.

Colt busied himself shoving his foot into the first of his pant legs.

"But we'll never catch him." Cain sniffled and wiped his nose on the back of his shirtsleeve. "He's too fast."

"No, he isn't." Colt said. "You just have to know how to catch him. It's just a matter of time. I'll show you sometime."

The little blond boy looked up at him with wondrous eyes, and Colt felt himself go a little cold. What had he just promised? He stood and pulled his pants up. Glancing out the window, he noted the sun outlining the small cabin in the distance. The blinds were drawn, the place dark and quiet. "Where's your brother?"

"Layin' into that stack of Horseshoe's pancakes. One the size of Cooper's Bluff."

At least he wasn't still out there, Colt thought to himself. Not that he cared. It was just that his brother had a lot of work to do and Colt needed him wide-awake and on the job. Along with learning about women, the boy needed to learn to keep his priorities straight, too—and so much sex that a man couldn't get his work done was, well . . .

"Can I go out with you this morning?" Cain's question brought him back from his musings. It was the same question that Colt heard day after day, for his little brother sought him out every morning.

As usual, he shook his head and reached for his boots. "I've got a lot of work to do today. And you've got your lessons and your own chores." And a life that really shouldn't include Colt, the wild and unpredictable brother. The brother who didn't deserve to be a part of this household.

That was the very reason Colt was taking things so slow, why he was living out here in the bunkhouse. His stepbrothers had lost so much in the past six months: Their ma to sickness and their pa to . . .

Colt didn't want to upset things by rushing in and trying to save the day. He was little more than a stranger, he'd been away for so long that who knew if they'd even benefit by his return to the household. Certainly changing their routine wouldn't help. And taking the bedroom they offered him in the house—his Pa's bedroom—

that wouldn't solve anything. No, it was better that he stayed out here, in the bunkhouse. And it was better that his brothers went about their chores as usual, without him.

He would simply take up his father's burdens silently, providing for them and expecting nothing. Let Horseshoe do all the real raising. He'd likely do that anyway; the man was crusty, but he had a paternal streak in him a mile wide.

No, Colt wasn't here to change any of that. He was here only to pay his debt to the man who had given him his life.

"So, where did you disappear to, Colt?" His little stepbrother was asking. "We've missed you." He said this as he trailed along after Colt, who was making his way up into the main area of the bunkhouse. There, a group of ranch hands were gathered over cups of pitch-black coffee.

"Galveston."

"Why'd you go there? To bring back candy?" Cain asked hopefully. He climbed onto a stool and watched Colt pour himself a mug of coffee.

"Do you think I'd go all the way to Galveston just to fetch candy?" Colt asked. He sat down beside the boy. "That seems silly, doesn't it? When we have a town just a short ways from here?"

Cain gave him an unconvinced look.

"I was fetching a friend." He hadn't given much thought to explaining Sinful's presence to the younger boy, but the minute he opened his mouth, the lie flowed out. "She's the sister of an old friend of mine. She's taken a teaching job in the next town, but they don't expect her for a few more weeks." That wasn't an out-and-out lie, exactly. She *was* here in an educational capacity. "I told her she could stay with us until she's ready to move on. She's out in Horseshoe's old cabin."

The cabin had once housed not only Horseshoe but his wife—a stern older woman who on her deathbed had made her husband promise to help raise the Durango children right. She'd left behind not only her biscuit recipe but that commandment. And Colt was somewhat glad, considering that Horseshoe was doing a fine job.

Although, Colt had to admit that the woman's idea of "right" probably didn't include Colt hiring a stripper to tutor Cameron in the arts of love—but then she had never seen the look of pure desperation on the boy's face each week when they walked into Carlisle's Emporium and got a glimpse of the owner's daughter Caroline.

"Did she bring any candy?" Cain's voice asked, pushing past Colt's thoughts.

He sipped his coffee and tried not to grimace at the taste. "Who?"

"The teacher lady."

"You think she came all this way just to bring you candy?" Colt echoed his earlier question, giving his little stepbrother a stern look.

"Maybe," Cain said, giving him a tough look. The boy's out-thrust jaw and posture made Colt think of himself as a child, and it sent a rush of longing through him. For all he'd missed. For what he was missing now.

He stifled the thought. He wasn't missing anything. He was right here. Right now. Any time he wanted, he could—

"Well, did she?" Cain's voice had softened, hopeful. "Did she bring me any candy?"

"No." Colt said. "And don't you go pestering her, either. She's tired from her trip and wants some peace and quiet. I promised her both. Now, run along to breakfast." He reached for his gun belt and his hat.

"All right," Cain said. He scrambled off of his stool and out the doorway toward the house. Colt's voice stopped him in mid-scurry.

"Take a look in my saddlebags after you eat." He fought back a small smile as the little boy's eyes lit with excitement. Seeing the look, he added, "But only one piece at a time, or Horseshoe will tan my hide for making your teeth fall out."

The boy nodded vigorously, then skipped off down the hall. Colt's first urge was to sink back down at the table, close his eyes, and go back to sleep. He had to finish that dream. After all, it was just a dream. There was no harm in dreaming about things, just so long as one didn't actually act upon them. Right?

Wrong. The thinking would lead to doing,

and the last thing Colt intended to do was bed a wild woman like Sinful Sinclair. Despite his sudden urge to stomp outside and wake her from her own sweet slumber just to see if she looked every bit as good spread out on a patch-work quilt as he imagined.

An image popped into his head, but he managed to push it right back out before it could do any more harm. He was already too hard, too hot.

He drew in a deep breath and tried to calm his racing pulse. He had work waiting, his daily chores. There were several new foals to help nurse and Beelzebub, the most stubborn, most ornery piece of horseflesh he'd ever had the misfortune to have to break. Colt needed to focus, to keep his perspective, neither of which involved one sexy-as-all-get-out redhead with sweet-tasting lips and a sass that drew him like a tinhorn to a poker table.

His life was all about responsibility now. About getting up in the morning and contenting himself with the same routine day after day. About forgetting the past and concentrating on the future. About getting Sinful and her red hair and her luscious lips out of his head.

There was only one way to do that. Distance. Colt was keeping his distance and his perspective and he wasn't going within a stone's throw of Sinful Sinclair, even if it was well past sunup and her cabin still sat dark and quiet in the distance.

She was obviously tired after last night.

The thought bothered him a lot more than it should have.

But that was only because her languishing in bed all day undermined the story he'd just told his young stepbrothers. No way would a fine, respectable teacher be lazing about in bed. She'd be up and about, doing the fine, respectable things that teachers usually did when they weren't teaching school.

Maybe keeping his distance wasn't such a good idea just yet, not until he'd set some ground rules, starting with the fact that Miss Sinful had to earn her money during the day, as well as at night. He had his younger, impressionable brothers to think of. Not to mention, the less time she spent in her bed, the less he was likely to picture her there.

At least that's what he hoped. Otherwise, these were going to be the longest three weeks of his life.

Chapter Six

". . . rise and shine!"

The words pushed into one of Elizabeth's favorite dreams involving the tall, dark and delicious cowboy and a banana split.

She ignored the footsteps creaking around her and concentrated on the mountain of whipped cream covering Colt's chest, his stomach, his—

"Get up!"

The words burst past the wonderful haze of her dream of seduction and snatched her back to the lumpy mattress and scratchy blanket upon which she lay. She frowned, cracking an eye open to the shadow looming over her bed.

"I was beginning to think you were dead." The deep, familiar voice slid into her ears, causing her senses to jolt into awareness.

"You have rotten timing," she grumbled. Her senses might be stirred, but she'd spent too many hours on the trail, followed by too many hours fantasizing. The only thing she wanted was to keep her eyes closed and sink back into the mattress.

He moved and one jean-clad thigh brushed her leg where it hung out of the bedclothes. Tingles of heat rippled through her.

Okay, so it wasn't the *only* thing she wanted, but a girl had to have priorities. Especially a tired girl with a sore rump and aching muscles.

"It's a good half-hour past sunup."

"What time is sunup?"

"Four-thirty."

"I hate you."

"You'll perk up once you get some breakfast. I brought you a plate of Horseshoe's pancakes."

"Save them for me and I'll eat later. I had a rough night." A night of tossing and turning and planning and dreaming. She rolled onto her stomach. "I'm going back to sleep."

Now *there* was an idea. Her eyes drifted shut and she searched for signs of her dream, hot fudge and mountains of ice cream and a banana. A big bana—

Smack.

The sound echoed through the cabin as a very firm hand made contact with her bottom. Sleep faded in a stinging rush of shock. Her eyes popped open and she bolted to a sitting position, training her most murderous glare on Colt Durango.

"What did you do that for?"

He grinned. "Because I didn't have a stick of dynamite. I'm beginning to think that's the only thing that's going to get your lily-white hide out of this bed." As if noticing the lily-white hide in question, his gaze drifted down and she became keenly aware that she wore only his oversized shirt—which had ridden up and tangled around her hips. His gaze made a sizzling trek over her legs, completely bare except for the garter on her right thigh. "I brought you some clothes." He indicated one of a pile of boxes. "They belonged to my stepmother, Grace."

"She outgrow them?"

"She passed away a few months ago." A wave of compassion swept through Elizabeth, quickly replaced by a rush of anger when Colt tossed a dress at her and barked, "Put this on. There's work to do."

She caught the calico outfit and glared, her backside still tingling from his hand. "Maybe for you, but Cameron and I don't have another lesson scheduled until tonight."

"I'm not talking about Cam. I've got another younger brother who is mighty curious as to what you're doing here. While Cameron's old enough to know about the things that go on between a man and a woman, this one isn't. He's young and impressionable, and I don't want him getting the wrong idea."

"What did you tell him?"

"That you're the sister of an old friend of mine, a schoolteacher passing through on her way to a job in the next town—which means you have to get up now. He's bound to show up any time."

"The teachers in this day and age get up at the crack of dawn?"

"This day and age? What are you talk—"

"All right, all right, I'll get up," she blurted, eager to cut off any questions. She had to watch herself, to play along and keep from stirring Colt's suspicions. She was Sinful Sinclair and this was the late 1800s. When had that book said Sinful had been in Galveston, 1892?

She drew in a deep breath and threw her legs over the side of the bed. The shirt rode higher, but when her gaze met Colt's it wasn't her legs he was staring at. The first few buttons of her shirt were undone and the shift in position had left a gaping V. The material barely covered the tip of one breast.

Colt's gaze had riveted on her cleavage and panic bolted through her.

Panic? No. This was excitement. Pure excitement, and she wasn't letting the opportunity pass. She had his attention and she was going to make the most of it.

She fought down a strange flutter of butterflies—strange because no bona fide wild woman would *ever* feel nervous—and concentrated on the heat pulsing through her, the way

142

her skin flushed hot and cold, the way her heart seemed to pause in that next instant, as if waiting to see what would happen next.

Whip off your shirt, prance over to him and throw your arms around his neck.

That's what she should have done. What she would have done in a heartbeat, but for years of watching her step, always conscious of others, always cautious; they refused to disappear just because she'd finally decided that she wanted to be the wild woman that she knew lurked inside.

Instead, she settled for something a bit more subtle. She lifted her arms overhead for a much-needed stretch. Her back arched, her chest lifted and heaved in a move that came so easily and naturally that it affirmed what she'd been thinking—she definitely had a side that was wild at heart. She'd simply never had the chance to flirt and tease, except in her most private thoughts.

Not in real life.

Not with a man watching her. Not with *the* man.

"Boy, am I stiff this morning," she murmured, before her courage could falter in the face of his silence and she dove back under the covers. She focused on the heat pulsing through her, on the rampant lust in his eyes.

"Actually, Peaches, *I'm* the one who's stiff." A grin twisted his lips before he seemed to realize what he'd said. Then he froze. "I mean, that is,

143

my muscles are aching." He rolled his neck for emphasis, as if to work out the kinks. "That is, my body is throbbing. I mean, damn but my mattress was hard. I'm really paying for it this morning."

She patted the spot next to her, feeling a lascivious thrill. "Mine is just right."

"Glad to hear it." His gaze swiveled to a box near his feet. Apparently he wouldn't go for an early morning seduction. "I also brought a few other things. Some stuff to keep you busy during the day."

Her mind rushed back to the fifth grade, to her teacher and the woman's dreaded math box. "If it's flash cards, I'm going to have to kill you."

"Flash cards? What in tarnation is a flash—"

"I, um, meant *flesh* cards." Okay, she was reaching, but they sounded provocative, whatever they were. And a woman like the woman she was supposed to be—correction, the woman she *was*—would certainly say something ripe with innuendo. "Yep. If you've got flesh cards, I'm liable to kill you . . . um, with kindness. Yes, that's what I'm liable to do."

He gave her a look of mild amusement. "I'm afraid to ask."

"They're these cards," she rushed on, focusing on the intensity of his eyes; they never failed to feed her courage and make her feel every bit as daring as the real Sinful would be. "That have different positions written on them. Sexual positions," she added for emphasis. "They're my absolute favorite and I would be forever grateful for a box of them."

For a few moments, a grin played at his lips and her heart pounded with excitement. Maybe she'd punched his buttons. Maybe—

The thought died as his mouth eased into a frown and he was, once again, all business.

Darn it.

"I also brought you some books and a few samplers." He tossed several leather-bound volumes along with a sewing circle and a bag of various colored thread onto the sawbuck table near the door. "You should rise and shine at a respectable hour and keep yourself busy with this stuff during the day. That way, if anyone's of a mind to notice, you'll look like any other school miss keeping herself occupied in between study sessions."

"So what you're saying is, you want me to suppress my true passionate nature and pretend to be something I'm not." In reality, the reading and needlepoint were much too close to what she truly was. How was she supposed to loose her inner vixen and be Sinful Sinclair when during the day she was forced to act like plain, boring Elizabeth Carlton? And what was the point of living in the past for that? "I'm afraid I can't do that. I need to languish in bed." The words slid out before she could stop them. The way he looked at her then truly made her feel sinful.

"You can languish in that rocker out there on

the front porch, but make sure you're fully dressed when you do it."

"That's no fun." Hey, when you're on a roll, you're on a roll, and with Colt Durango's dark, assessing gaze burning holes into her, she was moving right along. Her heart was pounding, her blood humming, and her nipples hard and needy.

He gave her a stern look. "Just behave yourself during the day."

"Which means nights are for misbehaving?" She wiggled her eyebrows and could have sworn she saw a glint in his eyes. Maybe she *was* wearing him down.

His mouth stretched into a taut line. So much for the wearing-down theory.

"Fine. You can do whatever you want at night, so long as you do it in private. But days, I want your word that you'll be on your best behavior."

"I swear," she said, crossing her heart. "On one little condition."

"No conditions. I'm paying you to do a job."

"And you're paying me quite a lot," she quickly agreed, her gaze drifting to the pouch of gold coins he'd handed her when she'd first accepted his his proposal. "But to be fair, when we made the deal, you didn't mention any pain and suffering. Just pleasure." She fingered one of the books he'd brought. "I mean *it's* not like we're talking Emmanuelle or *9½ Weeks* here."

"What—" he started, but she cut in before he could finish.

"This is *Moby Dick*. I get the willies just looking at frozen fish sticks, and you brought me a book about a whale."

He stared at her as if to say "What planet did you come from?", but then he shook his head and muttered, "City women." He gave her another deep, assessing gaze and a stern frown. "So what do you want?" he finally asked.

"*You.*" The word was out before she could stop it. Not that she would have. It was the wild woman in her talking, the part that needed to talk, despite the fact that her hands were trembling so badly she had to clutch them to keep from tugging the hem of her shirt down.

"I'm not available."

"You're married?"

"No."

"Engaged?"

"No."

She shrugged. "Then you're available."

"Hardly." He picked up the empty box that had contained her books and turned toward the door. "I told the boys to leave you alone, but I give them five full minutes before curiosity sets in and they come peepin' around here. When they do, just tell them you're tired and send them home. Don't encourage them. The less time they spend with you, the better." He gave her another frown before turning toward the door.

"What's this?" She held up a small container.

The grin returned, crinkling his eyes at the corners and making her heart pause. "Smelling salts."

"Good thinking. I'm liable to pass out with boredom from reading this stuff you brought me."

"They're not for you. They're for Cameron."

She raised her eyebrows. "He doesn't like *Moby Dick* either?"

"He doesn't like girls."

Her eyebrows inched even higher. "You didn't tell me that. I'll have to charge extra."

His grin widened, and warmth spread through her. Then he shook his head. "No. Not like that. He likes them, but the idea of them, of doing anything with them, gets him a little crazy."

"He gets crazy talking about sex?"

"He gets sick. Faint. And not just about sex. About Caroline, too. She's the girl he's after. The girl you're going to help him get."

She met his stare. "And what do *I* get?" The question was ripe with challenge and innuendo and she waited for him to respond. She wanted him to respond. To stare at her with that hungry gaze that made her go weak in the knees, and tell her she would get him.

Colt stared at her long and hard, his expression unreadable before he frowned. "A hefty load of gold." He nodded toward the table, then to the salts. "Keep them handy." With that, he turned toward the door.

Talk about running hot and cold.

"You don't like me very much, do you?" Her question brought him up short. He turned and eyed her, and she prayed that the floor would swallow her up. The last thing her ego needed was for him to start ticking off things about her that made his skin crawl.

"I like you too much, darlin'," he finally said, and she let out the breath she'd been holding. "That's the trouble."

She grinned. "Doesn't sound like trouble to me."

"I don't want one night."

"Good, because I'm here for three full weeks."

His grin was full and heart-stopping and so unexpected that heat bolted through her. "Temporary," he told her. "You're temporary, darlin', with a capital T, and I gave up temporary a while back."

That's what he said, but the look in his eyes told an altogether different story. That maybe Colt Durango wasn't entirely the permanent guy he was trying so hard to be.

For a quick second, admiration welled inside her. He was trying to be a man of principles. But the heat in his gaze was too powerful to ignore. He wanted her, and while part of her was tempted to leave things alone, to say good-bye to Colt and his world and return to hers—the last thing she wanted was to tutor Cameron Durango, verbally or otherwise—she couldn't abandon this one chance without even trying.

The chance to really live, to free the wild woman inside her. She'd blown it the first time, let the opportunity slide by—but never again.

Chances were rare, and second chances even more so.

Tonight, she promised herself as Colt turned on his heel and left her sitting on the edge of the bed. Starting with number one of the Naughty Nine, she would uncover Colt's deepest, most erotic fantasy, or at least move things in the right direction by eliminating one and leaving only eight to put to the test.

"I am Sinful," she told herself as she fingered the garter and adjusted it firmly on her leg before getting to her feet. "I am beautiful and desirable. I am every man's fantasy, including Colt Durango's."

That's what she told herself. She just wasn't one-hundred-percent sure that she believed it.

Colt was wrong about his little brother. He didn't come to investigate her right away. Elizabeth spent most of the day walking around the front porch, nibbling food from the basket he had brought and being bored out of her skull. It wasn't until late in the afternoon, after a dinner made up of beans and biscuits and what looked something like chili, though she wasn't about to place any bets, when she got her first glimpse of Colt's youngest stepbrother.

She was just returning from a very eye-opening experience in the outhouse when she opened the cabin door and found a small boy sitting at her sawbuck table.

He wore faded overalls and a plaid work shirt and looked at her with a mixture of wariness and excitement.

"Hi," he said, sticking out his hand just the way Cameron had for a shake the night before. "I'm Cain. I brung you dessert." He held up a sweet-smelling apple turnover. "One o' Horseshoe's turnovers."

She stared at the tart. "It looks triangular to me. Last time I looked, horseshoe meant u-shaped."

"Not horseshoe turnovers. *Horseshoe's* turnovers. He lives with us and helps out with the ranch. He made them. He loves to cook. Colt said not to bother you, but they're so good, I figured you might want one. But I won't," he added. "Bother you, that is. I ain't s'posed to bother nobody. I just thought you might be hungry."

Her stomach grumbled its appreciation and Cain smiled, his ears turning bright red the way Cameron's had the night before. The shy thing definitely ran in the Durango family.

With one tall, dark and delicious exception.

"Thanks, Cain." She cleared her throat and started to recite the name that had been echoing in her head for the past two days. "I'm Sin—Sinclair." Sinful, even as a name, didn't seem like an appropriate word to say in front of a five-year-old. Particularly such a nice, polite, *proper* five-year-old. "*Miss* Sinclair," she said, drawing out the *ess* sound the way Miss Gorman always had. "I'm a teacher." She said the words more to remind herself than Cain. "Yep. A bona fide reading and writing dynamo. That's me."

The boy turned to the table and fingered one of the books Colt had brought her. "I can't read yet, but I love books. My ma used to read to me, but she's dead now."

"I'm sorry."

"Me, too. She smelled good. Like cookies." His gaze met Elizabeth's. "She used to make cookies. And cakes, too. And tarts. Hers were even better than Horseshoe's, but I ain't s'posed to tell him that. He thinks he cooks the best."

"Then it'll be our secret."

He opened the copy of *Moby Dick* that was on top of the pile of books and fingered the pages. "Are you reading this one?"

Moby Dick. Just looking at the book brought back memories of her high school library where she'd hibernated in the corner by herself while her best friend, Katy Smiley, had flirted and teased and done everything Elizabeth had ever wanted to do when it came to boys.

"Are you?" Cain's question stirred her from the sudden rush of memories.

"Not unless someone pulls a gun and . . ." Her words faded as disappointment flared in his eyes. ". . . holds it to my head am I *not* reading it. I was just starting it." She'd always been a sucker for disappointed faces. "You can sit in and listen if you like."

Excitement brightened his expression for a brief moment before he shook his head. "I'm not s'posed to bother you."

Here it was, an easy way to do as Colt said and get rid of the little boy. She had to plan, to prepare, to *fantasize* about tonight's plans for Colt and number one of the Naughty Nine. That was what she was here for, right?

"Then you'll definitely sit in, because it's no bother."

So she'd figure that stuff out later. *Moby Dick* was a classic, after all.

A few pages turned into a few chapters. A full hour passed before Elizabeth finally closed the book and stifled a yawn.

"You'd better get going. It's dinnertime."

Cain nodded. "Thanks, Miss Sinclair."

"Elizabeth," she blurted out before she could stop herself. "My name—er, that is, my *nick*-name is Elizabeth. You can call me that. And you should come back every morning, so I can read to you."

"Thanks, Miss Elizabeth." And then he smiled a sweet, gap-toothed grin that left her warm inside for the next few minutes as she sat there staring at the sun as it sank below the horizon.

Now this was a scene straight out of her fantasies. The brilliant orange glow. The peaceful ambiance. The shadowy figure topping the horizon, headed straight for her.

Cameron.

She fought down a wave of disappointment and tried to calm her pounding heart. Drawing in a deep breath, she rose from the chair, a set of notes she'd prepared in hand. On the way to the door, her gaze rested on the bottle of smelling salts and she paused.

Nah. They weren't actually going to *do* anything, just discuss the subject in very nonthreatening terms. The doing wouldn't come until later tonight, with a different partner, and only if she lucked out.

Visualize.

The positive reinforcement echoed through her head as she pictured Colt and herself, them together, with lots of breath-stealing heat. Yes, that would come later tonight. In the meantime, she would have to take care of his brother. But surely she wouldn't need the smelling salts.

Colt was probably jumping the gun with Cameron the way he had with his youngest stepbrothers, expecting too much from them too quickly. Five minutes? It had taken Cain an entire day to work up enough nerve to visit her cabin. Sure, Cameron might be a little shy, but . . .

The thought faded as she remembered last night, the boy's bright red ears and his embarrassed flush. Okay, so he was very shy. But all shy people did not faint at the mere mention of sex. After all, they were just going to talk about it. Not *do* it.

"Cameron?" Elizabeth passed the smelling salts beneath the young man's nose and lightly slapped his chalky-white cheek. Score one for Colt; he'd been right about his stepbrother's squeamishness. "Can you hear me?" Another whiff of the salts, another slap and his eyelids fluttered. "Are you okay?"

"What happened?"

"You fainted."

"Fainted?" The boy's disoriented gaze scanned the dim interior of the cabin before colliding with hers.

"Swooned," she clarified, wishing she'd paid more attention to Mrs. Gorman's six-week section on word origins. "Fainted. Keeled over. You were doing okay when I mentioned sex. And when I mentioned Caroline. But when I mentioned sex and Car—"

"Don't." He clamped his eyes shut. "I think I feel sick."

"There's nothing to be scared of. You're a boy. She's a girl. What happens is natural."

"Caroline is not a girl."

"She's not?" A dozen possibilities raced through her mind as she remembered Colt's earlier comment. Of course, he'd been teasing though.

"She's a *woman*," Cameron rushed on, quickly setting the record straight. "A beautiful, desirable, wonderful woman and I'm just a . . ."

"A man?"

"A boy. A kid. So far below her that I might as well be gunk on her shoe."

"I think you're exaggerating a bit."

"No, I'm not. My mama used to read me these stories when I was little, about princesses and princes and all that stuff. That's Caroline. She's a princess—but I ain't no prince. Colt should never have brought you here. I'll tell him to forget it."

"Let's not be too hasty," she said, spurred on by the sheer desperation on his face even more than the notion of losing her chance with Colt Durango. She knew what it was like to be Cameron, to want something just out of reach. To feel that you just weren't going to live up to expectations.

Of course, she had different reasons for her feelings. She wanted to reach out, she knew what she could be, but she'd been held back by her loyalty to her family. It was fear that held Cameron back. But were they really so different?

She patted his back. "You can do this. You can sweep that girl right off her feet. You just need to have a little confidence in yourself."

"I don't know."

"Confidence," she stressed again. "That's the key. You're a good-looking boy—man," she corrected. "You have a lot to offer a woman. The trouble is, you're idolizing this girl. She's only human."

156

"No, she ain't. She's a—"

"Woman," Elizabeth cut in. "No more. No less. Forget the princess thing completely. Believe me, she puts on her pantyhose like everybody else."

"Her what?"

Open mouth, insert foot. "Never mind. Look, just rest assured, she may be pretty—"

"Beautiful," he cut in. "She's plumb beautiful."

"Beauty's only skin deep. She's still flesh and blood like the rest of us, and probably has an addiction to chocolate and at least a few cellulite dimples."

"A few—"

"Visualize," she cut in, eager to distract him from her tongue slips. He not only had to think she was Sinful, but he also had to believe she was from his time period. She couldn't imagine having to explain her current predicament. "Just visualize this girl in her underwear and you'll realize there's nothing to be scared of. She's just like the rest of—Cameron?" He'd gone deathly pale again, his Adam's apple bobbing as if he were perilously close to losing his dinner. "What's wrong?"

"Caroline," he choked out. "Underwear?" Another choke and a gasp, and then he hauled open the door and stumbled out into the yard to be sick.

Elizabeth grabbed a cloth, shoved it into the wash bowl, then followed him. She definitely had her work cut out for her.

He clutched the base of a nearby tree and leaned over it, and something twisted inside her. She knew what he was feeling, the fear, the desperation, the longing. And how powerful those emotions were.

She'd spent her entire adolescence longing for what she could never heave—Chase Parker, the handsomest, sexiest, most daring bad boy ever to ride his Harley down the halls of Cherryville High.

She'd wanted him so badly, but she'd never been able to do anything more than talk to him. He'd been hot and hunky and *bad*, and she'd been the mayor's daughter—prim and proper and pristine. She'd had circumstances that prevented her from acting on her feelings, but the only thing standing between Cameron and the hot-to-trot Caroline was fear.

And fear could be overcome with a little help.

"Here." She handed him the cloth a few minutes later when he leaned back against the tree, gulping for air.

"Thanks." His chest heaved as he held the cool cloth to his forehead. "It's no use, Miss Sinful. I cain't do this."

"Can't," she corrected. "And sure you can. Why, we've only had two lessons and I can already see progress."

He let the compress slip, one eye peeking over the edge at her. "How do you figure that?"

She patted him on the back and gave him her most encouraging smile. "At least you didn't faint this time."

Chapter Seven

Elizabeth was the one who felt like fainting now.

She stood outside the barn door later that night after she finished up her lesson with Cameron and listened to Colt's deep, rumbling voice. Apparently, he was talking to his horse as he rubbed it down. Her body flushed hot and cold and butterflies swarmed in her stomach.

Excitement, girl. Butterflies are for tame women.

"I am Sinful," she murmured, gathering her composure and pushing open the door. Wood creaked, hinges whined and her footsteps slid across the dirt floor.

I am Sinful.

I am Sinful.

I am—

"What are you doing out here, Peaches?"

"Sinful." She finished the thought out loud before she could stop herself. "That's my name. You called me Peaches," she pointed out, her brain spinning, her heart pounding.

"You look more like a Peaches to me." He didn't so much as glance up from his horse, and she wondered for the umpteenth time if maybe she weren't wishing for things that could never be. That she was destined to live the rest of her life reaching for the stars when she couldn't even manage to get off the ground. That time and circumstance would forever stand in her way.

But then he turned his dark, intense eyes on Elizabeth and the flash of raw desire she glimpsed there convinced her that he wanted her as she wanted him, he just wouldn't admit it. The time was now to uncover his wildest fantasy. Or at least narrow the list.

Naughty Nine number one—sex talk—here I come.

She stepped toward him, keenly aware of his hot gaze trailing over her. She was fully clothed in a yellow dress covered in tiny white daisies, yet she might well have been naked. She felt every bit as exposed as when she'd been wearing nothing but his shirt and the garter. As turned on.

She focused on the feeling and let it feed her courage. Her fear—er, that is, her inhibition— slipped away, leaving only desire in its wake.

"What can I do for you?" he asked. "You need more smelling salts?"

"Actually, yes."

He grinned. "I told you. That boy is—"

"Tell me something else," she cut in.

He eyed her. "Like what?"

"I don't know . . ." Her hand reached out and Colt's steed skittered backwards. "How did you get into training wild horses?"

"I've always loved them, from the moment I saw my first mustang." He smiled to himself. "That was something. She was as ornery as old Horseshoe and ten times as mean, but I just had to get close."

"I bet it was some kind of ride the first time you climbed on." The statement didn't come out quite as breathless and sexy as she'd intended. It hung in the air between them and her courage faltered. Maybe this wasn't such a good idea. Sure, she wanted to loose her inner wild woman, but if he wasn't a willing recipient of so much wildness, she couldn't very well force him. At least not unless that was what he secretly wanted. Wasn't that number five on Isabella's list? "But maybe not." She started to turn, her dwindling courage getting the best of her. "It is kind of late. I'd better head back—"

He cut her off. "It was wild and rough and scary." His gaze locked on hers. "And I loved every minute of it." He stroked his horse's flank and stared off into the distance. "So much power beneath you, surrounding you." He

161

turned and his gaze fused with hers once again. "Once you get a taste of that, you can't help but want more."

Boy, did she ever. She licked her lips, remembering the sweet whiskey taste of Colt the night she'd kissed him in the hotel. His eyes followed the motion of her tongue and undisguised want flashed in their dark depths.

He wanted her. An unquestionable sureness sang through her for a few seconds before he broke the spell by turning away.

"I'd love to take a ride," she said.

"So would I." His words, soft and bone-melting, echoed through her head as he stared at her, into her. Then, as if he realized what he'd just said, he shook his head and turned away. "I mean, I do. Love to ride, that is. Horses," he blurted. He let out a deep breath. "Particularly that black beauty out in the corral. It's all I've been thinking about since Horseshoe brought her in."

"Want to know what I've been thinking about?" Before he could reply, she rushed on. "I've been thinking about how much I'd like you to kiss me again." She touched his hand, her fingers closing over his. His skin seared hers and every nerve in her body felt the blast.

"About how your lips would feel against mine." She searched for every erotic word she'd ever read and tried to voice the need coursing through her. "How you would taste, how your tongue would feel sliding against mine." His muscles rippled and flexed beneath her touch. "What are *you* thinking about? What are you imagining right now?"

His gaze shifted from where her hand rested atop his and his deep blue eyes caught hers. He simply stood there, the muscle in his jaw ticking, his nostrils flaring. "Chestnuts," he finally murmured.

"Come again?"

"Claybanks," he turned back to the horse and started rubbing. "Cremello. Dappled."

"What are you talking about?"

"Horses. Colors and markings."

O-kay. It wasn't exactly "I want your hot body," but then his life probably revolved around horses, so maybe he considered shop talk sexy. If he thought he was turning her on, she wasn't going to burst his bubble.

"I want you to kiss me," she went on. "I want to feel your lips on mine, your hands on my body, sliding down my neck, my breasts, my—"

"Time for bed." The brush hit the ground and he reached for her elbow.

"My thoughts exactly. I mean, I know you're feeling this, too. Unless that's a six-shooter in your pants pocket, but you appear to wear those in your holster, so I'm betting it's an altogether different sort of gun—"

"Dappled, dun, eel stripe, grulla," he called out as he ushered her toward her cabin.

"Look, I know all those terms are probably

stimulating to you and I'd love to say they do the same for me, but I prefer a few different adjectives. Let's see, grulla means smoky, which sounds much more seductive, especially when you draw out the s and lower your voice just a touch. I literally melt when you do that—"

"Here we are," he announced, steering her up onto the porch so fast she nearly pitched forward. A strong hand on her arm held her back, though, his fingers burning through her blouse to send a wave of heat rushing through her, consuming her.

She turned toward him, her lips puckered and raised. This was it. They were finally going to do it. Finally.

She cracked one eye open in time to see him turn away.

"Hey, where are you going?"

"To bed," he called over his shoulder.

"You're going the wrong way. The bed's in here."

"*My* bed."

"Isn't that a little risky with your family in the house? I mean, I can get off to the forbidden thrill fantasy as much as the next person, but I've read *Moby Dick* to your kid brother. I just wouldn't feel comfortable in there so soon. Besides, the Forbidden Thrill doesn't come until number seven."

His grin slashed open the darkness, and she could make out his bemused head-shake. "Sweet dreams, Peaches."

"But what about your six-shooter?"

"I leave it sitting on the nightstand while I sleep."

"Not *that* six-shooter." He kept walking and disappointment sluiced through her.

I told you you should have recited a few lines from Patty does Pennsylvania.

"I was getting to it," she grumbled to herself as Colt disappeared into the darkness and she was left trembling and alone. After all, for all her wild notions, she'd never actually put any of them into play before. She'd never walked up to a man and whispered a four-letter word. She'd never laughed and giggled as some hunk whispered them to her. This was a first time, and she'd needed a little encouragement to get her nerve up. A few kisses and she felt certain she could have blurted out enough dirty words to make a sailor blush.

Not that it would have done much good. Sure, his gun had been loaded and ready to fire, but he'd still walked away without so much as a draw. He obviously wasn't a talker.

So much for fantasy number one.

She ignored the stab of disappointment. Tomorrow was a new day. A new fantasy. She would move on to number two of the Naughty Nine.

And if he's not interested?

She would keep going. She was bound to hit a weakness sooner or later, then he'd be putty in her hands. He would, she told herself for the hundredth time, because she was Sinful Sinclair—and Sinful wasn't a woman to take no for an answer when she wanted something. And she wanted him.

Boy, did she ever.

She wanted to slap him.

Forget slap. She wanted to shoot him. To slide a noose around his neck and hang him from the nearest rafter.

Better yet, she'd like to pop him on the rump and see how he liked it.

Her hand itched at the thought as she stared at Colt. He loomed over her bed, her blanket draped over one arm, a challenge glittering in his eyes. "Good morning."

"I really hate you."

"Sure, Peaches. Rise and shine, and don't make me come in after you."

Her body ached from a night of tossing and turning without relief. "I should be so lucky," she grumbled.

He grinned. And then he frowned. And then he did what she was fast discovering that he did best. He walked away.

"I'm not goin' to throw up anymore," Cameron vowed that night when he arrived for his lesson, quill pen and paper in hand, a determined expression on his face. "I'm *not*."

"You're thinking positive. That's great."

"No. It's not that, really. I had Horseshoe mix

me up some of his all-cure. Guaranteed to fix everything from a bad case of hives to an aillin' stomach." He sat down at the table, set up his pen and paper, and drew in a deep breath as if bracing himself for a dose of cod liver oil. "Where do we start?"

"Talking."

His head snapped up and his surprised gaze met hers. "But I thought I'd be closing my eyes again and thinking about . . . I mean, you wanted me to picture Caroline in her . . ." He licked his lips as his cheeks flushed. "I mean, we were picturing people in their, um, unmentionables last night when I got sorta sick and blew it, so I figured we'd pick up there."

"That was just to help ease your fear, but I think the best thing to do is just to tackle this entire thing head-on. We're not going to give you any time to be afraid." She wasn't sure she wanted to put Horseshoe's all-cure to the test. "We'll just get right to the nitty gritty of seducing this woman, starting with step one."

"But I practiced the visualizing thing."

"Good, you'll use it later, but for now it all starts with talk."

"Says who?"

"Cosmo."

"Cosmo?"

"A magazine. *The* magazine when it comes to sex and today's woman."

"What's a mag—"

"Now," she interrupted before he could finish

his question. She had to remember where she was. *When* she was. "You want this girl, right?"

He drew in another ragged breath and gave a stern nod.

"Then you have to learn to talk to her." Even if it hadn't been exactly successful for Elizabeth the night before. "Courting is not just about rolling around in bed with a woman." Cameron's ears turned bright red at that. "Breathe," she said, eager to keep him calm and clear-headed. When his chest had relaxed to a somewhat natural rhythm, she went on. "You have to get to know her, talk to her, listen to her. Foreplay is the key to any woman's heart."

He gave her a puzzled look. "Four-play?"

"All the stuff that comes before the actual consummation. Most men think that foreplay is just a little petting and a few kisses once everyone's undressed and ready to go, but it starts way before that. The foreplay starts the moment you look into her eyes and say hello. You're stirring her, seducing her using your words. If you really want to get a girl, you have to learn to *talk* to her."

He looked startled before shaking his head. "Geez, Miss Sinful, I don't rightly know . . ."

"You want this girl, don't you?"

" 'Course I do. If she'll have me."

"You'll never know if you can't get past hello."

He stared at his boots. "I said hello once."

"And?"

"She didn't hear me. I sort of got this lump stuck in my throat."

"Then you'll have to swallow it back down and talk louder the next time you greet her. And when you tell her how pretty her eyes are and how nice she looks and how much better your day is just because she's in it and—"

"Wait." He held up a hand as he dipped his quill and started to frantically write. "This is some really good stuff."

"And then there's her smile. You have to mention her smile. And her hair. And whatever she's wearing. And . . ."

The next forty-five minutes passed in a blur as Elizabeth gave Cameron pointers on what to say, how to say it, and how to pull back just enough to stir Caroline's interest once he'd delivered a few carefully chosen compliments.

"There," she said when he finished scribbling the last piece of advice on how to be sure to compare her skin to fresh milk. The line was cheesy, but Elizabeth knew that sometimes even the most cliched lines could work if delivered with the right amount of sincerity and reverence. Oh, and it didn't hurt if their deliverer was a tall, hunky, wild-eyed cowboy.

Her heart pounded as she thought of Colt in the stables, then about what she'd do tonight. She drew in a shaky breath and tried to keep her attention on Cameron. "This wasn't so bad now, was it?"

He breathed a sigh of relief now that the third

night of his training had come to an end. Cameron packed away his extensive notes and gathered up his things. "Horseshoe mixes up the best medicine. Why, I don't even feel sick." Wood scraped as he pushed his chair back and got to his feet. "So what are we covering next?"

"Kissing," she said, watching his smile fade and his mouth go a suspicious shade of green around the edges. She gave him an encouraging pat on the back. "Better tell Horseshoe to make it a double dose tomorrow night."

What Elizabeth wouldn't have given for her own double dose of Horseshoe's all-cure right about now.

She drew in a deep breath and tried to calm her pounding heart as she stood in the shadows and stared at Colt's silhouette atop the wild horse. He'd been out in the corral for hours now; dinner long since past, the moon high and vivid in the pitch-black sky. He twisted and turned and jerked, and she knew that any minute now he would hit the dirt and the session would be—There!

He slammed into the ground, rolled and then he was staggering to his feet, his deep, calm voice soothing the shaking animal.

Goosebumps traveled down her arms and anticipation bubbled up inside her. It was time.

She turned and bolted, racing the few yards to her cabin. Inside, she lit every lamp, filled the wash bowl with water and positioned herself in front of the large front window that gave full view of her from the thighs up.

And then she waited.

With the barn behind her and the bunkhouse in front, Colt had to round the cabin to get home, and she intended to use that fact to her ultimate advantage.

The barn door slammed shut in the distance. Boots crunched on gravel, moving closer.

She felt his gaze even before she caught sight of him turning the corner of the cabin.

"He's just a man," she murmured to herself, the words meant to soothe and encourage and unleash. Yes, unleash was what she needed to do, but it felt more difficult than she'd expected. She'd kept her wild woman locked up for so long, the locks seemed to have rusted shut. Her stomach jumped and her heart double-thumped. Okay, now she could understand why that strategy hadn't worked for Cameron. As for visualizing Colt in his underwear . . .

She wasn't even going there. Instead, she closed her eyes, pictured Colt's face in her mind's eye, the wildness in his gaze, the heat, and started to hum one of her favorite tunes. The footsteps paused and she didn't waste any time reaching for the top button on her blouse.

She was on her eighth chorus of Cheap Trick's "I want you to want me" when she finally reached the last button. Where was a simple piece of Velcro when a girl really needed it?

Giving a heavy sigh that lifted her chest considerably, she chanced a quick peek to make sure he was watching.

Was he ever.

He stood off to the side, his body froze, his gaze fixed. It was working. He was falling hook, line and sinker for number two of the Naughty Nine—I see you. He liked to watch, and she intended to give him an eyeful. If she could just get the hooks on the back of her skirt undone . . . *There*.

Material slithered and pooled, until she wore only a camisole and drawstring underwear. Panic beat through her, but she closed her eyes and found strength in an imagined picture of him, so attentive and wild. He made her feel sinful with his deep, dark gaze, and she slipped more easily into the charade.

She fingered the ties on her camisole, let them fall away one by one until the material parted. Cool air swept over her nipples as they became exposed. They pebbled and swelled. She dunked her hands into the wash basin, submerging them in the sudsy warmth for a long moment as she found the washcloth. Then she arched her neck, tilted her head back and lifted the dripping rag to her throat. Water sluiced down her skin, over the tips of her breasts and she relished the sensation for a long moment before drawing the washcloth down. Over her neck. The slope of one breast. She paused, circling the nipple and wringing a low moan from deep in her throat.

The sound surprised her and her eyelids fluttered open, and her gaze collided with Colt's. Even as she stared deep into his eyes, she knew she shouldn't. This was supposed to be his fantasy. He liked to watch, and one of the titillations of such a fantasy was that the object wasn't supposed to know that someone was watching. It was supposed to be voyeurism at its finest.

Colt's eyes, fierce and primal in the darkness, glittered back at her, feeding her courage, urging her on.

Her eyelids drifted closed again and she gave the same attention to her other breast, circling, rubbing, until she ached for more, for him.

Damp fingers worked at her drawstring pants until the waist loosened and the garment puddled at her feet. The air seemed lodged in her throat as she dunked the washcloth again before touching the hollow between her breasts. Water trickled down her, over her navel, caught in the hair between her legs. The feeling was unlike anything she'd ever felt before. Delicious. Decadent. *Sinful*. She slid the warm rag down, caressing her skin, circling her belly button until her entire body hummed, and then she proceeded further.

Don't look.

Colt's brain issued the command, but damned if his traitorous eyes would listen. They were having too good a time on their own, watching every detail—from the glide of water down her skin, to the steady heaving of her luscious breasts, the suds clinging to her ripe nipples, the subtle touch of her hand as she drew the cloth to the red downy thatch at the apex of her thighs. Her neck arched, her mouth opened and his need overwhelmed his thoughts of propriety.

Focus, a small voice whispered, the last thread of sanity in the face of his overzealous band of hormones that were frantically chanting "Go get 'er, Cowboy!"

He wanted to. He wanted to pull her into his arms and feel her luscious mouth against his own. He wanted to lave her nipples with his tongue and pull her hand away and replace it with his own. She'd be so warm and soft. So damp. So ready.

His body throbbed with awareness. He was ready, too. It had been so long and she was so tempting. He was just a man. Flesh and blood. Weak.

"Blood bay," he murmured, drawing in a shaky breath, willing his feet not to move toward her. He'd worked too hard, sacrificed too much to lose it all now. "Buckskin, buttermilk, calico, California sorrel . . ." He ticked off the colors and markings of horses he knew, focusing on thinking rather than feeling the heat in his groin, the need firing his blood, the hardened flesh of his sex threatening to burst free from his pants.

Don't look.

His brain issued the command again and surprisingly, the rest of his body listened.

Footsteps crunched, pushing past the pounding of her heart, the sound making her ears ring. Elizabeth's eyelids fluttered open in time to see Colt's back as he stormed off toward the bunk house.

Without the heat of his gaze, knowing he was no longer watching, reality intruded. She became acutely aware of her compromising position, the cool night air sweeping over her naked, wet, deprived body.

She yanked the curtains closed and snatched up her clothes. Okay, so Colt apparently wasn't an I-see-you fan, even though she'd been convinced that she'd found his secret weakness.

She tried to calm her pounding heart and ignore the hurt that stabbed through her. She was not going to take this rejection personally. Everyone had their hot button and she simply hadn't punched Colt's.

Yet.

But where there was a will, there was a way, as the saying went. Actually, where there were desperate hormones, there was a way, and she was determined to find it.

"Number three, here I come."

In the meantime, if Colt Durango thought he could simply walk away and forget her so easily, he had another thing coming. Elizabeth Joanna

Carlton was many things, but unforgettable wasn't one of them. She would simply have to get closer to him.

And that would start first thing tomorrow morning. No more waiting.

He couldn't sleep.

Hell, it wasn't surprising. Not after what Colt had just witnessed not less than two hours and three minutes ago. Why, he'd seen the sweetest, warmest-looking woman ever to tempt a man, and he'd walked right on by her.

Not only had she been sweet and warm looking, but she'd been naked as well. *Naked*, for Pete's sake.

It just wasn't fair.

The last thing he needed was a naked woman in his life. Or any woman for that matter. He had his hands full as it was.

He shoved off the horsehair blanket, threw his legs over the side of the bunk and reached for his pants. Sliding on the denim, he grabbed his boots and headed through the bunkhouse. He needed some fresh air and a drink of water.

Hell, what he really needed was some common sense, because he was sorely tempted to march back out to Sinful's cabin and take her up on her blatant offer.

He willed his body to relax and headed past rows of sleeping cowboys, through the adjoining cookhouse and—

"Now this here's a woman." Horseshoe's

voice stopped him cold in the middle of the kitchen where he found the old man sitting at the sawbuck table, a steaming cup of coffee in one hand and a turkey leg in the other.

Colt passed a hand over his face to wipe away his exhaustion. "What are you doing out here?" he asked the man.

"Buck shot a turkey and the boys roasted him up. They invited me down for dinner, but I'd already cooked up a mess of pan-fried steak for your brothers. I was pretty full myself up until a little while ago. I was layin' in my bed, trying to go to sleep and so's I started countin' sheep. Only they didn't look like sheep. They looked like turkeys. So there I was countin' turkeys and I got to thinkin' about Buck's turkeys. Why, I could practically smell the dadblamed critters, taste 'em even." He smacked his lips. "So here I am." He took a bite and said around a mouthful, "Ain't as good as mine, though." He bit off another chunk and chewed.

"I can see that." Colt eyed the picked-clean bones sitting on the plate in front of Horseshoe. "What's that? Your third or fourth piece?"

"Fifth, not that it makes no nevermind. I didn't say it wasn't good. Just that it wasn't as good as mine." He eyed the turkey leg, turned it over in his hand a time or two. "Needs more seasonin', maybe a little salt and some molasses to give it a twinge of sweetness." Horseshoe shifted his attention back to the newsprint laid out on the table next to his plate. "Yessirree, this here's one hell of a woman."

Colt leaned over the man's shoulder and glanced at the listing of ingredients for a dish called Apple Strudel Delight. "I hate to break it to you, but that's a recipe, not a woman."

"Yep, but it's a woman's recipe. It's from Cookin' and Courtin', this here column the Dallas Star runs in their newspaper."

"And how did you get your hands on it?"

"I got my ways, boy. Ernest from the mercantile in town imports these things 'specially for me."

"Import means it comes from out of the country."

"Exactly. Comes a clear hundred miles from Dallas. I get it a few weeks later than the folks there, but it makes no nevermind. Still as good as a cured Christmas ham come spring." He grinned. "Pretty interestin' column, here. Lists gals lookin' to find themselves a husband."

"Mail-order brides?"

"Somethin' like that. Only these gals ain't your typical mail-order merchandise. They can cook. At least this one can. Listen to this, boy. You take soft, succulent apples and dip 'em in molasses 'afore you start slicin' . . ." Horseshoe went on for a few more lines that had him gnawing on the turkey leg in between sentences. "Lordy, this gal sounds good."

"You need to think with your head and not your stomach."

"At least I'm thinkin'."

"What's that supposed to mean?"

The old man eyed him. "That if you had an ounce of sense, you'd be fightin' me for this here column and findin' an Apple Strudel Delight for yourself. You ain't gettin' any younger."

"I'm young enough, and I've got my hands full with this ranch. I don't need to muddy things up with a woman."

"Not just any woman. A woman who can cook. Why, these gals are salt-of-the-earth types. They ain't nothin' like that fancy city gal you got holed up in that there cabin."

Colt narrowed his gaze. "You know about Sinful?"

"I know everythin' that goes on here, and I'm tellin' you right now, don't go gettin' any ideas about her. She ain't your type anymore."

That's exactly what Colt had been telling himself ever since he'd first set eyes on Miss Sinful Sinclair.

The funny thing was, telling it to himself and hearing Horseshoe say it were two very different things. He didn't much like the latter.

He frowned. "She's here to help Cameron. End of story."

"I hope so."

His frown deepened. "Don't you have more vittles to eat somewhere?"

"Actually, Buck also mentioned some venison stew he cooked up tonight." Having finished his turkey, Horseshoe got up from the table and headed for a cast-iron pot hanging near the stove.

"I was thinking of up at the house."

"I like it down here. Nice and quiet this time of night." Horseshoe eyed him. "Usually. What are you doing up this late?"

"I couldn't sleep."

Horseshoe grinned. "City gal already keepin' you up?"

Yes. "No." His mind scrambled for a plausible excuse that would get him out of another knowing look. "A fox in the chicken coop. There's a fox after Cameron's chickens and I thought I'd see about catching it."

"I'll bet," Horseshoe said as he spooned stew into a bowl.

"Best time is at night when the critter's up and about."

"I'll bet." The man topped off the cast-iron pot and headed back for the table.

"I'm not going near the cabin or Sinful Sinclair."

"I'll bet."

"I'm not."

"You ain't got to convince me, boy. I know you got willpower. The question is, are you goin' to use it?"

"Would you just eat and hush up?"

"I'm eating," Horseshoe said around a spoonful of venison stew. "But you really ought to think about this here column. You could use yourself a good woman."

"A woman's the last thing I need," Colt said as he headed outside into the crisp night air.

The *very* last thing.

At least that's what Colt wanted desperately to believe.

It was first thing the next morning and Elizabeth was standing as close as possible to Colt Durango.

Unfortunately, a fence separated them, not to mention a wall of silence that had dropped the moment she'd shown up that morning—after he'd given her his usual wake-up call right on the rump and dragged her out of bed.

Her bottom still stung, but she was up and about and ready to get close to Colt Durango. And she knew just how to do it.

She watched as he crooned to the fidgety horse stomping around the corral and moved in, the harness in his hands.

"So I was thinking," she said when he reached for the horse. At the sound of her voice, his hands dropped away and the animal danced out of his reach. "I've always been fascinated by ranches and since this is a real one, I was hoping you could show me around."

"No time. I've got work to do."

"Maybe I could help."

He shot her a glance over his shoulder, his gaze moving from her face to the tips of her toes and back up again. "I doubt that, Peaches."

"I *could*, too," she insisted.

"We'll see." Silence fell over them as he moved toward the horse again. He reached out.

"I could pitch hay," she suggested. The horse danced and his hands fell away again. "You do pitch hay around here. I saw you doing that yesterday."

"Which means I'm finished doing it."

"Oh."

More silence as he moved forward again. He lifted the harness.

"What about collecting eggs?" The minute the question was out, every muscle in his body tensed. The horse moved and he let out a vicious curse.

He turned on her. "I've got work to do. Why don't you run along?"

"What about the eggs?"

"I don't gather eggs. Cain does it."

"Well, what do you do? I think you'd be a fascinating resource and I'd really like to see what you do firsthand."

"A what—"

"Never mind. I'm just interested and eager to help. I'm sure you can use another hand around here."

He eyed her for a long moment. "Eager, huh?"

"Very eager. Just tell me what I can do and I'll be right there by your side, ready, willing and able."

He studied her for a long moment before he finally spoke. "Meet me at the barn in a half-hour," he told her. "And you can help."

She smiled and climbed off the fence. "Agreed." Excitement rushed through her. This was it. Her chance. They would be working side by side. Arm to arm. Sharing the same space. Breathing the same air. It was time to learn his interests and get close. Very *close*.

The last thing Colt intended to do was let her get close to him. But since she was so hellbent on learning the workings of a ranch, the least he could do was oblige her.

"Here." He handed her a shovel and indicated the first stall.

"I thought you pitched all the hay yesterday."

"It's not for hay pitching, Peaches. It's for shoveling."

He watched as she glanced into the stall and wrinkled her nose. "You mean . . ."

"That's exactly what I mean." He glanced toward the open doorway. "You'd better get started, too. It's nearly lunchtime and there are twenty more stalls just like this one waiting."

Indecision played across her features and for a few seconds Colt thought he might actually have won the battle before the first shot had been fired. No way was she going to hike up her skirt and walk into the dung-filled area.

"I guess if you can do it, so can I." She hiked up her skirt, revealing trim calves and slender ankles that tapered into a functional pair of boots that had belonged to his stepmother.

183

There wasn't a danged thing sexy about her getup. Yet he felt his groin stir in response. Worse, something shifted in his chest as she lifted the shovel, drew in a deep breath and walked into the stall. Something dangerously close to admiration.

Crazy. She was only doing it to get close to him. To seduce him. Still, the women he'd known would never have gone to such great lengths to seduce a man. The women he'd known in his past wouldn't get their hands dirty, even for a tumble with a sexy cowboy.

This one was definitely one of a kind.

Not *his* kind, he told himself yet again. Not anymore.

"Where's your shovel?"

"I'm not shoveling. I've got a batch of strays to round up."

"But I thought I'd be helping you."

"Actually, Peaches, you're going to be helping Buck. He's in charge of shoveling the stalls and he's been feeling a mite poorly lately." He pointed to a short, round man sitting near the barn doorway. He wore dirty overalls, no shirt and a stained cowboy hat. He smiled, revealing a toothless grin before he went back to the whittling in his hand. "His old arms aren't what they used to be. I've been promising to get him some help, so your offer came at the perfect time."

"Buck?" Her face fell as she stared past him at the toothless man. "But—"

"I'll see you later, sugar," he cut in. "You need

anything, you just ask old Buck, here, and he'll help you out."

Because Colt Durango was *not* going to help her himself. He was going to discourage her as best he could, despite his sudden urge to take the shovel from her hands and do the work for her.

After all, it wasn't his idea to put her to work. She'd come up with that all by herself. The least he could was oblige her.

She was stupid, that's what she was.

Elizabeth decided that later on, after eight hours shoveling poop and praying for a can of Lysol.

Her back ached, her nose burned and her feet cramped at the mere thought of the boots she'd yet to get used to. So much for spending time with Colt Durango.

He'd appeared later that day, much later, cast one glance at the stalls, commented on a decent job and walked away. He hadn't even so much as glanced at her.

Not that she'd wanted him to. She'd been filthy and smelly and about as attractive as a pile of the poop she'd been shoveling. She fought back a wave of tears and concentrated on pulling on a fresh dress. Her muscles screamed with each movement, but she was determined. She had a fantasy to carry out tonight and she wasn't going to be discouraged just because her get-close-to-Colt plan hadn't worked.

She would simply chalk today up to experience and forge ahead.

She drew in a deep breath and eyed the boots for a long moment before shucking them off. If all went as well as planned tonight, she wouldn't be wearing shoes anyway. She might as well skip the formalities and cut right to the chase.

"Fantasy number three, here I come."

Chapter Eight

Six days and an equal number of fantasies later, and Elizabeth had yet to effectively punch even one of Colt Durango's hot buttons. She was beginning to wonder if he had any.

She'd not only undressed in the window for him, but the following night she'd touched herself in a very blatant demonstration of number three—sex without contact. Sex as in "bringing herself to orgasm." That was the difference between numbers two and three. Number two implied watching sexy things. Three implied something a little deeper.

Elizabeth had intended to get down and dirty and have an orgasm, but before she could so much as get herself into the mood, Colt had stomped off toward the bunkhouse. She'd spent another night alone and frustrated.

The next night she'd fashioned a mask out of the lace of one of her chemises and met him in the barn in a very obvious number four—the faceless stranger—and promptly found herself abandoned in a haystack.

The night after that had been even more humiliating. She'd cornered him out behind the barn with a very lethal-looking pitchfork after everyone had gone to bed, and ordered him to undress. It was the classic force fantasy and number five of the Naughty Nine. Before she'd been able to blink, he'd disarmed her, tossed her over his shoulder and toted her back to the cabin. There, he'd left her with strict orders to behave or else.

Yesterday, she'd actually approached him while he'd been inside one of the horse stalls with a rowdy looking chestnut for a little number six—the audience fantasy. Okay, so a horse didn't really qualify as a roomful of people, but at least it had looked when she'd undressed for Colt, which was more than she could say for the cowboy. He'd busied himself doing anything and everything but looking at her.

She had all of three fantasies left and her hope was fading. Not to mention she was getting more calluses than she could count, thanks to that shovel and the ridiculous sense of obligation she felt to Buck. She'd actually gone back for more smelly torture.

But the man had been so appreciative, not to

mention he'd wittled her the cutest horse figurine. She couldn't let him down.

As for Colt . . .

Something was wrong.

You, a voice whispered. *You're not sexy or desirable or daring. You're just not any of the things you're pretending to be and he just isn't turned on.*

Maybe. Then again, it took two to tango. Maybe it was Colt himself who was causing the problem.

"Your brother does like women?" she asked Cameron on Friday evening when he arrived for their nightly lesson, his notes in one hand and Horseshoe's all-cure in the other. They hadn't made a ton of progress, but she wasn't unhappy with the boy's growing comfort level.

"Sure." Cameron settled in at the table for his lesson. "Colt likes everybody."

"I mean *like* like, as in romantically."

He stared at her blankly for a long moment, then his ears reddened. " 'Course he does." He nodded. "He loves women."

"Of course." So much for salving her bruised ego. Colt was as straight as an arrow, which meant he just wasn't interested in her. That was the only explanation for the way he'd brushed her off for the past week. She sighed.

"Let's get started. Do you have your kissing notes—"

"Then again, I've never really seen him talk to any in particular," Cameron cut in, still stuck on her first question. "When we're in town, I don't really pay him no nevermind. That's when I get to see Caroline. I'm usually trying so danged hard not to get sick that I forget all about him."

"That's understandable. You certainly don't want to toss your cookies in front of—"

"But I'm sure he does," the young man went on. "Why, he probably sweet-talks every woman within spittin' distance and I just ain't of a mind to take notice—but I will, if you like. First thing tomorrow."

"What's tomorrow?"

"Town."

"Town? As in people and buildings and *stores?*" Her frustration level was at its peak. She needed some satisfaction in the worst way and there was nothing like the sweet smell of shoes or clothes or *anything* to fill the ache inside her. Shopping was a wonderful cure-all.

"There's McCrory's Mercantile."

"I'm there." Hey, it wasn't Saks, but beggars couldn't be choosers and she needed a shopping excursion in the worst way.

"You're going with us?" He eyed her warily. "It's a few hours away and we usually leave afore sunup. You sure you can get up that early?"

"I've been dragging myself up plenty early the past few days. I'm going. Besides, I can't very well send my prize student out on his own. Tomorrow's your first test."

"Test?" The word seemed to sink in and the meaning of what she was saying hit him. "You mean . . . That is, because I'm gonna see Caroline?"

"That's right. And you're going to sweet-talk her right into a kiss."

"I'm gonna sweet-talk her right into a kiss," he repeated. The knowledge seemed to sink in and his eyes widened. "I'm gonna sweet-talk her into a kiss?" He shook his head. "I can't."

"Sure, you can."

"I'm not ready."

"You've got a stack of notes. You're as ready as you'll ever be."

"But I just *can't*. I'm . . ." He seemed to search for words. "I'm busy. I mean, I will be busy. Looking out for Colt, that is. He's my step-brother. Kin. I can't just leave him to fend for himself, especially now that I know he might have a problem. You don't think he has the same problem as me, do you? That maybe he ain't comfortable with the ladies either?"

"I'm sure that's not a worry." With those eyes and that body, she had no doubt Colt Durango was very comfortable with the ladies. Any woman would go out of their way to make him so. He just wasn't too comfortable with her. "You just keep your mind on Caroline. I'll see to Colt."

"You gonna give him lessons like you're giving me?"

If only. "I'm sure Colt is fine." That was the

191

trouble. He was fine, which meant something had to be wrong with her.

Geez, where was a hot pair of shoes or some naughty lingerie when a girl *really* needed it.

Tomorrow. The thought of a break the next day eased the disappointment she felt. She wasn't going to worry over Colt, to wrack her brain trying to figure out what she was doing wrong. It was time to retreat and regroup and treat herself and her efforts to a little shopping extravaganza with some of the gold she'd earned. Then she could jump back on the horse and ride out the remaining three fantasies she hadn't yet tried.

In the meantime . . .

Her gaze shifted to Cameron, to the panicked light in his eyes, the tightness around his mouth, and the paleness of his face. She grabbed a hand mirror and handed it to him. She gave him an indulgent smile.

"Pucker up, honey. We've got work to do."

Where the hell was she?

It was past midnight. A full quarter past.

Colt stood in the barn doorway and scanned the dim interior for the countless time. There was no sign of Sinful. No flame-red hair peeking out from behind a hay bale. No creamy thigh visible just beyond a stall wall. No lush lips blowing kisses at him from the haystack. Nothing.

Not that he cared.

It was just that he'd gotten used to seeing her these past few nights, wondering what she would come up with to tempt him, worrying over whether he would have the strength to resist.

Each night grew harder and harder. Each night *he* grew harder and harder. Like tonight.

He glanced down at the prominent bulge stretching the crotch of his pants. And that was just from the anticipation.

He hadn't even seen her yet.

Maybe something was wrong. Maybe she'd gotten sick.

The minute the thought hit him, he turned, his boots pounding in the dust as he headed for her cabin. That was it. She was too sick to get out of bed and play her wicked woman games.

Or she was too busy.

The thought hit him, along with a rush of anger and he halted mid-stride. That was probably what was going on. She was probably too busy with tonight's lesson. With Cameron.

The idea sent him stomping back toward the bunk house. But he would make a brief detour by her cabin, of course. After all, she *could* be lying in bed with a raging fever and no one to hear her delirious cries for help.

The place was quiet—so much for delirious cries—and completely dark. Just dark enough for two people who wanted some privacy. Cameron and Sinful!

Not that he minded a single bit.

He forced himself past the cabin, toward the bunk house and the quiet solitude of his bed. He *didn't* care. The only thing he cared about was his family, this ranch. He had chores in the morning, then also was the ride into town. He needed some sleep. Some real sleep. Not the tossing and turning he'd been doing the past week thanks to Sinful and her bedtime seduction attempts. Lying awake wanting a woman was no way to get rest.

But not tonight. There had been no seduction attempt, which meant he wasn't nearly as worked up, which meant he might even be able to get some actual shut-eye.

Inside the bunk house, he grabbed a bottle of whiskey and headed past the other cowboys— all fast asleep in anticipation of another work day—toward the rear of the building. No sirree. He didn't give a rat's ass if she and Cameron were too busy to come up for air and—

"Cameron?" The boy's name burst from Colt's lips the minute he reached his bunk and saw the young man standing in front of his chest of drawers. The kid was staring into a small shaving mirror propped on top.

"What the heck are you doing?"

Cameron whirled. "I, um, was just waiting for you. And, um, practicing for tomorrow."

Relief rushed through Colt and he actually smiled. His brother was right here in the bunkhouse, not anywhere else getting into who knew what.

Not that Colt would care if he did.

It was the principle of the thing. They had to get up awful early tomorrow after all, and Cameron had chores to do before they set off for town. Just because the boy was learning a thing or two from a beautiful, desirable woman was no cause for him to be allowed to lag behind on his work.

That's what Colt told himself. Now if only he believed it, life would be sweet.

Or at least bearable.

"I thought you might want to borrow this." Cameron handed him the shaving mirror. "For tomorrow."

"I already have a shaving mirror."

"Yeah, but you don't know how to use it. See, it ain't just for shaving. It's for kissing."

"You're kissing a mirror?"

"I'm exercising my lips. Miss Sinful says strong lips make the most kissable. She also says it's good to stretch them out before you do any serious mouthwork."

Colt tried to ignore the jealousy that went through him at hearing "Sinful" and "kissable" in the same sentence, and from his kid stepbrother of all people.

"She ought to know," Colt said as he yanked at the buttons on his shirt.

"Boy, she does. She knows everything."

He didn't need to hear this.

"All types of kissing."

He *really* didn't need to hear this.

"And all about what to say and where to touch, and about forepl—"

"I think that's enough puckering for tonight." Colt reached over and turned the mirror face-down. "We're up early tomorrow, so you ought to be getting up to the house."

"She could probably give you a few pointers," Cameron said. "If you need them. And I'll be glad to show you them lip exercises. Or she could show you. All you have to do is ask—"

"I'll pass."

"I'm sure she wouldn't mind. Then you would feel right comfortable talking with the ladies."

"Pass."

"That is, if you *want* to talk to the ladies." Cameron eyed him while he shrugged off his shirt. "You do, don't you?"

"What are you talking about?"

Cameron's ears turned red as Colt turned on him, and he thought the boy was going to back down. Instead, the kid pulled back his shoulders and stood his ground. "I never see you talk to any women."

"And?"

"And—I just don't, that's all."

"That's because I'm busy when I'm in town." His mouth curled down into a frown. "Turn in."

"All right," Cameron said. "G'night."

Once his brother had left, Colt shucked off his boots. Lessons? Why, of all the crazy, insane, ridiculous things. The last thing, the *very* last thing he needed from Sinful Sinclair was lessons. Especially regarding what she could teach. He had that area covered just fine on his own.

He paused in front of the shaving mirror Cameron had brought him, his gaze going to the thin scar that started at the base of his neck and wound down his chest. Yep, he'd known his fair share of lust, and it had nearly gotten him killed. He wouldn't risk that again. No more women who might have jealous boyfriends or husbands. When he did the deed again, it was going to be with the woman who was destined to be *his* wife. He needed a nice calm, tame filly to temper the stud in him. He wouldn't doom his own kids to the same wanderlust that raged inside him.

His father had managed. He'd saved himself from a life of wandering, and his boys, too, by making sure their mother was just his opposite. Grace had been shy, innocent, and calm. Those wholesome qualities had balanced out the bad boy in Sam Durango—and her sons were all sweethearts. Colt aimed to find himself the right woman to do the same for him.

And her name *wasn't* Sinful Sinclair.

She'd been wrong before. *This* was definitely the worst day of her life.

Elizabeth fought back a yawn and forced her eyes wide even though they fought to creep closed. They'd been doing that since she'd climbed onto the wagon seat well before sunup to wait.

She wasn't missing going into town for anything.

Okay. But she was on the seat now, ready to go. What could it hurt to shut her eyes just a little?

Elizabeth's eyes crept closed as she settled onto the seat. She would just relax a little. . . .

The thought faded as she drifted off. She wasn't lying on a hard bench, but a bed. A soft, fluffy mattress. Satin sheets caressed her back. Her bare back. Mmm . . . Yes, she was completely and totally bare, just like the man leaning over her, pressing into her—

"What the hell are you doing?"

The question snatched her from her satin sheet fantasy, to the smell of hay and horses and *him.*

Colt Durango peered down at her, his hat tipped back. Yesterday's five o'clock shadow had turned to the beginnings of a beard, and lines of exhaustion wreathed his eyes.

He'd never looked better, and her body gave a traitorous throb.

Shopping, she told herself. She needed something to build up her self-esteem before she went after Mr. Unattainable with the remaining three fantasies.

"What the hell are you doing?" he asked again. "It's barely sunup and you're awake. Without any coercion."

"Don't remind me." She scrambled upright, noting the chaos around her as Colt's stepbrothers piled into a second wagon, along with a scowling old man she could only guess was the infamous apple-tart-baking, cure-all-making Horseshoe MacAllister.

"Why are you up so early?"

"I'm going to town with you."

"No, you're not."

"Yes, I am."

"No." He shook his head. "The last thing I need is the people in this town seeing you. Especially looking so . . ." He eyed her. "Like that."

She glanced down at the simple calico dress. "What's wrong with the way I look? Okay, so it's a bit too *Little House on the Prairie*, but I didn't exactly have a say in the matter."

"It's too revealing."

"It buttons up to the throat."

"It's too tight."

"I could fit a family of four inside this skirt."

"It's too . . ." He shook his head. "Forget it."

"I'm going. You either take me with you or I'll hitch a ride on my own."

His grin was slow and provocative and she had the sudden urge to dip him in sugar and eat him whole. *If only*.

"I hate to say it, sweetheart, but there isn't anyone around here for miles."

"I'll hitch a ride in the second wagon."

"They won't take you unless I say the word."

"So say the word." When he didn't look the

least bit accommodating, she added, "Take me with you or I'll walk." At his doubtful expression, she added, "I will. I swear it. I walked a 10K back in college and while I don't exactly have a pair of sneakers, where there's a will, there's a way."

When he gave her a puzzled look and started to open his mouth, she rushed on, her voice ripe with sudden desperation. "Look, I'm going stir-crazy out here. I've read *Moby Dick* and *A Tale of Two Cities* and *Silas Marner,* and just yesterday I finished off *Twenty Thousand Leagues Under the Sea*. I'm this close to picking up the needlepoint sampler if I don't get a shoe fix."

"A shoe fix?"

"New shoes."

"What's wrong with those? Are they too tight?"

"No."

"Worn out?"

"No."

"Then why—"

"It's a woman thing. I just need a new pair. Maybe two. Three would be wonderful. Now please, take me."

"Okay," he finally muttered, pinning her with a stern gaze. "But keep the bonnet on. And the shawl. And behave yourself. I don't need any flashy city woman setting the tongues around here wagging." He climbed onto the seat next to her and grabbed the reins.

She glanced down at her simple dress and a

warmth spread through her. "You actually think I look flashy?"

His only answer was a fierce glare and a loud "Giddyup!"

The wagon jerked forward. Her arm brushed his and he stiffened, and for the first time in days, Elizabeth decided that maybe, just maybe, she might be wearing Colt Durango down.

She smiled, settling onto the seat. This might not turn out to be such a bad day after all.

Chapter Nine

"I'll take them."

The clerk smiled and added the lace-up leather boots to the already growing stack of items on the counter. Elizabeth's therapeutic shopping usually focused on shoes, but after sitting next to Colt Durango, feeling his thigh brush hers with every jolt of the wagon, hearing his deep, even breaths, smelling his delicious scent, she'd been desperate for relief.

For satisfaction.

She stared at the pile, everything from rose water and lavender soaps to a calico-print skirt. Nothing like a full-blown shopping extravaganza to give her that warm, fulfilled feeling inside.

Yet strangely enough, as she took the packages and left McCrory's Mercantile, she still felt unfulfilled. It hadn't helped that she'd seen a sign up in the mercantile that was advertising for an upcoming cotillion. A town dance. How she wished Colt would ask her to . . .

She pushed away the thought. There wasn't a man alive who couldn't be quickly displaced with a little buying frenzy. Her gaze snagged on the man standing several yards away in front of the livery. The sun outlined Colt's broad frame, making him seem even more dark and mysterious and sexy.

A pang of longing shot through her and she stiffened.

No, she wouldn't allow that! No longing. No lusting. Not for the next forty-five minutes, no matter how good he looked standing there in his cowboy hat and leather vest, his shirt sleeves rolled up to reveal tanned forearms sprinkled with sun-bleached hair. Nor would how his deep gaze snagged on her affect her, how he stared through her, how he smiled at her for a heart-stopping second that made her think he actually did want her.

Right. Six—count them, *six*. She'd gone through six of the Naughty Nine and she was no closer to uncovering his fantasy and seducing him.

Reality check! She had to face the truth. She sucked at this sinful business. *Attention everyone. Elizabeth Carlton is destined to die an old, shriveled-up prune like all the fine, upstanding Carlton women before her*. There would be no living life or walking on the wild side or tasting the forbidden.

It just wasn't in the cards.

"Howdy there, ma'am." The masculine voice drew her around to see a smiling cowboy tip his hat at her.

At first she glanced behind her, sure he must be making some mistake, but when she turned, she found she was the only one around. Her gaze slid back to his and he winked, and the woman on his arm gave a sharp tug on his shirt sleeve.

"Nathaniel Morgan Lewis Barnhart! You stop that carousing right now."

"Just bein' friendly, Ima Jean."

"Friendly my Uncle Nate's sweet patootie," the woman snorted. "Come along."

The cowboy's gaze captured Elizabeth's for a split second. She noted the gleam in his eyes and her mind drew her back to The Red Parlour Room. She remembered the clapping and chanting and the men. They had been surrounding her, staring at her, mesmerized by her.

Now, wearing a calico print dress complete with bonnet and shawl, she looked more like she was from *Little House on the Prairie* than *The Best Little Whorehouse in Texas*. Her garb was certainly a far cry from a sexy bustier, a feather boa, and not much else.

But his attraction wasn't due to her looks—

at least not the way her clothes looked. This was lust. Charisma. Sex appeal.

Because of the garter.

She felt the tightness around her thigh, the rub of silk and lace when she shifted her weight. Okay, so maybe she didn't totally suck at this sinful business. She couldn't. Not with the garter firmly in place.

Returning the cowboy's smile, she picked up her packages and started across the street to where the Durango wagon was hitched. Five cowboys and an equal number of smiles—including a few winks, some howdies and a full-fledged stare—later, and she reached the other side.

Okay, apparently she didn't suck. She definitely had it going on.

Sort of. Her gaze shifted once again to Colt, who was busying himself looking over his horse. He seemed to sense her. He turned and his gaze caught hers, but she got no smile or hat tip or lustful stare. Sure, she thought she had glimpsed lust on a few occasions, but she was fast coming to realize that it was more wishful thinking than any actual feeling on his part. Colt Durango was immune to the garter's appeal.

He wasn't just immune. He was turned off by her.

Because he sees through the charade. He sees the real you. The real, boring, plain you. Give it up, girlfriend.

She ignored the disconcerting thoughts. If he saw the real her, he'd see hot and sexy and wild. He'd see the woman she'd spent her entire life repressing. He'd see that she was sinful to the core.

He *would*.

"Are you okay?" Cameron asked. He'd come up beside her. Taking a few packages from her, he started placing her goods in the family wagon—the second one, farther from Colt.

"Fine. So how did it go? Did you talk to her?"

He shrugged. "Not exactly."

"But you smiled at her, right?"

"Not exactly."

"You winked?"

"Not exactly." At her frustrated look, he shrugged again. "I didn't exactly see her."

"I thought you said she was over at Carlisle's Emporium."

"She is. At least, I think she is. I didn't exactly go in. I meant to, but I just didn't have the time. I promised Colt I'd see to buying the chicken feed over at the livery. And then Horseshoe needed me to stop in at the blacksmith and pick up the brand he ordered—Hey, where you going?"

"To Carlisle's," she called over her shoulder as she started across the street. "You can either stop being a baby and come with me, or stay right there and I'll bring you a piece of penny candy."

"I ain't no baby," he said, falling into step beside her.

"I'm not a baby," she corrected. "And I know you're not. You're a young man who's about to go calling on his sweetheart." She paused at the doorway to the Emporium.

"Are you ready?"

"No."

She smiled. "Come on, and remember, you can do this. You've been practicing, and you drank a triple dose of Horseshoe's all-cure." And then she pushed open the door.

The interior was similar to McCrory's Mercantile. There was a variety of everything, from sacks of flour and grain to pots and pans and bolts of material. A counter full of hats lined the far wall, attended by a very plain-looking girl with mousy brown hair and chubby cheeks. The opposite wall held jars galore full of various candies. Standing at attention amid all the confections was the most beautiful girl Elizabeth had ever seen. She had long blond hair and bright blue eyes. She was the sort of girl who would have been right at home in a cheerleader outfit, hanging on the arm of the captain of the football team, her skirt up to here, her chest out to there—the girl Elizabeth had always wanted to be.

"There she is," Cameron breathed, his voice trembling with fear and awe.

They were feelings Elizabeth knew all too well. She'd felt them every time she'd glanced at beautiful bad boy, Chase Parker. Every time she'd glimpsed him across a crowded hallway, seen him holding court in the middle of the cafeteria or riding off into the sunset on his Harley.

"Okay," she told him, stiffening with the memory of that one instance when Chase had asked her if she wanted a ride home. It had been one of those telling moments in a person's life. She'd been at a crossroads. Her heart had longed to jump onto the back of his bike, slip her arms around his waist and forget about the piano lesson waiting for her. Unfortunately, her head had reminded her of all the reasons she'd needed to stay on the sidewalk and head home, especially with half the school watching her, waiting to see what Miss Prim and Proper would do.

Of course, she'd done what was expected. She loved her father too much to ruin the one thing he loved—his career.

While she could sow her wild oats right here and now during this strange escape from the reality she'd always known, she could never undo that one decision that had shaped her life forever.

But Cameron hadn't made his choice yet. He was standing at that same crossroads, and Elizabeth was determined to give him a push in the right direction.

"Okay, take a deep breath, walk over and say hello." When he didn't budge, she added, "Relax. She's just a woman. She puts her undies on one leg at a time just like the rest of us. Just visual—"

"Don't," he cut in. "Or I'm liable to turn and run the other way." He drew in another deep breath. "Okay, I'm gonna do it." And then he took a step forward. "I *am*."

She watched as he crossed the room and by-passed Miss Nineteenth-Century Cheerleader. He was chickening out. He wasn't going to—wait a second.

Cameron was headed toward the candy counter.

"What are you doing?" Elizabeth hurried over and caught his arm.

"Going to talk to her."

"Aren't you going in the wrong direction? That's Caroline." She pointed to the opposite side of the store where the blonde modeled a large feather-plumed hat.

Cameron turned on her as if she were Dennis Rodman at a conservative Republican convention. "Are you joshin' me?" He shook his head. "That's her sister Nadine." He turned and stared longingly at the curtain covering the doorway. "Nadine can't hold a candle to Caroline. Did you see Caroline's face? Those eyes? That hair?" A dreamy look crept over his features. "She's a goddess."

The slim brunette turned to grab a jar full of rock candy. Her elbow caught a bag of licorice.

Candy scattered and she disappeared behind the counter.

Elizabeth pressed a hand to Cameron's forehead. "You're not warm, so I'll have to rule out the delirious with fever theory."

A lovesick smile lifted the boy's lips as he watched his beloved stand and fumble with the lid on the barrel-size jar of sweets. "One of them Venus de Milo's my ma was always talking about."

Elizabeth's gaze shifted from Cameron's smitten face to the uncoordinated girl who struggled to fill a small bag with rock candy. Well, she wasn't the knockout she'd expected to strike fear into the heart of Colt's brother, but she was cute in a plain, uncoordinated sort of way.

Sweet.

Elizabeth drew in a deep breath and tapped on the counter. "Miss Caroline, could you help us please?"

"What are you doing?" Cameron hissed.

"You were about to talk to her before I interrupted. I'm just helping you get back into the swing of things." Elizabeth's gaze shifted back to the girl who'd glanced up and, in the process, dropped a few of the jawbreakers she was taking out of a different jar. "Come over here, please." The glass container she held clunked down, the few jawbreakers that she'd dropped rolling farther away, and the girl started toward them. Elizabeth moved to the side to let her by, but Caroline's gaze snagged on Cameron as if seeing him for the first time. Her cheeks flushed a vivid crimson.

"Here's your chance," Elizabeth whispered to Cameron just before the girl stopped in front of them. "Don't blow it. Tell her hello."

"I . . ." His words faded as he swallowed. His Adam's apple bobbed. "That is, I . . ."

"What he's trying to say is, hello."

The girl's cheeks purpled further and Elizabeth felt sure she was going to make a mad dash for the stockroom. She couldn't let that happen.

"Nice weather we're having," she said, thinking fast. "Isn't it?"

"I . . ." The young woman licked her lips and Elizabeth could almost hear the sudden pounding frenzy of Cameron's heart. "I—I guess so."

"Great weather for a cotillion."

"A—a what?"

"The dance. You're going, aren't you? Because Cameron is going and I know he'd love to see you there—being of approximately the same age group. In fact, you two could go together. Wouldn't you like that, Cameron?" Elizabeth nudged the boy, but all he did was grunt. His mouth opened, but nothing came out. She covered for him. "He's got a touch of laryngitis. Otherwise, he'd be talking your ear off. So what do you say? Would you like to go with him to the dance?"

"I guess so." Caroline's gaze shifted and for

the first time, she stared Cameron square in the eyes.

Longing flashed in the young man's eyes and Elizabeth was sure this was it. His moment of reckoning. This was the crossroads she'd been considering earlier; and Cameron was not going to make the same mistake Elizabeth had made so many years ago. He was going to haul Miss Caroline across the counter and kiss the daylights out of her. She felt sure of it.

"Okay," Cameron said. "Bye." He turned and bolted.

Elizabeth blanched. What was he doing? Why was he running out now? She turned to the girl. "Nice talking to you. Cameron will see you Friday night." Caroline gave her an odd look, but Elizabeth just smiled at her. With that, she turned and chased Colt's brother.

She caught him out near the hitching post trying to make a fast getaway. "Where are you going?"

"I feel sick. I can't believe it." He grasped the wooden railing and leaned over it, gasping for air. "You asked her to the dance."

"No. *You* asked her to the dance, and she's going. Isn't that what you wanted?"

"Yes. No." He shook his head. "I can't do this. I'm not ready."

She touched his shoulder. "You're not giving yourself a chance. You're giving up before you've even tried."

Excuse me, but could you practice what you

preach, Miss Elizabeth? The self-condemnation rushed through her mind, prickling her conscience. It was true, she'd only made it through six of Isabella X's nine fantasies. There were still three more to go. One of them could be the answer, Colt's ultimate fantasy.

And I've got some swampland in West Texas.

She pushed the doubt aside and focused on Cameron. "You have to hang in there. Go after what you want. She likes you. I'm sure of it."

"She hardly spoke to me."

"You hardly spoke to her."

"That's 'cause I was nervous."

"Maybe she's just as nervous as you are." Elizabeth remembered how the girl had flushed.

"You think?" He shook his head in disbelief. "A beautiful woman like her ain't got no call to be nervous. She can have her pick of the boys around here."

"Maybe, but she's going to the dance with you."

"Now I really do feel sick." With that, he turned and bolted across the busy street, back towards the livery.

"Cameron, wait! There's no reason to be afraid—"

"What's wrong?" Colt's deep voice brought her whirling around. He had silently walked up behind her.

"—of snakes," she quickly amended. She couldn't let Colt know that her lessons with Cameron had not been as intensive and effectual as perhaps they could have been. Had she really been Sinful. "Because you're certainly not afraid of women. No sirree. You're doing just fine and dandy in that department." She looked up at Colt. "What were you saying?"

"Something's wrong with him."

"Of course there is. He has a full-fledged snake phobia. You should have warned me."

"There aren't any snakes around."

"There's no rhyme nor reason to a phobia. Hello again, Mr. Barnhart!" She called out to the man she'd met outside the mercantile. He was no longer accompanied. Elizabeth smiled, eager to divert her attention from Colt's dark, assessing gaze.

"Howdy, Miss Sinclair. Let me help you with those." He bent to pick up the packages that Cameron had abandoned.

"No need. I'll get them."

"Thanks a heap, Colt. That leaves me free to escort Miss Sinclair to her wagon." Barnhart took her elbow, but before he could help her down the steps, another man joined in.

"Howdy, Miss Sinclair. A purty thing like you shouldn't be going up and down the steps alone."

"She's not alone. She's with me," Barnhart said.

"That's a matter of opinion. Maybe she'd rather be with me."

"Boys, boys," she clucked. "I've got two arms." She slid a hand around each man's arm, all the while feeling Colt's gaze burn into her backside. If she hadn't known better, she would have sworn he might actually be a little put off that she was walking down the street with two admiring men.

Of course, she knew better. Colt Durango wasn't the jealous type—and if he had been, he certainly wouldn't be jealous over her. He barely spared her a glance. He had repelled all her advances. No, the jealous theory was too much to hope for.

That's what she told herself, but after the long walk to the wagon, she wasn't so certain.

She could still fell Colt's gaze drilling into her, hear the stomp of his boots, and there was no mistaking his growl when she laughed at something one of her escorts said.

He was jealous, all right, and Elizabeth loved every minute of it. Particularly when he pushed aside Mr. Barnhart and the other man to help her into the wagon. His hands closed around her waist and his gaze caught hers. Fire leapt deep in the dark blue depths and heat rolled through her.

She hadn't known much firsthand, but she knew lust when she saw it. He wanted her. He really wanted her.

Number seven, here I come.

But first, she had to make it back to the ranch without spontaneously combusting. And that was going to be very difficult if Colt climbed up and sat so close to her.

As if her thoughts spurred him into action, wood creaked and he joined her on the seat. His thigh brushed hers. His scent filled her nostrils, and she forgot all about her shoes and her new alligator handbag and snakeskin belt. The purchases she had made no longer brought her relief.

She wanted something altogether different, and she wanted it now.

"Maybe I'll just ride in back with Cameron."

He shrugged. "Do what you want."

She smiled and caught his smoldering glance. "That's exactly what I intend to do, cowboy."

And tonight was the night.

Chapter Ten

"Come on, baby. Take a lick." Elizabeth felt the warm roll of a tongue over her palm as the horse lapped up the sugar cube. "At least someone likes me." She scratched the horse behind the ears and frowned.

She only wished she could say the same for Colt. It seemed that his show of jealousy earlier that day in town had been just that—one great big show. She'd smiled at him and bumped against him and done her best to draw his attention during the wagon ride home, but it had all been for nothing. He'd barely glanced at her, and the moment they'd pulled up to the ranchhouse he'd promptly headed out to the barn to make sure that every other hand had finished his work. He'd given the entire staff—including Horseshoe—the evening off for some fun.

Of course, Horseshoe's idea of fun was a game of solitaire. Still, when Colt had approved it, the other boys had all headed off to town for some drinking and carousing. Now, Elizabeth almost wished she'd gone with them. After all, she wasn't having much luck here. The trouble was, she didn't want to carouse with just any cowboy. She wanted Colt.

He didn't just look the part, he made her feel the part. Wild and wicked and wanton. He was not only what made her lusty, but the man whom she lusted after. If only she made him feel the same.

The horse lapped at her empty palm, drawing her attention, and she smiled. "Too bad I don't have hooves, a massive overbite and a pretty tail."

"I don't know about that, Peaches. Your tail looks pretty enough from where I'm standing."

Elizabeth turned to find Colt Durango standing just inside the barn doorway, his back against the wall, his arms folded as if he'd been watching her.

If only.

"If I didn't know better, I'd say you were paying me a compliment."

His eyes gleamed with amusement and something else. Something hotter. "But you know better, right?"

"Considering you treat me like I've got a major case of cooties, I'd say yes. I won't bite, you know." A thought struck her regarding a certain fantasy she'd read about, and she came close to taking back her words. Would he want her to bite him?

Nah. Colt, with his gentle but firm hand and his crooning voice, was definitely not the sadomasochistic type. He was no different from the fifty thousand other males Isabella X had interviewed for her book, and so Elizabeth was sticking to the Naughty Nine and the last and final fantasy.

Full speed ahead. Gathering her courage, she pulled from her skirt the lollipop she'd bought at the mercantile. While this wasn't exactly dropping to her knees and unbuttoning his pants, her ego had been bruised enough. She was going to feel him out with the lollipop trick, see how he reacted, and then she'd go from there.

"You did a good job with Maddie." She could start by complimenting him on his work.

"Thanks." He walked past her, busying himself with the saddle he was carrying.

"She's as gentle as a baby."

"Not quite, but she'll get there. So will Justice."

"Justice?"

"The new sorrell out in the corral. Horseshoe brought him in this morning. I'd be careful with her. She's calm, but still a little nervous."

"Not around me. We're old friends. Right, girl?" Elizabeth gave the animal a pat. "Besides, I've got a bribe." She held up the lollipop and let the horse take a long lick, then she put it on a rail so that the animal could continue enjoying the sweet. "I haven't met a man alive who can resist raspberry swirl." She withdrew a second lollipop and put it to her lips. Her tongue darted out for a long slow lick.

Colt didn't so much as blink. He just watched, seemingly unaffected.

"What about you? You like raspberry swirl?" She pushed the lollipop into her mouth and twirled it a few times before pulling it out and wetting her lips suggestively.

"I've never been much for sweets myself."

"You've never tried these." She held up the lollipop so he could take a taste. He looked ready to refuse, but then his expression softened. His tongue darted out and he tasted the candy.

"It's good." He licked his lips and for a long moment, Elizabeth forgot that she was the one who was supposed to be enticing him. Her gaze followed the movement of his tongue across his sensuous bottom lip and she swallowed. Hard.

". . . bad for you."

Watching the play of his mouth was so distracting that she hadn't heard him talking.

"What did you say?"

"I said that too much sugar is bad for you."

"True, but sometimes you have to do things that are dangerous." She swirled her tongue around the edge of the sweet and watched Colt's eyes flare hotter. She had him. This was it. Number nine. Oral fantasies.

Judging from the way he was watching her mouth, the desire bright in his gaze, she'd hit a bull's-eye.

Finally.

"So?" She offered him the lollipop. "You take a taste." She licked her lips and let her gaze drop. "And I'll take a taste." Even as she said the words, she couldn't believe that they actually came out of her mouth. They were so daring, so risque, so *sinful*.

She smiled. "So what'll it be, cowboy?"

His eyes flared hotter, brighter, and excitement ricocheted through her insides, like a pinball racking up a high score.

"I . . . I should be turning in. It's late." And before she could blink, he turned and left the barn.

It took a few moments for the truth to register. She'd all but dropped to her knees and offered him pleasure and he'd walked away.

Forget walked. He'd practically run.

"What's wrong with me?" she cried out.

Colt's horse whinnied and she turned. The beast had finished its treat and wanted more. His tongue darted out and he lapped up her lollipop.

Crunch!

She looked down at the bare stick she held and gave a sigh of disgust. "Thanks a lot. That was my last one."

Not that she would be needing any more lollipops. Colt had turned down her offer. He didn't want her candy. He didn't want her.

Hence, number nine was a total bust. Isabella's book had failed her. And she couldn't imagine settling for someone else. Elizabeth apparently just wasn't cut out for a life of sex and wild times. Heck, she wasn't even going to be able to have one episode.

There was only one thing left for her to do.

It was time to go home.

He was crazy. Plum crazy.

That was the only reason a man—a hard, hot, hungry man—would turn down a warm, willing, sexy-as-hell woman who wanted him in the worst way.

It's called walking the straight and narrow. Being responsible. Growing up.

He clung to the thought, drew in a deep, ragged breath and picked up his steps. Otherwise, he was liable to turn around and head back to the barn, to her, to do what he'd been wanting to do ever since the first moment he'd laid eyes on Sinful Sinclair.

A vision pushed into his head, of fiery red hair spread out against white cotton sheets, and his body gave an answering throb. He paused at the watering trough and dunked his head. Ice-cold relief closed over him for a soothing moment before he came up for air.

He'd had enough women to satisfy a dozen

men during his lifetime. He shouldn't want any more.

Then again, that was precisely why he did. This woman reminded him of a past that still called to him. She was everything he'd left behind.

Sinful Sinclair was wild and wicked and exciting.

No more. He didn't need those things in his life any longer. He'd recognized the error of his ways and turned over a new leaf. He was a different man, certainly not the sort to get involved with a woman only interested in a night's pleasure. This was a woman who'd been teaching bedroom tricks to his younger brother.

Just the thought twisted a knife in his gut.

What the hell was he thinking, wanting someone like her?

He'd given up her kind for good. They were too much trouble. He'd come up against so many jealous husbands and lovers, looked down the barrel of too many pistols, and all for a pleasure that had been wholly fleeting. He'd never been satisfied. Not really. And that was why he'd always gone back for more. And more. Hoping that one day he'd find fulfillment.

Until he'd received Grace's letter and had come home to find his father on his deathbed, the victim of a bullet that had been meant for Colt.

He started for the cookhouse, the only place he could be assured was empty. With his brothers in the house huddled in front of the fire or asleep, Horseshoe cussing and fussing at himself over his solitaire game, and the bunkhouse full of the few hands who hadn't ridden into town, Colt was a man with few options. The cookhouse and some cold stew.

Or the barn and a warm, willing woman.

There was no question about it. He was crazy, all right. Crazy as a loon.

And from the looks of things, he decided, the minute he opened the cookhouse door, the condition ran in the family.

"I like you." Cameron sat at the sawbuck table, his elbows propped on top, a looking glass in his hands. "Oh?" He stared at his reflection, his expression expectant as if he listened to some silent voice. "You like me, too? I'm the most handsome wrangler you've ever seen? Well, shoot, darlin', you're as pretty as a framed daisy yourself." He smiled. "You want to what? To kiss me? Why, sure, honey. Don't be shy. I won't laugh—" Cameron's voice came to an abrupt halt as the door creaked shut behind Colt. His eyes flew to his stepbrother and a bright red flush stained his cheeks.

"I didn't know you were there."

"What are you doing?" Colt reached for a plate and tried to pretend he wasn't wondering what horse had walloped Cameron in the head.

Or what woman had loved him silly.

He shook off the thought and reached for a wooden spoon.

"Nothing." Wood creaked as Cameron shifted. "I was just talking . . . That is, I was practicing talking."

"You seem like you talk just fine to me." Colt retrieved the iron pot of stew from the icebox and placed it on the table. "What do you need to practice for?"

"For the town dance. I'm going with Caroline next Saturday night." He smiled for a full victorious moment before the statement seemed to sink in and his expression fell. "I'm going with Caroline next Saturday night," he repeated. Panic filled his eyes. "Hell's bells, that's just seven days away."

"You asked her to the Cotillion?" Colt asked, but Cameron didn't seem to be listening.

"In just seven days—count 'em—*seven*, I'll be with her. Close to her. Standing beside—"

"Looks like them lessons really paid off." Just saying the words left a bad taste in Colt's mouth and an ache in his gut. He focused his attention on shoveling a spoonful of cold meat and potatoes onto his plate.

"We'll be sitting together, drinking punch and eating cake and dancing . . . Landsakes, I can't dance!" His frantic gaze darted around the room as if he'd been locked in and was searching for an escape.

"If you can count, you can dance."

"But dancing means hand holding. Oh, Lord," he shook his head frantically. "I've never held any girl's hand."

225

"Just make sure to wipe your palms first. Girls don't like sweaty palms."

"And after the hand holding, she'll probably want to kiss." His eyes lit with panic. "Lordy, what if she wants to *kiss* me?"

"Kiss her back." He plopped the lid back onto the iron pot and hefted it back into the ice box.

"B—but it's not that simple. I've never kissed a girl before."

He straddled the bench. "No big deal. It's the same as kissing a grown woman." *The same as you've been kissing* my *woman.*

Colt forced the thought away and focused on the panicked boy sitting across from him, the mirror now lying forgotten on the table. Cameron was far from the picture of calm, cool confidence Colt had intended after a week of lessons with the infamous Sinful Sinclair. Then again, the bold redhead was a world away from shy, naive Caroline.

"With your eyes closed, a woman's a woman," Colt told his stepbrother. He fixed his attention on his plate rather than on the sudden image of Sinful, her lips full and red and wet as they laved the lollipop in the barn. "Just pucker up and do everything you learned."

He shook his head. "It's not the same. These are *real* lips."

"Sure, Caroline's not liable to have near the knowhow," Colt went on around a mouthful of stew. "But you like her and—" His words stopped as he choked. He finally swallowed with some effort and eyed his brother. "What did you say?"

"Kissing Caroline is gonna be different. She's got real lips. She ain't just a reflection in the mirror. I've been practicing, and while my lips are pretty loose, I don't know if I'm ready for the real thing."

Meaning he hadn't had the real thing? He hadn't . . .

Questions rushed through his brain as he tried to comprehend what he was hearing. He hadn't . . . She hadn't . . . They hadn't . . .

"Are you telling me you haven't kissed Sinful yet?"

Cameron gave him a shocked look. "We hardly know each other."

Anger. That's what Colt should have felt at his brother's words. After all, he was paying the darn woman a good deal of money for her expertise. However, the truth sent a burst of relief through him.

"It's too soon for kissing," Cameron went on. "Not to mention I don't want to kiss her anyway. I want to kiss Caroline, to be with her. That's why Miss Sinful taught me the lip exercises, and how to talk. Sweet talk. 'Cause that's what really lights a woman's fire—or so Miss Sinful says. What do you think?"

He thought about the past week and a half, about Sinful's sweet body framed in the cabin window, about her eyes filled with desire as she touched herself, about her face flushed with excitement as she proposed the most outlandish things to him, about the disappointment in her voice each and every time he refused her.

While she was obviously a schooled actress, a woman who made her living making every man feel special, she'd been sincere. She'd wanted him. She still wanted him.

Just me.

"So?" Cameron pressed.

"Lollipops," Colt blurted out as he shoved his plate of cold stew across the table at his brother. "Come to think of it, I could use one myself right about now. This stuff just isn't hitting the spot."

But he knew what would. Or rather, *who.*

Responsibility, a small voice whispered as he headed down the path toward Horseshoe's place.

It was a voice that urged him faster, because Colt had come to realize over the past week or so exactly how much he still missed his old way of life. Surely that was the reason he wanted her so badly. The reason he tossed and turned and burned all night, every night. The reason he'd damn near killed himself several times while he was breaking horses in the past few days. He couldn't think straight anymore. Not with Sinful at his ranch, in his life, in his head.

Those old desires called to him fiercely now— the wanderlust, the thirst for excitement, the need to lose himself in pleasure with a woman. Maybe, just maybe, if he gave in to his lust for

Sinful, for life, for *more*, he could sate his wild streak once and for all and find peace.

Maybe.

He clung to that hope and stepped up onto her porch. No more fantasizing, as she'd referred to it. It was high time for the real thing.

Elizabeth's fingers trembled as she sat on the edge of the bed and reached for the garter.

Trembled? No, she wasn't trembling. She could take a hint. It didn't take a Mack truck to get the message through to her. She simply wasn't enough of a woman—a *wild* woman—for a man like Colt Durango.

So? Who needed fantasies anyway? She shouldn't be wasting her time in the past when she had a great life waiting for her in the present. She had a business to run, albeit a lonely business. She had clients to help, people to bring joy to, seeing that all of *their* desires came true.

She also had a family who was probably wondering where she was right now. Even if it was a family who'd specifically asked her to stay out of touch for a few months, to remain at a distance until her father could win the gubernatorial race.

"We'll get together at Christmas, honey. I'll call you," she imagined him saying.

Okay, so she didn't have much of a life waiting for her, but it sure beat getting her ego trampled on by some guy from the past, a man

Kimberly Raye

whom she wanted more than anything she'd ever known. A girl could only take so much.

"I know when I'm not wanted."

Elizabeth reached for the garter at the same time the door clicked open.

Colt stood in the doorway, looking as dark and delicious as ever, his hat tipped low, his leather vest outlining his muscular shoulders.

"Leave it on. It's sexy."

Sexy. Just as the word registered, he stepped inside and kicked the door shut. "Cameron told me what the two of you have been doing. Or rather, what you haven't been doing."

"Physical contact isn't a necessity to teach a man how to seduce a woman. There's more to it than that."

"Really?"

"He has to be able to talk to her first. The physical stuff comes later."

"Would you have done the physical?" He sounded like he knew her reservations.

"Probably . . . not," she finally admitted. "I told you, he's just a kid."

"And you need a man." The door rocked shut and he came nearer. She felt his heat from where she sat on the bed.

"So, is that why you're here? To ask me about Cameron?"

"Nope."

"Then why are you here?"

"Why do you think?"

A dozen wonderful possibilities rushed

through her brain, but after nine rejections, she wasn't going to make the same mistake again. "To toss me out on my keister for bending our agreement a little?"

"Actually, I had other plans for your keister, Peaches."

"Oh, yeah?"

"Oh—" he said as he pulled her into his arms—"yeah." And then he kissed her.

Chapter Eleven

Lay one on me, baby!
  Come to mama, Big boy!
  It's about ever-lovin' time!
  The phrases echoed through her head as Colt's mouth covered hers. After nine days of endless sexual frustration, she was more than ready for this. For him. For the sweet pressure of his lips and the electrifying sweep of his tongue.

She'd been waiting for this, wanting it, dreaming of it.

Even so, only one thought rooted in her frantic brain with those first few moments of contact.

Wait a second.

It wasn't supposed to happen so fast, to be so explosive, so overwhelming. She couldn't breathe, much less think of what to do next or when or how.

"Stop," she panted when she finally managed to come up for air. "I . . . We need to slow down." Was that her voice speaking? Was she crazy?

No, Elizabeth, you're scared. Sure she'd imagined getting hot and heavy with Colt in her fantasies, but suddenly, this was the real thing. Strong hands burned into her back. Warm breath brushed her lips. Her heart pounded frantically inside her chest. His dark, piercing eyes stared down at her, into her.

"What's wrong? I thought you wanted this. I thought you wanted me."

The words sent a rush of heat through her. "I do, I just think that maybe . . . I mean, we haven't even really talked first."

"You want to *talk*?"

"Yes. I mean, no. I mean, maybe a little. We don't really know each other. I don't even know what your favorite food is. Or your favorite color."

"I've never been much for talking." One of Colt's hands swept the underside of her breast before his fingers grazed its tip through the fabric. Heat seared through her and before she could blink, he lowered his head. "I'm more a man of action."

Boy, was he ever.

He drew her nipple into the heat of his

233

mouth, suckling her through the thin fabric of her chemise.

After several long, heart-pounding seconds, he pulled away. "You still want to talk, Peaches?"

"Maybe later."

He chuckled and dipped his head, drawing her nipple into his mouth again. Sensation swept through her, pushing aside her fear until all she felt was need.

Not that she'd been *afraid* afraid. She'd wanted this her entire life. Wanted to let loose and get wild and crazy, fast and furious, and do *everything*. But she'd been repressing those urges, burying her wild side for so long, that it was only natural she'd feel a moment's hesitation when she finally let herself go.

But now she was free to be as sinful as she wanted.

She slid her arms around his neck, threaded her fingers through his hair and arched her back, pushing her breast further into his mouth. He suckled and tongued until she moaned. He caught the sound in his mouth as his lips closed over hers.

His mouth was hot and damp, entirely covering hers. He slanted his head for better access and made love to her mouth, pushing his tongue deep, stroking hers until she knew, absolutely, that nothing could be better than Colt Durango's kiss.

But then he touched her—his hands stroking

her back, gliding around her waist to cup her breasts—and that was better. He settled his leg between hers and pressed, rubbing his thigh against her . . . Mmm. Better. Much, *much*, better.

She didn't just stand there this time. Her body leaned into his, her now aching breasts rubbing his chest. Her lips opened wider, giving him better access to her mouth. Her tongue grazed his. Her hands joined in the play, roaming over his shoulders, unbuttoning his shirt and slipping inside to learn the hard contours of his chest.

"You feel so good." His voice filled her ear, gritty with the passion that was raging inside him. Heat rippled through her, calming her trembling fingers and building her confidence. She stroked the hard ridge at the front of his pants and a groan issued from his throat.

"You'd better slow down, honey. I'm not made of steel."

She stroked him again. "Could have fooled me."

A low growl rumbled from his lips as he hefted her over his shoulder and tossed her onto the bed. She'd barely managed to sit up when she felt hands urging her arms up, whisking the thin chemise she wore up and over her head until only her fishnet stockings and the garter remained.

She reached for him, but he stepped back.

"Wait, honey. I've been picturing you like this for a long time. I want to look."

In her fantasy, she would have tossed an arm above her head, given him a come-hither smile and struck an erotic pose. But this wasn't a fantasy. This was reality, and that made things slightly different. The mattress warmed her backside while cool air brushed her skin, pebbling her nipples and making her keenly aware that she was naked, completely *naked* for the first time in front of a man.

A real man.

For a moment she froze, all of her courage dissipating like so much smoke. This was the man of her fantasies, the one. Her terror was all-consuming. But then, his gaze locked with hers, his eyes burning so hot and bright that she actually felt the way she did in her fantasies. Suddenly she was bold and daring and desirable. Her grip on the blanket beneath her eased and her legs relaxed, parting slightly and drawing his intent gaze. She felt desire flood through her.

"You're wet." She wasn't any more prepared for the comment than she was for the hand that reached out to touch her. His fingertip swept the drenched flesh between her legs. Her thighs quivered and her nipples tightened and her body heated, but no longer with embarrassment. She liked him looking at her, touching her, wanting her.

He shrugged his shirt off his shoulders. Dark

hair sprinkled his chest, funneling to a thin line that bisected his muscular abdomen and disappeared inside the waistband of his pants. Long, lean fingers worked at the buttons and soon he was pushing his pants down and kicking them to the side.

Colt appeared above her then, tall and powerful and virile as he knelt on the bed. She'd felt his erection through his pants, seen the hard ridge, imagined what the real thing would be like, but nothing prepared her for the actual sight of him. His sex was long and hard and thick, its head a lush purple, and it seemed to tremble beneath her stare.

He leaned over her, once more touching her between her legs. One finger parted the flesh there and pushed deep. She gasped. He leaned forward and caught the sound, his lips claiming hers in another ravenous kiss. Then he was kissing her throat, her breasts. He rasped one nipple with his tongue just as he pushed a second finger into her waiting warmth.

The sensations were nearly unbearable; the steady draw of his mouth on her breast, the sweet pressure of his fingers sliding deeper, exploring, made her ache and burn and want more than she'd ever wanted in any fantasy.

The feelings coursing through her transcended anything she'd felt in her wildest dreams. She burned hotter, ached more fiercely, and acted more boldly.

For a moment she was wholly overcome by

erotic fervor. She arched her back and wiggled her bottom, drawing him deeper, wanting more, wanting that *something* she'd never experienced with a man before. That indescribable something that she knew only Colt could give her.

Then he touched something deep within her, and her lips parted on a sharp, pleasured gasp. Just a little deep—

His fingers retreated and she opened her eyes.

"Not yet, Peaches," he murmured. "Not without me." And then he positioned himself and thrust deep inside.

"Lord, you're hot," he said. Then he stilled for a long moment, as if relishing her warmth, and it gave her the chance to really feel him, every pulsing, throbbing inch. The sensation was indescribable, setting off a wave of emotion that swept through her, stirring her nerve endings and bringing her entire body to throbbing awareness. She knew a sense of completion unlike anything she'd ever known, and at the same time, she needed more.

He started to move, pumping into her, pushing her higher, and her restlessness reached a fever pitch. She lifted her hips, meeting him, making him cry out with every thrust, as if every sensation he experienced, every pulse of ecstasy were something that he had never before known.

She'd certainly never felt a man so hot and wild and deep, and the feeling unleashed something inside her. It made her want to move, to feel every inch of him inside her, around her. With each stroke, he burned her alive, until she ignited in a burst of flames. Her breath caught, sensation swept through her and she exploded. Spasms gripped her and her body began to milk his, so long and hard that he moaned. He drove deep one final time. His muscles turned to stone as he spilled himself, filling her, at last bringing her completion.

He collapsed on top of her, his head resting in the curve of her shoulder, his lips against her neck. His breath warmed her skin while his heart beat in furious sync with her own.

"Thank you." The minute the words slid past her lips, she wanted to snatch them back.

She braced herself for his response. He would rear his head back and look down at her as if she'd just grown a third eye in the middle of her forehead—or worse. He would look at her and know the truth, that she wasn't the infamous Sinful, but a poor substitute.

He stirred, but only to roll over and pull her into the curve of his shoulder, his arms solid around her, his head resting between her breasts. Relief rushed through her and she closed her eyes, thanking the Powers That Be for saving her from the ultimate humiliation.

Thank you? Of all the wimpy, boring, prim and proper and *virgin* things to say. She might as well have Clueless Ice Queen tattooed on her forehead. She was supposed to be bold and daring and sinful, for crying out loud. He should be the one thanking her.

Then again, she wasn't naive enough to think she was the first woman ever to bring him to completion. He'd had plenty of sex by his own admission, not to mention he'd known exactly how to touch her, to kiss her, to love her.

Physically, that is.

This was purely physical, and temporary. She had all of a week and a half until her time at the Triple-C came to an end. She didn't kid herself about Colt wanting to keep her once her usefulness to his brother ended. He would send her back. Then she would say good-bye to Colt and the past and return to her life with some really terrific memories—and the knowledge that she had truly lived. She had once been the wild woman she'd always believed herself to be.

Thank you.

Okay, so she'd been more polite than wild. And grateful. But it had been the first time she'd found release, after all, and she had truly felt grateful. Besides, there'd been no harm done. It wasn't as if he'd heard her.

On that note, she leaned down and pressed a kiss against his soft-as-silk hair. Closing her eyes, Elizabeth let the warmth of his embrace seep through her.

Thank you.

The soft words followed Colt as he left a very naked, very sated, very tempting Sinful sound asleep and headed out to the barn well before sunup.

He'd heard a damn sight many things from women before, during and after a good tumble, but never anything as rousing, as heartfelt, or as damned sincere as her soft, breathy *thank-you*.

It was as if he'd given Sinful Sinclair more than just a good roll between the bed sheets. As if what had happened between them had been something special. As if he'd been someone special.

He shook away the thought. Last night had been great, but surely nothing out of the ordinary for a woman like her. An experienced, fantasies-are-my-business woman like her would have had plenty of earth-shaking sex.

As for his reaction to her—the pounding of his heart, the trembling of his body, the fierceness of his climax . . . Hell, those things were easily explained. He'd been out of the saddle for so long, that once he climbed back in, he was bound to feel as if he was taking the wildest, most exciting ride of his life.

Six months without a woman could do that to a man, especially a lusty, healthy, virile man who in his prime had never gone more than six days without. He'd been so overwhelmed the past few weeks he hadn't been able to think straight. It only stood to reason that his reaction would be stronger, more intense than ever before.

A few more times, and it wouldn't seem like anything out of the ordinary.

In the meantime, today was just another day. He had work to do. And so he'd traded the warmth of Horseshoe's cabin and Sinful for the dark chill of the barn and a snorting, ornery Maddie.

"Easy, girl."

Perspective. That's what it was all about. While he'd made up his mind to enjoy Sinful and her generous charms, he wasn't about to let that rearrange his priorities. There was a time and place for everything. Last night had been the time for getting hot and sweaty, and this morning was about work, about doing his duty and repaying his debt to his father.

"Don't recall hearing you come in the bunkhouse last night." Horseshoe's voice cut through the early-morning silence.

Colt glanced over his shoulder to see the older man standing in the barn doorway, a tin cup in his hand. Steam rose as he sipped the contents.

"I got held up."

Horseshoe chuckled, the sound mingling with the crunch of straw as he walked inside. "Finally got yore hands on that redheaded critter, didya?"

"Yep." His hands and every other inch of his body.

"Finally. She's been keeping you up too much lately."

"You're telling me." His body throbbed as a

memory rushed through his mind of all he'd done to her. All he still wanted to do to her. "I haven't slept decent a single night since she showed up."

"That's 'cause you worry too much. Take me, for instance. Sure, I don't like critters sniffing around what ain't theirs, but I sure as hell wouldn't spend all night freezing my patootie off just to catch a sneaky old fox."

"Actually, I didn't do much freezing. It was pretty warm. And I have to warn you, she sure as shootin' would have your hide if she heard you talking about how old she is."

"My hide? What are you . . . ?" The question trailed off as a knowing light lit his eyes. "You weren't sittin' in the chicken coop all night, were you?"

"Nope."

"And we ain't talkin' about a fox, are we?"

"I don't recall ever saying we were. You said red-headed critter. She's definitely got red hair." Soft, silky red hair that had tangled in his hands as he'd held her head and kissed her mouth.

"Land sakes." Horseshoe snorted. "You mean to tell me, you gave up a good night's rest over a woman?"

"Actually, it was still a good night." He grinned. "We just didn't do much resting."

"Well, you sure as shootin' wouldn't catch me sacrificing my shut-eye over some woman, especially a citified, painted-up, man-pleaser like that. No sirree. Why, I'd rather drink turpentine and piss on a brush fire. It's about as safe."

Colt couldn't argue with that. He knew first-hand how dangerous taking up with a woman like Sinful could be.

But this was different. He wasn't half-drunk, tumbling her up in her room while a saloon full of admirers played cards downstairs. He wasn't pushing the limit, living dangerously, shirking his responsibility.

He was right here at his ranch, living up to his promises.

"Unless she can cook, that is," Horseshoe went on. "And I ain't talkin' just mixin' up a batch of biscuits. I'm talkin' the buttermilk kind, with fresh whipped butter and jam." He licked his lips. "Now that's the kind of woman I'd lose a night's sleep over." He eyed Colt. "You need to get your priorities straight, boy."

But Colt was clear on those, too. He might be taking up with Sinful, but it was only tempo-rary. A business arrangement. He'd hired her for her expertise in bed, and while he hadn't intended to be the beneficiary, he was damned tired of fighting the attraction between them. She wanted him and he wanted her. They might as well make the most of that.

Not right now, though, of course, despite the heat rushing through his veins, warming him from the inside out. He had work to do. Cattle to brand and a sick calf to doctor and an ornery horse to tame. Important stuff. Much more im-portant than walking back to the cabin, peeling off his clothes, sliding between the sheets and waking her up with his kisses.

This was just another day.

"You know what you need?" the ranch foreman asked with a smile.

Colt shook his head.

"You need yourself a proper woman, like that mail-ord—"

Colt cut him off in mid-sentence. "We've been over this, Horseshoe. That's not going to solve any of my problems. Right now, I have everything I need right where I want it. As for the future . . ." The last thing he wanted to do was think about the future.

Elizabeth kept her eyes closed and her breathing even as she listened to Colt's footsteps on the hardwood floor. While she considered herself an expert when it came to fantasies, she had *Virgin* tattooed on her forehead when it came to dealing with the morning after.

With *now*.

What had she done?

She'd slept with her first man, that's what. Actually *slept* with him, too, which made for a world of complications she hadn't anticipated. After all, while she was wide awake, she might have kept up her Sinful facade, but asleep . . . What if she'd snored? What if she'd drooled? What if she'd sang in her sleep? Then there was the whole morning-breath issue.

Sinful was surely not the sort of woman to

snore or drool or sing off-key, much less wake with anything less than a minty fresh, kiss-me-now taste in her mouth. What now?

Elizabeth licked her lips and tried not to grimace. Where was a good tube of Colgate toothpaste when you really needed it?

Back in the twenty-first century with your common sense.

Okay, so she hadn't thought this thing through entirely, but it wasn't as if she'd had any experience to factor in. There'd been no falling asleep with, much less waking up with, any of her previous boyfriends—the ones from high school. She recalled Greg, that one time after her junior-year prom, when she'd let him do what he wanted, his hands trembling as he fumbled with her clothing and stressed about the thousand and one ways her father was surely going to kill him if he caught them in her basement.

However, the ten minutes or so they'd rolled around on the couch had been nothing to shout from the rooftops about. He'd been so nervous that he couldn't even deliver what he'd promised, at least not for long. And the lead-in hadn't even been all that thrilling, either.

If Elizabeth hadn't read all those fantasy books since that one and awful experience, she might have blamed herself entirely. But Greg hadn't exactly been schooled in the arts of making love. He'd been clumsy and quick, much too quick by last night's estimate. They'd both been at fault. It had been the wrong place, the wrong time—the wrong partner.

But last night . . . Mmm . . . last night had been everything she'd ever dreamed. The drawback was, she'd never included an *after* in her fantasies. They usually ended when she screamed in satisfact—

"Ouch!" The cry burst from her lips when a large hand landed squarely on her rump.

Her eyes popped open to see Colt drag the blankets down and bark a quick "Rise and shine," before he tossed a handful of clothes at her and turned away.

Wait a second. She wasn't positive, but she was pretty sure the morning after such a hot night of lovemaking should include a few wake-up kisses. Maybe some naughty whispering about the fun of the night before. At the very least, he should slide his arms around and simply hold her.

A large hand pulled the curtains back and sunlight poured into the room, temporarily causing her to be blind.

"Get up," he barked again, followed by another quick slap on the rump.

"An Uzi," she growled. "Just give me five minutes with an Uzi and you'd be Swiss cheese."

"I don't know what an oozie is, but it sounds unpleasant," he said, then chuckled. The door creaked shut, and she found herself alone and wondering if she hadn't simply imagined the past night.

Surely not. She had a good imagination, but it had never been *that* good.

But as the day progressed and Colt Durango did little more than look unemotionally at her— much less jump her bones, wink or give that wicked little smile that said he had sinning on his mind—she began to wonder if maybe, just maybe, she *hadn't* imagined the entire thing.

Last night *had* been hotter and wilder and more intense than anything she'd ever felt in real life.

She admitted that to herself that night as she closed the door behind Cameron after a long, lengthy discussion of kissing. They'd gone over the hows and whys and whens, and she'd given him pointers as she'd watched him share a mean liplock with his mirror in anticipation of Saturday night and the cotillion.

At least he had something to look forward to. As it was, the only thing in front of Elizabeth was a long, boring week. While she'd struck out with Colt—he apparently wasn't interested in her anymore—she'd hit a home-run with Caroline and Cameron. It was her duty to stay and support Colt's brother in his time of need. But for her, the future looked bleak. No longer with any purpose she was smack dab in the middle of *Bonanza* hell. No electricity. No running water. No TV. No computer. Nothing but a cookstove and a sawbuck table and a half-naked man standing in her doorway—

The thought stumbled to a halt as her gaze riveted on Colt, minus his shirt. The cowboy leaned on the doorjamb, his shoulders broad, his chest covered with the dark silk hair she'd felt the night before.

Correction—*thought* she'd felt the night before. That had been just another fantasy. Right?

This was just another fantasy. She had to be dreaming.

He pulled a lollipop from his pocket, pulled off the wrapper and took a lick.

Need surged through her, her nipples puckering. Elizabeth felt her heart speed up and her loins flood with anticipatory desire.

She tried to gather her control. She was losing it. In a place that seemed like a fantasy, brought by a magic garter, Elizabeth was fantasizing further. The fresh air, the crystal clear water, the non-processed food—they were all starting to wreak havoc on her system. This all-natural lifestyle would drive even the sanest modern woman to the edge. She simply wasn't thinking or feeling or seeing clearly.

Okay, nix the seeing clearly, she was doing that. Her gaze traveled over Colt's face, noting the shadow stubbling his jaw, the sensuous curve of his lips, the thick column of his throat. His pulse jumped at the base of his neck and she couldn't help herself. She licked her lips, wanting to taste him, to feel his skin beneath her tongue.

She blinked and tried to gather her wits. "This is not happening."

"What isn't?"

"You. You're not really here."

He stepped inside. The door clattered shut as he closed the distance to her. "Now I'm here."

"I mean here as in *here*. You're not real. You can't be real." He couldn't be, no matter how real he felt when his fingers closed over hers and touched her hand to his chest, to where his heart pounded in a frantic rhythm. "You're just a figment of my imagination."

"Really?" The fictitious Colt nodded and slid her hand down his chest—his very hard, very warm, very *real* chest. Hair tickled her palm and muscles rippled and quivered beneath her fingertips. "And what about this?" He pushed her hand down until it covered the long, hard length straining to be free of his pants.

"That's a very big figment of my imagination." And getting bigger by the second.

"I'm real, Peaches." His deep voice slid into her ears.

"And I'm here to take you up on your offer."

"What offer?"

"You've been trying to seduce me for a week." Her heart pounded at his blunt words. They were true, oh, so true.

"You have been flaunting yourself before me.

But that's what you do. You make fantasies for people. Now you can make mine."

Her pulse leapt at the prospect. "Which one of the Naughty Nine is it?" Her voice was a little breathless.

"The Naughty Nine?" Colt grinned and the devil himself danced in his wicked brown eyes. "All of them, darlin'. Every last one."

Chapter Twelve

"This is supposed to be *your* fantasy." Elizabeth arched her body as Colt's lips trailed down her neck. His warm, wet mouth slid over her collarbone, trailed over the slope of her breast. What did he have in mind? "Which means I should really be doing this to you."

His lips closed over one sensitive nipple, his tongue laving and flicking until she moaned. Then he drew the tip deep into his mouth, pulling on her, sucking so hard she felt the pressure between her legs.

"But this works, too," she gasped, threading her fingers through his soft hair. She held him close as he sucked and stroked and worked her into a frenzy until, at last, she didn't think she could take any more.

But then his hot mouth trailed to her other

breast, and she could. She took the sweet heat of his mouth and the play of his tongue, and she begged for more.

And he gave it to her.

He trailed his strong hands over her body, caressing her breasts and her stomach and her hips. Then he slid his hand between her parted thighs and touched her wetness. A sharp ache radiated from his touch and she squirmed.

"Please," she gasped.

"I aim to, Peaches." He slid down her body until his face was directly between her thighs. "I surely do." His hot breath bathed her swollen flesh and sent an electric current shimmying across her nerve endings. She nearly lost control as his strong hands stroked along her inner thighs and spread her legs wider. And then he spread *her*, his fingers parting her sex, opening the folds. He dipped his head and took a long, heart-stopping taste of her with his tongue, and she screamed.

"Are you pleased?" he murmured, his voice a vibration that sent pulses of pleasure through her already throbbing body.

"No," she said on a gasped. "I mean, yes. Sort of." She fought for a breath. "I—I don't know."

He lifted his head and flashed her a wicked grin that stopped her heart even faster than the feel of his mouth between her legs. "Let's see what I can do about making up your mind."

His grin disappeared as pure intent carved his features. "I've been wanting to taste you for so long." But he didn't. He simply stared, as if she were a giant chocolate cake and he a barely recovering sugar addict.

"I guess this qualifies as number nine," she heard herself saying, eager to fill the strained silence with something other than the frantic rushing of blood in her ears. Surely he could hear her heart pounding, and then he would know that she was excited beyond belief. And how could she explain that from a woman like Sinful Sinclair? A woman who'd undoubtedly done this, felt this, too many times to count.

Elizabeth had never been so exposed. So needy. So turned on. Not even in her most wicked fantasy.

"Number nine?"

"Oral fantasy," she blurted, then wished she could snatch the words back. The heated look Colt gave her sent heat pulsing through her body, making her feel even more open and exposed. "That's number nine," she rushed on, eager for a distraction from the self-consciousness whirling through her. She was being silly. Wild women didn't feel self-conscious.

Then again, pent-up wild women probably did.

"And if you're into number nine," she went on, "your fantasy is oral sex. That means you dream about it."

"I've definitely dreamed about this."

"That's not exactly—" she started to say but

254

then he lifted one of her heels to his shoulders and tilted her hips, pulling her more fully against his mouth, and she forgot all about books and lists and everything else. She found herself caught up in the here and now, in him, and everything else faded away.

His tongue slid into her slick core and he made love to her with his mouth, stroking and sucking and nibbling. The pressure built, higher and higher, until at last she cascaded over the top. Heat flushed her body, and she cried out Colt's name. Ecstasy washed over her. Flooded with pleasure, Elizabeth could hardly move. That had been everything she'd dreamed and more.

Several heart-pounding moments later, she floated back down from the heavens. Opening her eyes, she saw Colt looming over her, his eyes dark and intense.

She reached for him then, boldly, taking his erection into her hands in a move that surprised her. But with her body still throbbing, she felt forward and daring—and needy. Yes, she definitely still needed him in the worst way, and judging by the size of him, he needed her as well.

The realization sent a burst of confidence through her and she ran her hands down his length, drawing a low hiss from his lips. "You didn't let me finish earlier. See, if you're into number nine, you dream about *receiving* oral pleasure. Is that what you dream about, Colt?"

His nostrils flared and fire leapt in his eyes. She had her answer.

She kissed his lips before working her way down beneath him, kissing a decadent trail until she reached his waist. She licked the voluptuous head of his arousal, tasting the drop of moisture that had beaded there.

Her hands slid around to cup his buttocks, to draw him into her mouth, and then she was driving him wild in the way that he'd done for her. He pumped into her mouth for a few frantic seconds before he pulled back. "Enough."

"I thought you were into this."

"Darlin', the only thing I *really* want to be into is you." He slid down her body and, with a quick thrust, filled her with his hard, hot length.

She was already so excited that it only took a few quick pumps before he again pushed her over the edge. Her fingernails dug into his shoulders as he plunged deep—so deep she wasn't sure where he ended and she began, and then she didn't care because she was floating again, and Colt Durango was right beside her as they both shattered in a mind-boggling release.

From then on, the night passed in a heated blur. Despite her intensive reading on the subject, Elizabeth never realized there could be so many variations on one particular fantasy. But Colt Durango gave new meaning to the concept of oral pleasure with his delicious mouth. He paid homage to every inch of her body and she, in turn, worshipped him. The entire experience was wild and wonderful and downright wicked—and she loved every moment.

The wickedness came to an abrupt end the next morning, however, as Colt woke her with a slap on the rump. She quickly realized that he might want to warm her bed at night, but during the day, it would be business as usual, despite the softness in his touch and the reluctance that flashed in his gaze as he left the cabin.

Business as usual. He went about his ranch chores, and she went about hers. She had Cain to read to. She'd promised Buck she'd help him with the stalls the way she'd been doing every day. And she had her lesson to plan with Cameron.

She didn't have time for a full-blown relationship with Colt. More importantly, she didn't want one. The last thing she wanted was to wake up to Colt's soft kisses, his warm body wrapped around her, his touch lingering on her flesh and making her want more. This wasn't about the morning after. It was all about the night before. About living a fantasy.

It was important she remembered that.

This was *not* a good idea.

"What did you say?" Colt's deep voice pushed

into her thoughts, and Elizabeth's head snapped up.

"I, um, said this was not a good idea."

He frowned. "Why's that?"

"Because it's a great idea. The best you've ever had. I can't wait."

He grinned and she fought back a wave of anxiety. Being nervous was not a part of her wild woman persona. At least, it wasn't a part of the wild woman she wanted to be. Besides, there was nothing to be nervous over. Sure, they were in the barn, just a stall away from a handful of cowboys playing poker, and sure they could hear everything, from the raunchy jokes, to the slap of cards hitting the table, to the clink of a whiskey bottle whenever someone took a drink. But still, these men were nothing to be truly worried about. None of the ranch hands could actually *see* them. This wasn't truly an audience fantasy, was it? Darkness enveloped the small corner where they stood, shielding them from prying eyes.

It was here that, five days ago, she'd intended to strip naked and seduce Colt. In this very spot.

Okay, so she hadn't actually stripped. But she would have if he would have given any hint that he'd wanted her to. If he had looked at her with his eyes so dark and hot and intense as they were now, if he had reached out and trailed his fingertip from her pulsebeat at the base of her throat to the ripe tip of one breast the way he was doing right now . . .

Heat sparked through her, shunting aside all doubt and filling her with a longing that superceded the fears she had of being caught.

A soft moan vibrated out of her throat, and he caught the sound with his mouth. He kissed her deeply, his tongue plunging inside, stroking and coaxing as his hands began undoing the buttons of her dress, peeling back the material. Fingers stroked her skin through the thin chemise before he found his way inside and his warm hand cupped her breast.

He dipped his head, laving her nipple through the material, drawing the pebbled tip deep into his mouth with a delicious pressure that wrung another moan from her.

"Ssshhh." He pressed his fingertips to her lips, an amused gleam in his dark brown eyes. "They're liable to hear us, Peaches."

She became keenly aware of the sudden silence, as if the cowboys had, indeed, heard something and were now listening. Her heart revved faster, but instead of frightening her, it fed the excitement. She became cognizant of the picture she made leaning against the barn wall, her back arched, her breasts in full view, her nipples puckered and wet from Colt's wondrous mouth.

She should cover herself. She would have, but she couldn't move. The blood pounded so hard through her veins that she could do little more than hold her breath in fear of discovery.

A slap of cards burst through the heart-

Kimberly Raye

pounding silence and a round of laughter went up as the men went on with their game. And Colt went on with his seduction.

His hands caught the hem of her dress, pushing the material higher, higher, scorching her bare skin as they passed. His fingertips stroked her thighs and caressed between her legs.

When the tip of one finger found its way past her bloomers and trailed along her slick folds, she sank her teeth into her bottom lip and fought back a scream of ecstasy.

She reached for his pants, tugging at the buttons. Within moments, he sprang hot and hard into her hands and she stroked him from root to glistening tip and back.

He groaned this time, and she pressed her fingertips to his lips, echoing his earlier words. "Careful. They'll hear us." He smiled against her skin, and then the expression disappeared as he urged her legs farther apart. He rubbed his straining erection back and forth against her aroused flesh.

With a quiet grunt, he lifted her and she wrapped her legs around his waist. Reaching between them, he guided himself into her slick opening. One thrust upward, and Colt buried himself deep with one thrilling motion that wrung a low groan from both of them. The air went still and silent around them, but Elizabeth was past the point of caring.

She was too wound up, too desperate, too wild.

260

She wiggled and his grip on her hips tightened. He withdrew, then plunged into her again. And again. Elizabeth's legs tightened around his waist and she moved with him. Her raspy breathing echoed in her ears, her heart pounding as he hammered into her, building her tension, lifting her higher than she'd ever been before. Another thrust and she exploded, caught up in a torrent of pleasure that rolled over her and turned her every which way but loose.

She barely caught her scream of pleasure, but she did, and fought it back down as her muscles contracted, gripping him tightly inside her body. Tremors rolled through her.

A few heartbeats later, his release followed. His body turned to stone and he growled, sinking into her one last time as pleasure overcame him.

But as wonderful as it had been, she still didn't feel one-hundred-percent satisfied. As he eased himself out of her and lowered her feet to the ground, Elizabeth was still restless, still shaky, still off balance as she pushed her dress down and worked at its buttons with trembling fingers.

He reached for his pants and pulled them up to his waist, eyeing her keenly the entire time.

She couldn't seem to get enough air into her lungs, to calm her pounding heart, to reach the end of the ripples of pleasure that were still throbbing deep inside her.

Colt finished dressing and his hands closed over her shoulders. "Are you okay?"

She shook her head, barely managing a breathy, "Not yet." And then before she could think better of it, she drew in a deep breath, turned, and let loose a loud Tarzan yell the way she'd been itching to since the moment she'd peaked. Her vocal cords vibrated as she shouted her release, her joy, her happiness.

She sighed, then.

Within a second, footsteps sounded, boots scrambling as a dozen cowboys rounded the corner.

"What the hell . . . ?"

"Who the hell . . ."

"Colt? Is that you?"

"Yep. It's me." And despite Colt's wild and wicked nature, despite his devil-may-care attitude, he actually blushed beneath the men's speculative glances.

Elizabeth was beyond blushing. She felt a hundred feet tall. Powerful. Invincible.

I am woman, hear me roar!

"Ma'am? Is everything all right?"

She smiled. "As right as rain." Before she could think better of it, she planted a kiss on Colt's stunned mouth and murmured a heartfelt "Thank you." Then she turned and walked away.

He was *loco*. Plum loco.

That was the only explanation for the warmth

spreading through him as he watched her disappear. The feeling didn't have a danged thing to do with the fact that she'd said it again.

Thank you.

He knew it was all just an act. The trouble was, as much as he tried, he couldn't seem to shake the feeling that he was more to Sinful Sinclair than just another man.

Not that he wanted to be more. No sirree. No matter how she looked at him with the biggest, greenest eyes he'd ever seen—so full of wonder, as if every kiss, every touch were something totally unique and new. No matter how softly or how sweetly she kissed his cheek when she thought he was sound asleep.

He was just a man and she was just a woman and this was all about lust. Ever since they'd first made love, that's all it had been.

She was leaving in four days, their agreement concluded. They hadn't discussed any other options, so he had to assume that's what she wanted. Then Colt would get on with his life—with looking after the ranch and his brothers, and eventually with finding a wife. A nice, calm, settled woman who didn't scream like a banshee when he made love to her.

A grin tugged at his lips, but then he frowned. Four days and it was over. Until then he would keep his head on straight and ignore the damnable notions that struck him every time she gave him that wide-eyed, I've-never-been-kissed look.

"She's something, ain't she, boss?"

The question drew him back to the present and the half-dozen men standing around him, knowing smiles on their faces as they stared at Sinful's retreating figure.

"Don't you boys have work to do?"

"It's a quarter past ten and darker than a batch of tar."

"Well, shouldn't you be sleeping then? We've got an early day tomorrow." Without waiting for a reply, he turned on his heel and stomped from the barn. He passed her on the way.

"You headed to bed?"

"Sure enough." He couldn't hold back the smile this time. He was headed to bed, all right, but not to sleep. As mixed up as he felt, there was one thing Colt was clear on. They'd made a deal and Sinful Sinclair was his. He would make use of that.

For the meantime.

And after that?

Colt ignored the strange loneliness that the question stirred.

She was here right now and she was his, and he still had a mess of fantasies he wanted to live out. And the next would be his all-time favorite.

"You want me to *what*?" The question escaped her lips before Elizabeth could think better of it.

"It's a simple request, Peaches. One you've probably heard too many times to count."

"I have? I mean, yes, of course I have. I just thought we'd moved past this. I mean, it's a little tame compared to what we've been doing."

His grin was slow and wicked and sent her pulse racing. "I've been thinking about this ever since I saw you step out onto that stage in Galveston."

Ever since she'd chickened out. Of course, she was different now. She wouldn't be afraid to do a striptease in front of a room full of stunned, mesmerized men. Would she? And certainly not in front of the man she was sleeping with.

But she was. Colt was different. He wasn't stunned or mesmerized or dumbstruck. He was hungry. Very hungry. And the intensity of his attention was a little bit unnerving.

"You said you wanted to give me my ultimate fantasy. Well, that's it."

"But there's no music." Not to mention the all-important fact that her dancing ability was limited to a little fox-trotting at political galas and some very minimal aerobics.

Sure, she'd dreamed of bumping and gyrating to some techno rhythms while a bad boy lover looked on, but she'd never actually done it. She'd never even practiced alone in front of her mirror. She'd *never*—

The thought made her pause. She had come here and been able to do all the things she'd feared to do. That prickled her conscience and prodded her courage, almost as much as the fierceness in his dark brown eyes.

"You're sure this is your ultimate fantasy?"

"It's haunted me every night."

"That does qualify as ultimate," Elizabeth said. She drew in a deep breath and lifted her trembling hands to the top button of her blouse.

Trembling? She'd been naked in front of the man. Naked and panting and *screaming*, for heaven's sake. What was a little dancing?

That's what she told herself, but as she moved to the center of the cabin floor while Colt settled into his chair to watch, it was that night at the Green Turtle all over again. After the prom.

The place had been packed, every eye fixated on her to see if she would take her friend, Mark, up on his bet. Mark had been one of her best friends in high school and a major bad boy in his own right. Her father had hated him.

Too bad. He'd tempted her and teased and coaxed, and she'd been so close . . . *this* close . . .

She'd stood up on the table and stripped off her blouse. But when it had actually come down to unhooking her bra, she'd chickened out. Her father, that's what she told herself. She'd held back because of him, because she hadn't wanted to tarnish his reputation and cause a citywide scandal. She could imagine the headlines still.

But as the same insecurity rushed through her now and her hands faltered on the third button, she started to wonder if she wasn't in over her head. There was something exposing in taking off your clothes in such a manner, something more dangerous even than sex. When you stripped for a man, you were putting yourself there entirely for him, and that was perilous.

Maybe it had been the beer, she told herself. She'd had too much to drink, that night—otherwise she might not have felt so nervous. She felt sure that's what it had been, but for a few crazy seconds, she actually panicked that she might not overcome her fear. Would she always be a girl who couldn't dance or flirt or take her top off in front of a dozen chanting strangers?

Colt wasn't chanting, but right now the feeling was every bit the same, if not more powerful, and this time there was no beer to take the blame. There was nothing to blame but fear. A desperate fear that she wasn't worthy, that for some reason she couldn't even play at being wanton.

Stop that. You are Sinful. You've wanted your entire life to be sinful. To take it all off and enjoy every moment.

"I can do this," she murmured. "I . . ." The rest of her affirmation quickly faded as a shout came from outside.

"Colt! Come on out, boy. I got a surprise for you."

"I'm not up for any surprises tonight."

"You've got a visitor."

Colt started to protest, but Elizabeth was

quicker, desperate for an exit. She hauled open the door.

Outside, she found Horseshoe and a small brunette wearing a white bonnet and a deep blush, a cake plate clutched in her gloved hands.

"Miss Sinful." Horseshoe tipped his hat, a smile as broad as the Mississippi on his face. "Allow me to introduce Miss Lucy Mae Waltrip and her prize-winning pineapple upside-down cake." His gaze swiveled to Colt and his grin widened. "She's Colt's fiancée."

Chapter Thirteen

"She is *not* my fiancée."

"Shore she is." Horseshoe grinned at the young woman. "Aren't you, darlin'?"

"Well, I did come here to—"

"I didn't invite you," Colt cut in, keenly aware of Sinful and her rigid posture next to him.

"Shore you did." Horseshoe clapped him on the back.

"You didn't?" the woman asked.

"Shore he did." Horseshoe squeezed the woman's shoulder.

"But the letters." The woman shook her head. "You sent me all those letters and in them, you said—"

"I didn't write any letters."

"Why, shore you did," Horseshoe said, squeezing Colt's shoulder again.

"You didn't?" Lucy Mae asked.

Colt shook his head before his gaze swiveled to the man standing next to him. The old, ornery, stubborn, you-need-to-settle-down-and-get-hitched old coot had been riding him for the past six months about landing himself a mail-order bride. Apparently, this one. No wonder he'd been disapproving when Colt had told him he was spending time with Sinful.

"You wrote the letters," Colt said. "*You.*"

"You wrote the letters?" The woman's gaze shifted to Horseshoe. "You?"

"Landsakes, I declare, there must be some kind of echo in here."

The ranch foreman was cut off as Sinful squeezed past with a choked sound. She fled into the darkness outside.

"You wrote to this woman and used my name," Colt said accusingly.

" 'Course I didn't. Why the hell would I write such dadblastit nonsense? Sure, yore too damned pigheaded to see how perfect this little filly is fer you, but it ain't none of my concern. So what if she can cook and crochet and smiles as pretty as a Texas sunrise."

"You like my smile?" Lucy Mae's surprised gaze lifted to Horseshoe's. "You really think so?"

"Shore 'nuff, missy." Horseshoe stared at her for a long moment before he noticed Colt's disapproving stare. He frowned. "That is, if you're inclined to be taken in by such things as a purty little sunset—which I ain't." He made a big pretense of yawning. "Got to be up early." Before Colt could say anything, he turned on his boot heel and disappeared.

"I'm sorry about all this," Colt told the woman. "I'll pay for your passage back."

"Back?" She turned bright eyes on him and seemed to come to some monumental decision. "I'm not going back. I'm staying here."

"We really don't have—"

"Not here at your ranch. In town. Except for tonight. It's too late to head back. Do you think you could spare a room?"

He nodded. "Sure."

"And I'm sorry for you, too. I didn't realize that you weren't the one who'd written to me. Is she somebody special?"

He shook his head, but damned if the question didn't stay with him as he walked outside and set off in search of Sinful. He had to explain this mix-up to her. Obviously, his hormones were talking. No way was Sinful Sinclair really somebody special to him—not emotionally, at any rate. She was just good in bed. And in the barn. And out by the river.

Sex. That's all she was to him. And all he wanted.

Fiancée. The truth followed Elizabeth as she walked away and even when she went back to her cabin. She knew it would haunt her the rest of the night. Not because she was jealous. It was

271

purely disappointment in Colt's morals. How could he not tell her?

He had a fiancée. Of all the lowdown, dirty, snake-in-the-grass—

Excuse me? Her conscience prodded. *Since when do you care?*

She didn't, of course. Not in a possessive, you're-my-man-and-I-need-you sense. No way. What she was feeling was only disappointment. They still had lots to try, not to mention that she'd been really looking forward to attempting some variations on the basic Naughty Nine.

Still, there was no caring involved. Or jealousy. At least, that's what Elizabeth told herself as she trekked out to the barn. She would go out and work off some of her disappointment there. She took some pride in the fact that she was helping Colt with the horses now—she'd started several days earlier after she and Cain had finished reading *Moby Dick*. It gave her something "reputable" to do during the daytime, and truth be told, she'd become somewhat attached to Colt's animals.

But why, then, if there was no caring involved in her reaction to Colt's impending marriage, did she have an insane urge to smack him in the face with her shovel when he walked through the barn door a short time later and gave her a wickedly charming smile?

Fatigue.

Yes, that had to be it. She was tired after a

restless night, the barn smelled awful and . . . *fiancée*.

"She's not my fiancée," he said as if he'd read her mind.

She forced her gaze away from his intense blue eyes and concentrated on shoveling a rather large present from one of the horses into a wheelbarrow. "Who?"

"Lucy Mae. She's not my fiancée."

"It doesn't matter."

"She's not."

"It really doesn't matter."

"She's *not*." He caught the shovel she held and pulled it from her hands, then forced her to face him. "This is all a big misunderstanding."

She shrugged and tried to ignore the heat from his hands as they burned into her upper arms. "It doesn't matter." It didn't, she told herself for the umpteenth time. Still, his denial sent a rush of warmth through her, and his fingers . . . his warm, strong fingers sent fiery tingles running along her nerve endings.

"It was Horseshoe's idea," he went on. "He's been writing to her in my place. He's trying to settle me down. But I'm already settled."

"That's why you still sleep in the bunkhouse with the ranch hands, I suppose."

"What's that supposed to mean?"

"Just that you're settled here, living here, staying here, or so you say, but you haven't even moved into the main house."

"I didn't want to upset things. My brothers

were already settled in, used to a certain way of living. I didn't come back to upset things for them." He shook his head. "What with Grace and my father gone now, I know things are tough for them. I know that firsthand."

"How's that?"

She watched as he turned and started shoveling for her.

"I'm waiting."

"It's not important."

She caught his arm and forced him around to face her. "How do you know?"

"I know what it's like to have everything you've ever known disappear in the blink of an eye. I've known it several times. It isn't easy. My mother wasn't exactly the tame sort. She was once a saloon girl. One of the most popular. Unfortunately, her line of work didn't lend itself to a nice little farmhouse with a white picket fence. My dad was here, settled with the boys and Grace, but I was with my mother, going from saloon to saloon. When things slowed, we picked up and moved to the next town. One day, she just picked up and moved without me."

The sudden bleakness in his eyes struck a chord inside her. "She left you?"

He shrugged. "It was tough on her having a kid, especially in her line of work. She told me I'd be better off with my dad, but he was already married to Grace, trying to build up this ranch and start a family. She left me enough money to take a stage here, but I didn't do it. I had only seen him twice in my life, and I didn't know if he'd want me." His gaze met hers. "I mean, if he had wanted me, he would have taken me from my mother. He didn't, so I figured that was that and I was on my own."

"How old were you at the time?"

"Ten." The softly spoken word echoed through Elizabeth's ears.

"*Ten?* And you were all by yourself?"

"I had a little money and enough sense to know how to get by. While my mother worked, I roamed the streets and learned the basics. I could play cards and dice and shoot as well as any man."

"But you were only *ten*. You should have been playing with G.I. Joes, not cards or dice or a gun." She tried to absorb the enormity of what he'd faced at such a young age.

"What's a G.I. Joe—"

"You were just a baby," she cut in, eager to cover her slip. "You shouldn't have had to face life on your own."

"That's the way the cards fall sometimes. I survived." His gaze locked with hers. "But it wasn't easy. It was an adjustment, going from something to nothing, even if it was a little something in the first place. I want that same adjustment to be easier for my brothers. I want them to realize they're not going from something to nothing. They still have me, but I didn't grow up with them. Hell, I didn't even meet them until I came home six months ago. I knew of them." A far-off look touched his eyes. "And I thought about them, pictured them. I even pictured this place, but I never thought I'd get a chance to actually see it all in person. I never thought they'd need me."

"I think you're the one who needs them." At the comment, he gave her a sharp glance, but she continued. "You can't go it alone forever. You have to let people in. You have to open yourself up."

"I am."

"By sleeping in the bunkhouse and keeping a wide berth from everyone around you? Sounds like you're hiding to me." She watched the emotions race across his face—everything from surprise to anger to an umistakeable loneliness that told her her instincts were right on the mark. "You're hiding because you're scared."

For a long second, she watched the fear play across his expression before his features smoothed and a gleam lit his eyes. "Is that right?" The question came out with a slow drawl that slithered into her ears and spread through her body, setting her nerves ablaze and making her think of lots of sweet breath-stealing heat rather than the subject at hand.

Which was undoubtedly his intention.

He was turning the tables on her, trying to avoid the subject and put her on the defensive. She knew that and she vowed to hold the upper hand. But when he stepped closer, she found herself inching backward.

"You're afraid to get too close," she rushed on, eager to keep the conversation on track. "For all your talk about staying, you're afraid to get close to anyone because you're not so sure you can stay. And if you're close, it'll make leaving that much harder."

"You think so, huh?" Another step forward and another inch back.

She held the shovel up between them. "Would you just stop?"

He took the tool from her hands. "What are you doing this for anyway? You don't have to keep shoveling the stalls. That's Buck's job."

"I gave my word. I told you I wanted to help, so I'm helping, and don't try to change the subject."

"What subject?"

"You and your intimacy problems."

"I don't have intimacy problems. Hell, I don't even know what intimacy is."

"My point exactly. You've been shying away from intimacy for so long, that you don't know how to let yourself be vulnerable."

"No, Peaches. I really don't know what it is. Can't say as I've ever even heard the word. How'd you learn such big, fancy talk?"

She wanted to say in the future. In fact, the need to tell the truth hit her so quickly, so fiercely, that it surprised her. Crazy. The last thing she needed was to blurt it out to Colt Durango. It was unbelievable. "My, um, speech pattern is of no concern now. The matter at hand is that you won't let yourself get close to anyone."

He glanced down at the handspan that separated them, barely a few inches. "Looks like I'm close to you right now."

"That's physical. Emotionally, you're miles away." Which was a good thing, Elizabeth told herself. A very good thing. Because when this was all over and she was done collecting all the fantasies she wanted, she'd go back to her own life and her own time. It was what they both wanted, wasn't it? "You, um, really should consider Lucy Mae." Was that her voice? "If you really want to settle down, she's definitely the right type." Oh, God, it *was* her voice sounding so waspish. But she couldn't help herself. He was so close and a small part of her still couldn't erase the feeling that had consumed her the moment she'd heard the word *fiancée*.

"You're my type."

His words sent a rush of excitement through her. Her heart pounded. "You like girls who know how to use a shovel, do you?"

"Just one girl." And then he pulled her close and kissed her. She let herself be swept away.

Afraid of intimacy.

Sinful's statement haunted Colt the rest of the night and early into the morning when he headed back out to the barn to work.

Why, he'd just spent the entire night making love to a beautiful woman. He was not afraid of getting close to someone. He'd been as close as a man could be. Hell, he'd been buried so deep inside Sinful, he'd lost track of where he ended and she began.

He could get close to people. He *was* close to people. He damn well was.

"Can I go with you today?" Cain's voice shattered Colt's thoughts. He turned to find his youngest brother peeking past the slats of the stall.

"No," he began to say. It was the same spiel he recited every morning to keep Cain at home where he belonged, safe and sound and at arm's length. It was the same reason Cameron worked side by side with Horseshoe rather than with Colt himself. Because Colt worked alone; his own work was more dangerous.

You're afraid of intimacy.

In an instant, the truth of what Sinful had said crystalized. He was afraid—afraid to get too close, to get attached. She was right; he feared he wouldn't be strong enough to stay, to fulfill his duty. He was terrified of leaving his brothers the way his mother had left him. And he didn't want them to feel the same pain, the same loss. But he had to try sometime.

"Come on, cowboy. Let's saddle you up."

"That's okay—what?"

"You're coming with me."

"Really?"

"I said so, didn't I? But you'd better hurry up before I change my mind." But he wouldn't. Not when his kid brother smiled so brightly that it made his chest ache. Colt knew then and there, that all his fears had been for naught. He'd been holding back, keeping everyone at arm's length, trying to protect his feelings. But somehow, some way, Cain had slipped past and right into his heart, and it felt right. Perhaps he'd been there all along.

He fluffed his younger brother's hair. "Come on. Let's go. And tomorrow," he said with a smile, "I'm going to show you how to catch a redheaded critter—we're gonna bag that fox that's been eating Cameron's chickens."

Elizabeth's life couldn't get much worse.

She came to that conclusion as she watched Colt hoist his brother up onto a horse and warmth spread through her. What was so awful was, this wasn't a sexual warmth, but something that went much deeper. She liked seeing Colt Durango like this—as much as she liked seeing him poised above her, his eyes fierce with passion, his muscles taut and his expression intense.

Maybe she liked it more.

She closed her eyes as dread overcame her. These thoughts felt close to the truth. She *wasn't* like the daring Sinful. She was really only Elizabeth Joanna Carlton, a woman who liked puppies and longed for happily ever after. She'd been masquerading all this time. She was an ordinary woman in love with an extraordinary man.

Love. Even as she fought the idea, it solidified and grew inside her, refusing to be ignored.

Colt smiled down at her and Elizabeth's heart double-thumped. He touched his brother and her breath caught. His gaze caught hers and her insides fluttered.

Oh, no. She *was* in love.

The realization sent her rushing back to Horseshoe's cabin, running from the truth and from Colt Durango before she did something she would surely regret. Like slap his face for being so wonderful. Or worse, kiss him.

No, she couldn't kiss him. No more kissing. That's what had gotten her into this mess in the first place. His tender kiss. Kissing was the ultimate act of intimacy and while she'd enjoyed it with Colt—loved it—she should have remembered *Pretty Woman*. No kissing and a girl could keep her emotional distance.

Yes, it had been his lips that had gotten her into this mess. His lips, and the garter.

She became acutely aware of it rubbing against the inside of her thigh. The scrap of cloth had almost become a part of her.

But it wasn't.

She wasn't Sinful Sinclair, no matter how many cowboys tipped their hats or smiled or stumbled all over themselves trying to help her with the water pump.

She was a fraud. In reality, she was more like

prim and proper and buttoned-up-to-here Lucy Mae than any red-hot bombshell nineteenth-century stripper. If Colt knew how far from his type she actually was, he would send her packing in an instant.

Which wasn't such a bad idea, considering the circumstances and the all-important fact that she was falling in love with him.

Yes, she needed to leave. Now. Before things got even more complicated—

"I've got it." Cameron's voice shattered her thoughts as he came up behind her, and she jumped. "You'll see. She'll be eating out of my hand tomorrow night. Guaranteed."

"Tomorrow night?"

"The dance."

"About that . . ." She summoned her courage and faced him. As much as she wanted to see Cameron overcome his fears and wow Caroline, Elizabeth couldn't risk falling even further for Colt. That was the key. She was falling at the moment. She wasn't actually there. Yet. But the more time she spent with him, the more she watched him with his brothers and Horseshoe, the more he smiled at her . . . She had to leave now before she sunk deeper into the big L.

This wasn't supposed to have been about love. It was about lust. Fantasies.

"I just want to say thanks," Cameron rushed on as she paused to gather her courage. "I wouldn't be going if it weren't for you taking charge like that. But I'll make you proud. You'll see for yourself that I been taking real good notes and listening to what you said."

"That's good. All you have to do is remember everything, and you'll do just fine by yourself."

"Maybe, but just knowing you're going to be there is the only thing giving me the courage to go through with this. Otherwise, I'd be liable to stand Caroline up and blow my chances for sure. So what about the dance?"

"I—um—that is, I couldn't decide what to wear. Green or yellow." She smiled at Colt's brother. "So tell me about *it*. What have you come up with?"

"This. Guaranteed to make me stand out from all her other beaus."

She watched as he raised his hands, did a quick lip exercise before forming his lips into a pucker, then planted a big sloppy kiss right on the back of his hand. And then he swirled his tongue over the spot and licked it.

"What do you think? You think she'll be impressed if I do that?"

"I think she'll slap a dog collar on you and call the pound." When he gave her a confused look, she rushed on, "You need to think subtle."

"Subtle?"

"You know, soft and understated. You're trying too hard."

"Maybe. It does hurt a little when I twist my tongue so far sideways."

"Exactly. It shouldn't hurt. It should come naturally."

"Subtle," Cameron repeated, a thoughtful look on his face. "I guess I could think up something else." He turned on his heel and strode toward the barn.

"You're a sucker," she told herself as she started for her cabin again. "A big, soft sucker."

But she *had* gotten the kid into this. She'd mentioned the dance to Caroline and pushed her into going with him. The least she could do was see him through to the last waltz.

But, until then, it was all about keeping things in perspective. The wild side of Colt she'd been able to handle—the touching and kissing and red-hot sex. It was the gentle side of him that was throwing her for a loop, making her crave something deeper.

However, that was not a problem. Luckily, the man reserved that side of himself for his brothers, which meant Elizabeth was safe.

Even so, she wasn't taking any chances. From this moment forward, Colt Durango was completely off-limits.

"Stay back." Elizabeth made a cross with her fingers and held it out as Colt stood in her cabin doorway later that evening.

"What's wrong with you?" His eyes narrowed, and if she hadn't known better, she would have sworn she saw true concern glimmering in their dark depths.

It's just lust, she told herself. Raw, unchecked lust. Nothing more.

Unfortunately, that was enough to send her heart into palpitations and make her seriously rethink the distance thing. One more night. One more sweet night of . . .

She summoned her courage and inched backward. "I'm sick." She faked a loud, grumbling cough. "You really should stay back."

"You were fine this morning."

"It hit me all of a sudden." She gave another strangled cough. "My throat's itchy and my chest feels tight."

He studied her with keen blue eyes. "You do look a little flushed."

She nodded frantically. "A fever. A high one. I need to lie down."

"I'll help—"

"No." She shrugged away from his reach. "I could be contagious and then you'd be sick and the boys would get it from you, and then the whole ranch would come down with it. I wouldn't want to be the cause of a full-fledged epidemic."

"Peaches, I think you're getting a little too worked up over nothing."

"Nothing? We're talking an epidemic, here." She shook her head frantically and pushed him back toward the door. "You just keep your distance and go. I need to lie down. I'll see you tomorrow." Before he could protest, she pushed him out and slammed the door.

As she leaned back against the wood and listened, her heart paused, waiting for him to knock again, to beat down the door and toss her on the bed and make wild, passionate love to her. Or better yet, slide his arms around and simply hold her.

Ugh. Her priorities were definitely getting mixed up.

Her heart echoed loudly in her ears as she waited, her breath bated. Finally she heard the creak of wood and footsteps. Relief rushed through her. There would be no coddling or holding or anything remotely resembling soft, warm, cuddly and . . .

She did not want to think about the *and*.

Her only salvation was that Colt still had his perspective on their relationship, or lack thereof.

Otherwise, she'd be a goner for sure.

She was a goner, all right.

Elizabeth stared at the cast-iron pot in Colt's large hands and a strange warmth spread through her. It was a heat that had nothing to do with the fact that he was standing in her doorway looking handsome and sexy with a day's growth of beard on his face, and everything to do with the concern glittering bright in his scintillant cobalt eyes.

He set the pot on the table. "Horseshoe makes some of the best soup around these parts. Since you're feeling low, I thought I'd bring you some."

Elizabeth stared at the pot. Her nostrils flared

at the enticing aroma of chicken and broth and vegetables.

"What's wrong?" His deep voice drew her attention and she found him studying her.

She blinked against the sudden moisture in her eyes. "Nothing." *Everything*. He'd brought her *soup*, for crying out loud.

Or all the lowdown, dirty, rotten, *nice* things to do.

"You don't like chicken soup?" he asked in disappointment. "I told Horseshoe to make veget—"

"I *love* chicken soup," she croaked past the sudden lump in her throat. "It's just that no one's ever brought me any before." No one had, either, because there had never been anyone there. Her parents had always been off at some political fund-raiser or something, usually with her perfect brothers in tow, while she'd been stuck at home with a housekeeper whose best efforts involved handing her a can of Campbell's and a can opener.

"I'm usually on my own when I'm not feeling well," she admitted. She remembered the bleakness she'd seen in his eyes when he'd talked about his own childhood, about being on his own for so many years, and before she could think better of it, she asked, "What about you?"

He shrugged. "I always feel good."

"Always?"

He shook his head. "Yep."

"That's ridiculous. You can't feel well *all* the time."

"Sure you can."

"You mean to tell me you've never had a cold or a fever or *anything*?"

"I didn't say that."

"You said you always feel well."

"Me and a shot of whiskey."

"Whiskey can't cure a cold."

"No, but it can make it so you don't feel the cold. Or anything else for that matter." The sudden sadness in his eyes sent a rush of sympathy through her and before she realized what she was doing, she reached out a hand to touch his arm.

"*I'd* bring you soup." At his sharp glance, she added, "If you were sick. I'd bring you some." What was she saying?

The truth. She'd bring him chicken noodle soup and tuck him in and fuss over him and give him all the love and attention he'd missed while growing up. The very same affection that she'd missed.

The thought sent a thrill through her, followed by a rush of panic.

"What's wrong?" His deep voice drew her from her thoughts. "You don't look so good, Peaches."

"I don't feel so good." Love and attention. *Love.* Of all the crazy, ridiculous things . . .

She stared at Colt, read the concern in his eyes, and her blood pressure rose tremendously. Crazy. They were worlds apart. To make matters even worse, they were a full century apart. He was a bona fide, roping and riding, nineteenth-century wild man and she was a prim and proper, twentieth-century tame woman.

And never the twain shall meet.

Not to mention, she shouldn't be feeling these things for a man who'd never made any mention of love or commitment. Heck, he'd never even said he liked her. They just shared an intense chemical attraction. Otherwise, he wasn't her type. She wasn't his type.

She couldn't wouldn't, fall for him.

"Come on." He touched her and heat sizzled along her nerve endings, but more compelling than the sexual overtones of his touch was the flood of warmth that went through her at his gentleness. "Let's get you into bed."

"That's okay." She shrugged him away. He's not warm. He's not gentle. *No.* "I can do it by myself. You've done enough already."

He'd done more than enough because now she could no longer ignore the fact that she was falling, headfirst, for Colt Durango.

Falling, but not quite there. Not yet.

Not ever.

Not without a fight.

Chapter Fourteen

"Dadblame it. This waiting is bad for my digestion."

"Just hush up and tell me what to do."

"But Lucy Mae made chocolate creme pie."

"You can eat later. I need your help."

"But the meringue's warm right now," the old man protested. "It's warm and firm and melt-in-your-mouth sweet." Horseshoe's stomach grumbled and Colt frowned.

"I could keep it hot for you," Lucy Mae said from the kitchen doorway. Horseshoe turned a gaze on the young woman and they exchanged smiles.

"Why, thank you, darlin'. I'd be much obliged."

"You're welcome."

"Can we get on with this, please? I've only got a few hours."

"I cain't believe you're going to all this trouble for a woman."

Neither could Colt, but he'd made his decision. He wanted Sinful. Not in a right-now, take-me-I'm-yours sort of way. If that had been the case, she would have been his the first moment he'd laid her on the bed. He would have slid fast, deep and sure inside her hot, tight little body, and her cold be damned.

But he wanted more than just that body. He wanted her heart, and so he needed to treat her in a way that no man ever had before. He needed to court her all right and proper.

Starting tonight.

"So what do I do?"

"Put your arms around me." At Colt's doubtful expression, Horseshoe glared. "We cain't dadgum well dance if'n you don't put your arms around me."

"He's right," Ludy piped from the sidelines. "You have to put your arms around him. Unless you're square-dancing. Then you just hook arms—but it's not nearly as romantic."

He thought of Sinful from the night before, the way her eyes had glittered and her mouth had formed that cute pout. How he'd had the sudden urge to haul her into his arms and just hold her close even more than he'd wanted to kiss her.

"I think I need romantic."

"I think you need a good kick in the head. The girl cain't even cook, for heaven's sake. Not like Lucy Mae, here."

"Oh, Eustice. You're too nice."

"Eustice?" Colt's incredulous gaze shifted from Horseshoe to Lucy and back.

The old man actually blushed. All at once, Colt knew then and there that the geezer liked more than just this young woman's cooking.

"What are you looking at? It's my given Christian name. And if Lucy and I are friendly enough to exchange recipes, we ought to be on a first-name basis."

"That's right," Lucy added. "I'll just leave you boys be and take this into the kitchen. You join me when you're done, Eustice. I've got a roast basting with your name on it."

"Did you hear that?" Horseshoe's eyes fired with excitement. "A roast? Sakes alive, I love roast." Horseshoe smiled after the woman. "Now that there is one fine lady." He stared at the empty doorway a few seconds longer before turning back to Colt.

"What?"

"You like her."

" 'Course I like her. She's one of the finest little cooks I ever had the pleasure of meetin'." The old man glared. "Yore damn lucky she's a lady in every sense of the word, or she would have slapped you upside your stubborn head by now for bringing her out on a wild goose chase."

292

"I didn't invite her out here. You did."

"A technicality, my boy. She was coming to meet you—and off you go and fall for some woman who cain't even cook a decent buckwheat cake. I don't think I'll ever understand yore thinkin', boy."

Colt quirked an eyebrow. What would happen if . . . "You know, you're right. Maybe I'll invite Lucy to the dance. It's the least I could do—"

"I already invited her to the dance, so you jes' never mind. I ain't givin' you a chance to break that gal's heart again. I'll handle things from here on out."

Guilt rushed through Colt. While he hadn't invited Lucy out here, the girl hadn't known that. She'd come to meet Colt Durango. A pot roast–loving, buckwheat-eating ranch owner. He hadn't invited her, but neither did he want to be responsible for anyone's upset. "She was really heartbroken?"

"Well, she said she weren't, but I know these things. Saw it in them sweet eyes of hers. Man, she's got the purtiest eyes."

Colt eyed the man. "I thought you were only interested in her cooking."

"I am. She's got some of the best damn recipes I ever seen."

"And the blue eyes to go along with them?"

Horseshoe glared. "Are you gonna learn yourself to dance, or stand there yacking?"

Colt held out his arms. "Just tell me what to do."

"Take a flyin' leap into Sucker's Pond . . . but since you ain't about to do that, just put one hand right here on my arm and the other— Ouch!" Horseshoe massaged his arm. "I ain't a steer, boy. If you want to dance with a lady, you've got to gentle your touch. There," he said when Colt lightened his hold. "That's better. Remember, a lady's like a fine piece of china. Delicate—Yowee!" Horseshoe screeched and glared. "Would you watch where you're puttin' them big ole feet of yours? I'm leadin', here, I ain't givin' free rides."

"Sorry."

"Just watch it, and remember. Delicate." The old man started to hum and move and Colt did his best to follow.

"So you really want to impress this gal?" Horseshoe asked later that day, after several hours filled with waltzing and two-stepping and even a few slow country swings.

"Yep." Colt practiced dancing the four-steps he'd learned, feeling very pleased with himself. Other than the occasional yelp, Horseshoe had been pretty silent for the past half-hour. Colt was obviously getting the hang of this courting stuff. "Got any last-minute tips for me?"

"Just one." Horseshoe limped to the nearest chair and collapsed. "Don't ask her to dance."

"Are you sure you're feeling up to this?"

No. Though it went unuttered, her reply echoed through Elizabeth's head later that evening

294

as she sat next to Colt Durango. The tall cowboy was steering the older Durango wagon down the dirt road away from the Triple-C, toward town. They followed the other wagon filled with Horseshoe, Lucy Mac and the boys, and a third that was loaded with the whooping ranch staff, which was ready for a night on the town.

"I could take you back if you're still feeling sick."

"And miss seeing Cameron's moment of triumph? I promised him I'd be there to support him. I wouldn't miss it for all the money in Silicon Valley."

"Which valley—"

"I'm up to it." She would see this business out with Cameron. She was up to seeing him, but looking at Colt, dressed in black pants, shirt and matching leather vest, looking as dark and delicious as a fudge brownie, was a horse of a completely different color.

The moment she'd hauled open her cabin door to find him standing before it, ready to escort her to their ride, Elizabeth had known she was in deep, deep trouble. He not only looked good, but he looked strangely confident, his gaze dark, mesmerizing and steadier than usual. As if he knew exactly what he wanted and he'd made up his mind to get it.

And he wanted her—not in a right here, right now, let's-drop-our-britches-and-go-for-it way, but a forever kind of way.

She'd known it the minute he'd placed her

hand in the crook of his arm. There'd been no passionate embrace. No soul-deep kiss. Instead, he was full of good manners and gentlemanly charm, and the realization sent warning bells clanging in her head.

The Colt who took her to bed, who stole her breath with his gentle kiss and ferocious love-making, she could handle. But this Colt . . . This man threatened to steal her heart.

She tried to force the notion away, but it stuck, setting her nerves on edge as she stared at the passing scenery, the wagon bouncing along up in front, the sky overhead—anywhere, everywhere but at him.

Her gaze strayed to Colt for a quick peek and she caught him looking at her. She felt her face flush and he smiled, as if he knew he was making her jumpy.

As if he was doing his damnedest to do just that.

"Can't this thing go any faster?" she snapped.

Snapping was good. That tone of voice indicated annoyance, which indicated dislike, which was such a totally far removed emotion from love, so that she didn't have to worry about dwelling on that awful realization and doing something totally insane like throwing her arms around him and confessing that she couldn't live without him.

She could live without him. And she would. After the dance tonight, she was trading in her garter for a one-way ticket back to her real life.

She'd be putting an end to what had quickly turned from her fondest fantasy into her worst nightmare.

Love. Of all the crazy, ridiculous, stupid—

"What's the hurry? It's a nice night." Colt's baritone drew her attention. The dark blue of his irises caught flickers of moonlight as his eyes found hers again, and her stomach hollowed out.

She was starting to feel sick.

"I just don't want to miss anything. Cameron's been working so hard." She glanced ahead at the boy who sat on the seat beside Horseshoe in the wagon that rode before them. The young man was ready to go, from his slicked-down hair, to his white Sunday shirt tucked into his tan britches, to his freshly polished boots, to the quart of Horseshoe's all-cure he clutched in his white-knuckled hands.

The wagon pitched, and Elizabeth's thigh bumped against Colt's. Heat flooded through her, infuriating the butterflies already fluttering in her stomach.

What she wouldn't have given for a quart of her own all-cure right about now. Maybe she could con Cameron out of some when they reached the Willow Farm house where the dance was to be held. Enough to get her through the evening, maybe, through a full five hours spent in Colt's company, gazing into his eyes, seeing him smile, wanting to throw her arms around him so badly that she ached inside. And knowing she wouldn't.

The sooner the evening was over with, the sooner she could whisk off the garter, forget the charade and get back to her old life. Her old self. Her business and her family and . . . *Ugh.* The thought didn't hold near the appeal it should have.

Her business, however lucrative and fun, was just that—a business. At one time it had been an outlet, a means to cut loose and live vicariously through her clients, but no more. She'd catered her last and final fantasy—her own— and now she was tapped out. It would never be the same again. She'd always thought that real life couldn't compare to the imagination. That her midnight musings were more than enough spice in her life. But she'd been wrong. Colt Durango had proven that to her. She didn't know how she could ever go back and settle for pretending once she'd experienced the real thing.

As for her family, they probably hadn't even missed her yet. Assuming time was progressing there as it was here, she was still a week shy of her monthly lunch with her mother. Until then, nobody was going to notice she was gone. Or care. Except Jenna. Jenna would care.

But Jenna would understand.

"Love makes the world go 'round, girlfriend." That's what she would say.

But not in this case. Elizabeth had lived too long on her own to go changing her ways now.

She liked making her own decisions and living by her own rules, however limited. She liked being in control and having her own identity. Experiencing her wild side had shown her that. She still had hopes and dreams and they didn't include the proverbial two-point-five kids, the house in the suburbs and the Suburban sitting out in the garage. Finding some guy she kind of liked and marrying him were not part of her plan. She wanted more excitement. She wanted . . .

Colt.

The truth echoed through her head, refusing to be silenced or ignored. She didn't just kind of like Colt Durango. She loved him. While he was an expert in bed, he was also a good, kind, strong man who valued his family enough to give up his prodigal ways and return home. That was a sacrifice Elizabeth admired and understood all too well. She knew what it was like to pretend to be something different to please your family.

The thing was, though, she wasn't pretending. Deep down inside, she was every bit the wholesome girl her father had wanted her to be. She'd tried to deny the truth, tried to pretend to be something different, but she couldn't. She'd failed.

Just as Colt was failing.

He was doing his damnedest to deny his wild streak, but it was still there, in the fierce glint in his green eyes and the wicked way he smiled at her. He was wild at heart, which was undoubtedly why he was so attracted to the bold, outrageous Sinful Sinclair.

Sinful, not Elizabeth. He was attracted to her charade, and if Colt discovered the truth, he would dump her faster than a hot potato.

No sirree. She wasn't giving him the chance to do that. She would end things first and at least salvage her pride—even if it was too late for her heart.

All she had to do was make it through the next five hours.

Five long hours of Colt acting like a gentleman, playing the gallant suitor, the charming date, the—

"We're here." His deep voice stirred her from her thoughts and drew her back to the moment, to the brightly lit farmhouse on the horizon and the festive music and the strong thigh pressed up against her own.

She realized in an instant that her own thigh had gravitated toward his during the ride, and she hadn't moved aside. He felt warm and right, and the sensation stirred the lust inside her.

Lust was good. Lust was what she wanted to feel.

"Sorry," he murmured, shifting his leg aside like the proper gentleman.

"That's okay. I liked it." She leaned toward him, eager for a kiss; maybe that would distract her from her emotional thoughts. Just one kiss and she could focus on the blazing heat of passion instead of the comforting warmth of love.

"We're here," he said. "We better get inside."

"What's your hurry?"

"I thought you were in a hurry."

"Maybe I changed my mind." She touched his arm and felt him stiffen.

"I'd like to change mine, but I told you I wanted more and I do. Tonight's going to prove that." She saw determination flare in his eyes as he moved away from her, and despite a feeling of disappointment, she couldn't help but admire him.

Ugh. She had to do something.

She debated between kissing him and jumping from the wagon. The former won out and her lips touched his. She opened her mouth, but surprisingly, he didn't open his. Instead, he gave her a quick peck. Nice. Warm.

And she loved it just as much as the hot, open-mouthed kisses he'd lavished on her before.

She pulled away and jumped from the wagon, her feelings a mixture of longing and relief. So much for focusing on the lust.

"Wait up." She'd barely made it two steps when she felt the warm press of his hand at the small of her back.

It was the barest of touches, so minimal she wouldn't have noticed if circumstances had been different. If she hadn't fallen head over heels for a man she couldn't have.

However, as it was, the few seconds of contact were more than enough to make her body react. Her pulse pounded. Her knees trembled. Her insides actually *quivered*.

And worse, she felt a rush of warmth. Not just passion, but the warmth of completion and the sweet joy of affection.

Five hours, she told herself.

She could do this. She would do this. She would live up to her promise to Cameron, then say good-bye. Until then . . .

She concentrated on taking steady, even breaths, all the while doing her best to ignore the man steering her toward the barn, his fingers warm and comforting on her. Despite the trying evening ahead, there *was* a bright side.

At least she didn't have to worry about dancing with him.

"I'm not dancing with you."

"Sure you are."

"I'm not." She tugged against his grip, but he was strong and determined as he tugged her toward the dance floor. "I thought you couldn't dance."

"I couldn't, but now I can. Come on." A few more tugs and they reached the dance floor.

A slow sweet tune played by a fiddler echoed around them, mocking the panic suddenly beating at her senses. They were starting with a waltz, and Colt wanted her to dance. With him. Now.

She tugged against his grip. "I can't do this. I really can't."

His gaze met hers and a slow grin spread across his face. "Trust me, Peaches. You can do this. This is simple compared to what you're used to."

"That's not what I meant. Of course I can do this—dancing, that is. I know how, it's just I can't right now." She winced and shifted her weight from one foot to the other. "My feet are killing me."

"We've been here all of fifteen minutes."

"And I still have to make it through four hours, forty-four minutes and fifty seconds. Or something like that. I'm tired already." At his questioning stare, she faked a cough. "I still haven't fully recovered my strength from that cold. I'm too weak. I'll never make it if I use what little energy I have left dancing right now."

"It's just one dance."

One slow dance, complete with swaying and touching and feeling and—

"No. I can't. Besides, I can do the solo dancing thing, but couples dancing is very different."

"I'll lead."

"You can't lead. You can't dance. You told me so yourself."

"I couldn't, but now I can."

"But I can't follow."

"Do the best you can."

"But I'm liable to step on your feet," she warned as he tugged her toward the hay-strewn dance floor."

"I'm wearing sturdy boots." Before she could

voice another protest, he swung her into his arms and started to move.

Elizabeth did the only thing she could the moment his solid arms closed around and his body pressed up against hers. She gave into the tingling heat. It lasted for a fraction of a second, but she came to her senses as—just as she'd warned—someone's foot got stepped on.

"Yow!" The squeal echoed above the music. It took all of a moment for her to realize that it was her own voice. Panic radiated up from her toes and her gaze snapped to Colt's.

"Sorry," he murmured, a sheepish expression on his face. "I guess it takes more than one lesson to pick this up."

"You took lessons?"

"One lesson. Today. So I could dance with you."

The pain faded in a surge of heat that swept her from head to toe. "You took a lesson for me?"

He nodded and then frowned. "But it obviously didn't pay off. We can sit down if you want."

"I wouldn't dream of it." *Would you shut up?* the voice whispered through her head as he stepped on her foot again. And again. *Why didn't you sit down, Elizabeth? What are you trying to do?*

"Sorry."

Pain splintered through her and she blinked back a sudden wave of tears. Her toes were surprisingly sensitive. "Don't worry about it. You're doing just great." No man had ever taken a dance lesson for her. The least she could do was appreciate it for a little while. Besides, the guy deserved some credit. He was doing pretty well for having had one lesson. She'd had to watch *Striptease* five times before she'd gotten Demi's strut down. And it was a good thing she had, she thought now with a grimace. Would Colt have really believed she was Sinful if she hadn't even began that routine? Perhaps all those movie marathons with Jenna had been worth something after all.

"Relax and don't think about the steps. Just listen to the music," she said to Colt and patted his arm. "All you need to do is loosen up and you'll be fine."

"You really think—Sorry."

"I'm sure of it." She ignored another bolt of toe-crunching agony, smiled and settled into his embrace—all the while her feet cried for a pair of steel-toe boots.

Stop that. What did she want, anyway? A guy who was perfect at everything? She had a hot, hunky man who'd actually tortured himself with a dance lesson just for her benefit. That should be more than enough to make her one happy woman.

But the fact that he suddenly had some ability, coupled with the obvious pains he was taking to make her happy, were only making things worse. All good things, as the saying went, had to come to an end, and her fantasy cowboy was only making himself a better thing. Suddenly Elizabeth was faced with leaving Colt Durango—just as soon as the evening ended.

All the more reason for her to enjoy the moment, to commit the smell, sight and feel of him to memory; to give herself some pleasant memories to warm her on all the cold nights to come.

To forget about her crying toes and focus on the here and now. To focus on him.

Maybe he wasn't stepping on her feet enough.

She couldn't feel her toes at all.

She'd passed excruciating pain about five minutes back during a very fast square dance and fallen straight into the land of the pleasantly numb for this last waltz.

Even so, she couldn't have been more pleased when Colt excused himself to go and fetch them some punch. Now if she could just hobble toward a table and collapse for a few blessed moments. . . .

The thought faded as her gaze snagged on Cameron. Colt's brother stood amid a group of teenage boys across the room in one corner, a cup of punch clutched in his hand. From him, her attention shifted to Caroline, who stood on the other side of the room, surrounded by girls.

Elizabeth watched as the two teenagers exchanged shy glances.

Shy, and after all her hard work. After all Cameron's hard work. With a determined sigh, and before she could give in to her crying feet, Elizabeth headed for Cameron, ignoring the whistles and greetings that followed.

"Howdy, miss."

"My, my, you look good, sugar."

"How's about a little dance?"

Obviously, the garter was still working. The knowledge should have sent a rush of pleasure through her. She'd always wanted to be noticed, to flirt and tease and be every bit as sinful as she had seen other women be. She had wanted to release the wild woman who had stayed like a shadow in her mind. She had heard it beg to be released.

But there was no wild woman. Just plain old Elizabeth, and while she did want to be noticed, it was only by one man.

The man she was leaving in three hours and forty-eight minutes and counting.

"What are you doing?" At the sound of her voice, Cameron's head jerked up and punch sloshed onto his boots. "This is a dance, which means you should be dancing."

"I'm getting to it."

"Not by standing clear across the room, you aren't. Why don't you go over there and ask her to dance?"

"I can't. What if she doesn't want to dance?"

"What if she does?"

"What if she doesn't?"

"Cameron, it's time you learned my last and final lesson."

307

"I hope it's not another kissing technique, 'cause it took me long enough to get down the ones we already went over. I don't think I can learn another on such short notice."

"It's not a kissing technique."

"Well, I hope it's not any more sweet talk, 'cause I ain't even had a chance to use the stuff I did write down."

"It's not more sweet talk."

"Then, I hope it's not about smiling a certain way, 'cause I—"

"Would you just be quiet and listen?" At his shocked nod, she took the cup from his hands and sipped.

"Ugh. What is this stuff?"

"The all-cure. I'm not feeling too well."

Her gaze flew over to Colt, who stood across the room in the line at the punch table and her stomach jumped. She downed the rest of the cup.

"Hey, I needed that!"

"Trust me, I need it more than you. Now." She set the empty cup on a nearby bale of hay. "The most important lesson to remember is that if you want something in this world, you have to go after it. You can't sit around waiting and hoping and worrying. You must square your shoulders, march over there, and take charge. Otherwise, one day you'll wake up and you'll be clicking your teeth, listening to Benny Goodman and playing ten bingo cards down at the local rest home. And you won't have gotten a single thing you want because you were always too scared to try."

"Rest home? What's a rest—"

"Just *go*." Before he could voice another protest, she gripped his upper arms, spun him around and shoved him in Caroline's direction. "Ignore your fear and doubts and just take a chance."

"She might turn me down!"

"And she might not. Now go. Go after what you want and don't look back."

As she watched Cameron make his way toward Caroline, her own words echoed in her head. *Ignore your fear and doubts . . .*

But she couldn't follow her own advice. Her situation was different. There was no maybe about it. Colt would reject her once he knew the truth. He was too wild to settle for someone so tame.

He was a mustang and she was a plow horse. They would never work. He would turn her down flat.

And maybe he wouldn't.

As she stood there and watched Cameron take Caroline in his arms, a smile of victory on his face, she realized that she couldn't leave without at least trying. Without telling Colt the truth, however shocking, and admitting her feelings for him.

She had to go for it, otherwise she'd be the one alone and lonely, sitting in a rest home, playing bingo for the rest of her life.

Her mind made up, she started for the punch table and Colt.

"Hold up, there, sugar. We've got business." A man's voice came from behind her.

"Look, my feet hurt and I'm not up to dancing, but thanks for asking." This business of the garter's sex appeal was starting to be a pain in the wazoo, particularly when she didn't feel like being Sinful.

At least, with anyone other than Colt. She finally realized that feeling sinful and being Sinful were two different things.

Which was why she was coming clean with Colt right now. He might reject her, but there was the chance, the slim chance that he wouldn't. That he would want her anyway, as much as she wanted him. After all, she had been the person he'd known—that was a part of her, if not the whole package.

She clung to the hope and kept walking.

"Hey, there." The voice came again and a hand clutched her arm.

"Sorry, buddy, but I'm not dancing with anybody. I'm really busy and—" The words were choked off by the sudden lump in her throat as she turned and caught sight of the man. He was one of the redheaded men—the biggest—who'd attacked her that night at the hotel.

"I'm not asking to dance, sugar. I want you to come with me."

"I don't think so."

"I do. We've got business."

310

She stiffened and began to back away. At least they were talking, which meant no one was going to just kill her. Yet.

"The only business you've got is with my knee. I have to warn you, I've been practicing my 'nutcracker' since the last time you saw me."

"I figured as much."

"What do you—" Before she could finish, a smelly rag closed over her face and cut off her circulation.

So much for the not killing theory, she thought. Blackness set in.

Chapter Fifteen

They'd ditched her.

Sadie Sinclair fought back a wave of disappointment and concentrated on her anger; that and the fact that she'd never in her entire life let anyone get the best of her. Not since she'd been five years old and her cousin Louisa May—eight years old and a witch extraordinaire—had challenged her to a frog-zapping contest. Make the frog sing. That had been the bet. Louisa had pointed her finger and zapped, and the frog had practically soloed like an opera diva.

Sadie's turn had come, she'd zapped her own frog. And zapped. And zapped again.

Nothing had happened.

She'd come to find out her frog had been magically muted by Louisa's older brother. The whole contest had been a joke, and Sadie had been the butt of it. But she'd gotten even; she'd resorted to a little old-fashioned revenge. Sadie had poured ink over Louisa's pale blond hair and then run like the devil was chasing her.

She'd learned a valuable lesson. When your magic fails, resort to good old-fashioned techniques. And that had been important lately.

Billy wasn't half the challenge Louisa had been, and he wouldn't make a fool of her by leaving her sitting back at the hotel like a good little woman.

His woman.

She quickly shoved aside the thought. She wasn't his woman. She'd be his worst nightmare when she caught up to him. She didn't like being made a fool of, which was why she'd spent the past four hours tracking him down. He wasn't getting away with this.

A drink? Had Billy Redd really expected her to believe such nonsense? Why, that was a lie if she'd ever heard one. If it was a drink he and his low-life brothers had really been after, they could have had one at the saloon and saved her feet the trouble of following them out to this homestead on the far edge of town. And all the way from the abandoned cabin they'd been shacked up in.

This here was a dance, a barn overflowing with people and music and laughter. There were no half-dressed girls standing on the front porch beckoning men inside. This was respectable.

And this was what Billy had lied to her about.

Her gaze went to one woman serving punch at a refreshment table set up beneath a large oak tree. A handsome cowboy stood across from her, his hat in his hands as he took the cup of punch she offered him. The woman wore a yellow dress with pale flowers, her hair swept up with a ribbon, not an ounce of face paint enhancing her features. She was simple and unadorned, and the cowboy couldn't take his eyes off her.

Sadie stared down at her own outfit, at the too-tight gaudy dress, the costume jewelry on her fingers, her black fishnet stockings. She'd spent her entire life wanting to be noticed, to be sinful like her sister, and still no one spared her the time of day.

Her gaze went to the couple again and a pang of jealousy shot through her. She was still on the outside, still looking in and envying what everyone else had. What she wanted.

Just once in her life, she wanted a man to want her, to really want *her*, to look at her with awe and respect and love. Yep, that's what it was all about. Love.

But not just any man. One man. Billy Redd.

The notion rushed through her head and she pushed it back out. Sure she might long for a handsome cowboy to love her beyond belief in a wholesome sort of way. But Billy, with his thug brothers, was far from wholesome. He didn't belong at this place any more than she did. Not to mention, he'd lied to her.

A drink.

Why, of all the cockamamie, two-timing, low-life . . .

The thought faded as she spotted Billy's horse tied to a nearby fence post and her suspicions were confirmed. He *was* here.

Anger rushed through her, along with another healthy dose of jealousy. Sure enough, the worm had gone out for more than just a drink. He was probably inside right now with a cup of punch in one hand and a woman in the other.

Forget the punch. He probably had two women in hand. Maybe three. He was awfully cute, especially when he smiled and showed his dimples. Then there was the way he looked in his britches. He had such a great behind. And he was polite. And he could really be sweet when he wanted to be.

Her anger fired hotter and brighter, and her hand started to shake. Her finger twitched of its own accord, wanting, needing something to zap, and before she could stop and think and revel in the feeling, she stepped from the shadows.

"Going out to get a drink, my aunt Fanny's hound dog," she muttered as she started for the festivities inside the farmhouse, oblivious to the attention she was drawing dressed as she was. "We'll see just how much you can drink when I'm done with you and those three floozies you're dancing with."

One curse. That's all she needed. One well-aimed curse and she'd put Billy and his cheating heart in their proper place once and for all.

And if her magic failed her—as it so often did—she could always dump a cup of punch over his head.

But first she had to find him.

"What'd you have to go and hit her fer?" The familiar twang pushed past the fog holding Elizabeth captive and she stirred.

She came to, feeling the hay beneath her back and smelling the pungent odor of horse. A rope bit into her wrists and a handkerchief was cutting into the corners of her mouth.

She was bound and gagged!

The thought brought her a brief terror before fading into the throb in her temples. Her head hurt so bad she felt sick to her stomach.

"I'm still limping from the last run-in." Another voice, just as twangy and just as familiar, sounded somewhere to her left and made her head throb all the harder. "The little gal's strong and I ain't risking my manhood on account of some feisty little thief."

"But she ain't no help to us if she's dead, and there ain't no way to know for sure if she's a thief." The third voice, twangy and familiar and a lot more hesitant than she remembered, slid past the heavy thud of her heart. It was Skinny, the smallest brother from the hotel that night, and the least threatening. "She could be innocent."

"You been talking to that crazy witch too much."

"I ain't been doin' no such thing—and she ain't crazy."

"Says you."

"You're just mouthing off 'cause she ain't here."

"And you're getting a little too friendly with her."

"That's right," the first voice said. "I shore seen you talkin' to her enough."

"So what if I was? Somebody had to, otherwise you'd both be sittin' here with your peckers out of order. You ought to be thankin' me."

"And you ought to remember who yore kin is."

"What's that supposed to mean?"

"That you been gettin' too friendly here lately, and it's gonna stop. We're almost done with this job and we're ditchin' her. We ain't goin' back fer her."

"We cain't just leave her in a strange town," said Skinny. "She thinks we just went out for a drink."

"A strange woman in a strange town. Makes sense to me, and if she really was a witch worth having around, she'd have known we was lyin' to her about goin' out fer whiskey."

"I still don't think we shoulda done that. She

317

don't know a soul in this town. Friends don't ditch friends."

"We ain't her friends. We're her damned hostages, or ain't you noticed her waggling that finger at us like it's a dadblastit pistol? Three weeks and we still ain't been able to get rid of her."

"And how come you think we'll get rid of her now?"

" 'Cause she's used to us. I talked to her three times yesterday and she didn't point her cursin' finger at me once. She trusts us."

"That's what I'm talkin' about. We cain't violate her trust. She's—"

"—a bully, that's what she is."

"She is not."

"Is too."

"Is not—"

"Enough," boomed Burly. Elizabeth remembered his voice, loud and authoritative and unforgettable. He was the leader. The biggest of the litter and the most threatening. "You boys keep it down, otherwise that whole barn full of cowboys is gonna be out here 'afore we can discuss our business, and Ripley ain't gonna wait any longer. Telegram said he's as antsy as an apple pie at a picnic and if we don't get some results, he's gonna take back the money he done paid us and hire the Bartlett brothers to do the job."

"That bunch of greenhorns? Why, they couldn't find a hole in their longjohns," Medium said. "Cain't even shoot worth anythin'. Heard that Mac Bartlett caught up to One-Eyed Sammy—that famous train robber—and he couldn't even nick him at ten paces. Ain't no Bartlett can outdo us."

"Ripley seems to think so, and he swears he's going with them if we don't get his ring back now. We got to take care of this, tonight."

Barn full of cowboys. Burly's words made Elizabeth keenly aware of the distant sound of music and laughter and *people*. Relief swept through her. She could get help. Somehow. Help might even be on the way. When Colt returned with her punch and found her missing, surely he would come looking.

Unless he thought she'd gone to the bathroom.

Or ditched him.

Or . . .

She killed the doubts. He *would* come looking.

Her captors were still arguing. "It ain't right you choosin' some woman over yore blood . . . and we didn't say no such thing. *She* said she was comin', and that if we didn't let her, she'd change us from bucks to does with one point of her finger. From the sound of you, she already done zapped you. Maybe that's why yore goin' all soft. She's zapped you into a woman."

"Like hell. I still got everythin' in working order—I'm one-hundred-percent man—and I ain't choosin her over my blood. I'm here with y'all, ain't I?"

"We'll see."

"Ain't nothin' to see. I'm here. That says it all."

"It don't say nothin' if yore still takin' up for her."

"I ain't takin' up for her."

"Are too."

"Am not."

"Could you boys keep it down? My head is killing me." The statement came out garbled and choked thanks to her gag, but it was enough to draw their attention and make them shut up for a few blessed moments.

"Looks like she ain't dead."

"I told you."

"Did not."

"Did too."

"Did—"

"*Shhhh!*" She was dying. Forget that. She was already dead and this was Hell. She was being tortured by the three redheaded stooges, Burly, Medium and Skinny, and—

Reality hit her as strong hands clamped around her ankle. *Tortured?* Definitely a poor choice of words; she hadn't even begun to be tortured. Fear slithered through her senses for a full moment before the situation became clear.

They wanted the ring they had been yapping about in the hotel. They still thought she had it. Which meant no blood was going to be shed until she revealed its whereabouts. Which meant she was safe as long as they thought she knew where it was.

She cracked one eyelid and fought against a sudden blur of tears. A few frantic blinks and she managed to focus. She *had* to focus, to find a way out. While Colt might indeed come looking, she wasn't sure how much time she had until then. Or before Burly, Medium and Skinny decided to wage another full-body search for their precious ring.

Like hell, they would.

They were in a barn, all right. A nearby horse whinnied. Elizabeth glanced to her right to see a spotted cow peering over the top of its stall, a cow she'd seen when they'd first ridden up to the farmhouse. The cry of a fiddle carried on the wind. They were near the dance, all right. She could hear the noises of the dance and if she could hear, it meant that someone could probably hear her—if she could just get the blasted gag off her mouth.

"Wake up!" A fierce slap on her rump punctuated the command and Elizabeth's eyes popped all the way open. "That's better. Now where is it?"

She mumbled a reply that met with a frown.

"Speak up, girlie," Medium said. "We ain't got all night."

"She cain't speak up past the gag," Skinny added.

"Oh, yeah." Burly tugged down the handkerchief. "Now we want some answers, missy, and we ain't gonna be nice like before."

She opened and closed her mouth and licked her dry lips. "Grabbing and mauling me was nice?" she managed, the question coming out so calm and controlled, she surprised herself. Her insides trembled and her mind raced.

But they didn't know that.

"If you had just handed it over, we wouldn't have had to grab you."

"That's right. We ain't grabbers," Skinny added.

"We *are* grabbers," Medium countered nastily. "When we need to be."

"For your information, I ain't ever grabbed anyone," Skinny told his brother.

"Yes, you have. I seen you."

"Have not."

"Have too."

They sparred back and forth for a few moments, forgetting about her, and she congratulated herself on the distraction. But her pleasure was brief.

Burly frowned at her. "You been causin' us a whole mess of trouble."

"We want that ring and we ain't takin' no for an answer." Large hands reached for her.

So much for the distraction.

She'd run out of time and so she did the only thing she could.

She opened her mouth and screamed.

The sudden sound shattered the night and

obviously caught the men off-guard. They swore, all three scrambling for her. One clamped a hand around her mouth and tried to tug the handkerchief up to silence her, but she was quicker. She bit down on his thumb. He yelped and snatched his hand back. She took the opportunity to scream again. Louder. Longer.

"Hush up, lady!"

"We ain't gonna hurt you," Skinny said. "Honest."

"Don't tell her that, you idiot!" Medium exploded. "We *are* gonna hurt her, and we're gonna enjoy every darn minute."

"Are not."

"Are too."

"Are—"

"Hell's bells, would you two shut up?" Burly reached for her again. "Now just stop—Ouch!" Another bite and he snatched his hand back, shaking it frantically to ward off the pain.

"We ain't gonna hurt her," Skinny insisted.

"Are too."

"Are not."

"I'm gonna hurt the two of you if you don't shut the hell up 'afore—"

"It's coming from out here!" The shout came from outside, stifling the bickering and sending another burst of panic through her captors.

Elizabeth felt it, too. Her heart pounded, her throat ached and her blood rushed. After all, they'd been considering a full-body search. Just the thought sent a wave of sickness through her, along with fear. Dread. Loathing. Were these men so dumb that, even if Sinful Sinclair had stolen the ring from their boss they thought she would continue to keep it on—in—her person?

She closed her eyes and kept screaming for what seemed like hours, her own voice ringing in her ears. If she was going down, she wasn't going quietly. No, sir. Not this girl. There was no way. She hadn't protected herself for so long, forfeited her wild and wicked tendencies, to be totally humiliated at the hands of three dumb clutzes.

"Stop it!" The command echoed through her head as strong hands gripped her shoulders and hauled her to her feet. She screamed even louder. She wasn't going down without a fight. Without at least trying to save herself. She didn't want to die or, worse, be strip-searched in a smelly old barn with an Elsie the cow look-alike staring down at her.

"Sinful!" The voice, so deep and strong and familiar, pushed past her frantic thoughts. Her eyes popped open and she found Colt Durango staring back at her.

Half of the people from the dance surrounded him, all of their gazes fixed on her. She realized in a heartbeat that she was still screaming. Her throat closed and her voice died as relief swept through her.

"What happened? What's wrong?"

"They were . . . they . . ." She fought for

breath but it wouldn't come. She shook her head frantically and buried her face in the side of his neck, inhaling his scent and sinking into his warmth.

He held her with strong arms for a long, heart-pounding moment before he pried her fingers loose and moved her back so she could talk.

"Tell me what happened. What are you doing out here?" He noticed her hands. "What are your hands doing tied?"

"I . . ." The reply faded into a choked sob.

"Somebody get the sheriff and search this place. Something's going on." Get yelled at the surrounding group. The group quickly dispersed as Colt reached around and worked at the rope binding her wrists.

"You really need to tell me what happened," he told her as he massaged her chafed skin. He held her hands so softly and tenderly, his eyes shining with a dozen emotions, that it thrilled Elizabeth as much as frightened her.

She buried her face in the crook of his neck and took another deep breath. Her mind rushed back to the dance, to the decision she'd made just before the men had captured her. To tell Colt the truth, to face up to reality.

"Tell me, Peaches. What happened?"

A dozen answers rushed through her head, but the only one that made it to the tip of her tongue was a frantic, "I'm not who you think I am. My name is Elizabeth Joanna Carlton, not Sinful Sinclair."

Immediately he put her away from him and stared down into her eyes. "What?"

She wanted to take it back, to pretend she hadn't said anything at all, but the moment of truth had finally come.

Maybe. The word echoed through her and she couldn't help herself. Maybe she should try to back out. *No*. She had to tell him the truth, regardless of the consequences.

"I'm not a famous stripper and I haven't slept with one thousand men," she rushed on. "I'm a caterer and I'm from the future."

The statement hung in the air a few long moment before Colt stared down at her, an unreadable expression on his face. "You need some air."

She shook her head. "Listen to me. I don't need air. I'm completely sane, and I'm from the future."

Disbelief carved his expression. "The future?"

"Over one hundred years, to be exact. I know I should have told you sooner, but I didn't know how to explain it. I mean, one minute I'm standing in this abandoned building and the next, I slide on the garter and bam, I'm back in time."

"A garter brought you back in time?"

"Not a garter, *the* garter. Sinful Sinclair's garter. It's magical. It's the source of her sex appeal—or it was before it came to me. Now it's the source of mine. It makes me attractive. Ir-

326

resistible." Her gaze locked with his. "It makes you want me."

"You think the garter is what makes me want you?"

She nodded. "I *know* it is. I mean, at first I thought that maybe it was a little bit me, because deep down I was this wild woman just dying to break free. I thought maybe you sensed that and it drew you to me, but now I know it was all just wishful thinking. Going to town last week proved that. I turned heads. I never did that before, because I'm not a hot babe. It was the garter. I'm not a hot anything. My father's a politician and I do needlepoint in my spare time and I literally know any other book besides *Moby Dick* by heart. I love you, but I'm not wild or wicked or even remotely exciting. I'm just me. Plain, old me."

"You're not— What did you just say?"

She swallowed the sudden lump in her throat. "I'm not wild?"

"After that."

"My father's a politician?"

"Keep going."

"I do needlepoint?"

"Keep going some more?"

"I know almost every book but *Moby Dick* by heart?"

"More."

"I'm plain?"

"Back the wagon up, Peaches."

She stared into his eyes and fought down a wave of fear.

Take the chance.

She would, but not because she expected it to make a difference or solve her problems. She would say the words because she needed to, because confession was good for the soul and when a person loved someone they didn't lie to them. And so far that's all she'd been doing. Lying to him, and to herself. She'd been hiding from the truth for far too long. No more. She was who she was—prim and proper and from the future—and she was in love with Colt Durango. And because of that love, she wanted to be honest.

They might not have a future together, but they could at least have some measure of honesty. She owed him. For bringing her fantasies to life and giving her a lifetime of sweet memories.

She'd spent her entire life running from the truth and making excuses for it. She'd been shy because of her father, repressed because of her duty. But in all honesty, she'd been shy because she *was* shy, and repressed because she was afraid. Not about embarrassing her father, but about seeing her true self.

No more. She knew the truth and Colt was going to know it as well.

She fought for her courage and stared him in the eye. "I said that I love you."

She expected a good many responses from

him, everything from excuses to laughter to anger—after all, she'd lied to him about so many things. Who she was and what she wanted and where she was from. All she'd been was one big lie.

He should be mad. Hurt. Cold.

She expected all three, but never in her wildest dreams did she anticipate his gruff, "I love you, too."

She relished the words for several moments, enjoying the rush of joy, the pleasure, before dismissing the crazy notion.

He loved her?

He didn't even know her. He loved the woman he thought her to be because of the garter. That strip of satin was clouding his thinking, making him stare at her with desire hot in his gaze, making his hands so strong and gentle as he caressed her.

And it was the garter that made him sweep her into his arms and head for his horse.

"Where are we going?"

"Home," he said as he unhitched the beast from the Durango wagon. He had obtained a saddle somehow, and now he placed it on the horse and cinched it.

"But what about the dance?"

"I can't dance." He mounted the horse. "It's time I stop pretending I can."

"What about Cameron?"

"Horseshoe will bring him home when he brings back the others." He leaned down and slid an arm around her waist to hoist her up in front of him.

"What about the buckboard?"

"Horseshoe can bring that home, too. He'll notice it's still here and my horse is gone." He settled her in front of him and drew her back into the cradle of his thighs, the musky scent of his body making her blood rush and tingle.

"I thought you wanted to take things slow, now that you're being a gentleman."

"We can take it slow, Peaches. We can take it any way you want it, as long as we take it home." And then he urged his horse to a gallop and they started for the Triple-C.

Chapter Sixteen

She was caught smack dab in the middle of a hot, steamy romance novel.

That's all Elizabeth could think of as she sat in front of Colt Durango, his powerful body framing hers, the horse beneath them. His hands caressed her wrists where the rope had chafed them, soothing her hurt away.

He was the hot, hunky hero cradling the shivering, frightened heroine who'd just had her brush with death. The moon glimmered overhead. Desire twined around them, stirring her senses and making her desperately aware of the way her dress rubbed against her breasts with the movement of the horse as it trotted toward the Triple-C.

Elizabeth leaned back, wanting to wrap herself in Colt. He smelled so good and she'd missed him so much last night. Why had she held herself back? It seemed so long ago.

"Lizzie Jo," Colt murmured, his voice sending a ripple of awareness from her head, clear to her toes. "I want you."

"I want you, too." She arched into the palm that sought out her breast and closed her eyes, relishing the heat that burned through the fabric of her dress.

Colt cupped the fullness of it before finding the nipple. With an insistent fingertip, he circled the swollen peak until Elizabeth felt her entire body burn for more. She rested her head against the curve of his shoulder and arched her back further. A tiny moan escaped her lips as he found the other breast and delivered the same delicious treatment.

Another fantasy. She had to be having another fantasy. Nothing real could feel so wonderful. He moved his hand across her abdomen and every nerve in her body rioted with pleasure.

His fingers burned through her stockings as he caught the hem of her dress and slid the material up, pushing past her undergarments. He touched the insides of her thighs. He stroked and coaxed until her legs trembled.

Through quivering lips, she gasped as he moved his hand higher, tormenting her, delighting her. When he touched the slick folds between her legs—she had stood in the stirrups, granting him access—a shudder rattled through her body. Her breath caught and she knew then that even if she had wanted to leave him, she couldn't. Not now. Not yet.

She needed at least one more night with him. A few more precious memories, because as much as she wanted to think she might find another man like Colt Durango, she knew she never would. He was one of a kind. There would be no one else like him in this time or any other.

She was ready to throw safety to the wind, to turn and wrap her arms around him despite the awkwardness of making love on a horse, when the ranch house appeared in the distance.

They reached the corral and Colt slowed the animal. Dismounting, he looped the reins over the hitching post and pulled Elizabeth into his arms, sliding her down the length of his hard body with exquisite slowness. The sweet friction sent spasms of need coiling through her.

"I want you so much," he whispered, his lips a sensual vibration against hers. "I've wanted you all night."

"You wouldn't even kiss me earlier," she complained.

"I wanted to take things slow."

"And now?"

"Now I can't help myself. You scared the daylights out of me when I couldn't find you."

The words sent a burst of pleasure through her. He'd been worried—because he cared.

Of course he cares. You know that. But love? Does he really—

The question was cut off as he dipped his head and captured her mouth with an urgency that took her breath away.

He moved his hands down her spine in a tingling sweep to grip her waist as he drank from her, pushing his tongue past her lips to delve deeply. Each velvet stroke set her senses ablaze until she burned hotter, brighter than she had before, like a brush fire blazing out of control. Locking her arms around his neck, she pulled him closer, afraid of the feelings he incited, yet desperate not to lose them.

Colt led her toward the ranch house, but they didn't quite make it inside before he stopped and pulled her into his arms. The next thing she knew, he was easing her down to the grass, his lips on hers. The kiss was deep, fierce, demanding, and Elizabeth gave of herself as much as she took from him.

Pulling his mouth away, he licked a fiery path down her neck. He traced his tongue across her collarbone, toward the deep hollow between her breasts, which pressed eagerly against the soft cotton of her dress.

When he leaned back, his legs on either side of her hips and his weight braced on his muscular thighs, she opened her eyes, her gaze locking with his for the space of a heartbeat. Then he unbuttoned the front of her dress and pushed the edges aside. His eyes darkened as he stared at her full breasts. They quivered beneath his attention.

Christ, she really *was* quivering. Like a virgin with her first lover. This was definitely the stuff romance novels were made of, complete with a heady dose of passion and enough romantic atmosphere to make even the stiffest, grumpiest woman lose her inhibitions.

"So beautiful," Colt murmured, reaching out to circle one dusky nipple with his finger.

The touch was sweet. So very sweet. Elizabeth inhaled, her breathing ragged, short, her heart skidding to a halt with each touch, then pounding forward at the pure longing that stole through her, as if she hadn't already touched him too many times to count.

He leaned down to flick his tongue across one aching tip. He pulled the ripe peak into his mouth and suckled deeply until she cried out.

Elizabeth buried her fingers in his thick mane of hair and held him to her. The cool wind whirled around them, lashing at her heated body but doing nothing to quench the fire raging inside of her—the fire Colt stoked with his feverish mouth.

"Please," she begged, eager for him to ease the frustration knotting her insides. She floated, and with each sensation she drifted higher, up through the murky rain clouds—

Rain clouds?

Her eyes opened and a fat rain drop caught her smack dab in the middle of her forehead. Then it was if the heavens opened up. The sky grumbled and the rain started.

Rain is supposed to be good in sexual situations. Isabella X said that it added ambience to many of people's fantasies. *So wet and slick and . . . cold.*

Yes, it was much too cold and stinging and not nearly as romantic as it would have been if she'd been curled up all warm and snug in her bed. Maybe this would be better—

"Colt," she sputtered, catching a mouthful of water. "I don't think this is going to work."

He leaned over, blocking the downpour for a few precious moments before he scooped her up into his arms and started for the house.

"So this is the main house," she said once they got inside. Her gaze took in the massive sitting room, from a huge stone fireplace to a small table set up with checkers, to the patchwork quilt gracing one wall. "It's nice."

Colt stopped and followed her gaze. "It is." His gaze locked with hers. "It's home."

"Is it?"

"It will be. I think I'm ready. Come on." He took her hand and led her down a hallway. "I want to show you something."

"What?"

"This." He opened a door at the far end to reveal a large bedroom with a huge four-poster bed. There was a wash stand, a fireplace and a huge rocker. "My room."

"But I thought you were staying in the bunkhouse."

"I was. But I moved in here this morning. I'm home."

The magnitude of what he was telling her hit her as she watched him walk into the room and begin to build a fire in the room's hearth. He looked so big and powerful and alone.

Lonely. The thought struck her and something shifted inside her. A feeling that forced her forward even when she knew she should turn and run. Colt had brought her to his home, to his room . . . because he wanted to show it to her, to show her he'd made peace, to show her he loved her. And to show her he wanted her.

When she walked over and touched his shoulder, every muscle in his body seemed to go rigid. She pressed her body up against him, traced the outline of one shoulder with her fingertips.

"I'm glad you're home, Colt. I'm really glad," she murmured, before pressing her lips to his shoulder blade and kissing him through the fabric of his shirt.

Her hands traveled over his shoulders, down his back to his waist. She hesitated for a brief moment. He never failed to make her feel so new to everything, as if they were touching for the first time. Kissing for the first time. Loving for the first time.

And yet it felt as if she'd loved him her entire life.

This was crazy. She was waxing poetic because of the mood and the rain and the fact that she'd finally admitted her feelings for him.

But it wasn't real. It was as if she'd stepped right into one of Isabella X's scenarios, or one of her own. She was in a fantasy, but one that Isabella could never sum up, could never explain.

This was her last and final fantasy with Colt Durango, and she intended to make the most of it.

She slid her hands around his waist, tugged at his shirt until it came free and she could slide her hands underneath. Warm, hair-dusted skin met her fingertips and Colt groaned. And she groaned because he was so hot, so real, and her senses went into major overload.

She ran her fingers up over his chest, down his stomach—so flat and hard, and quivering beneath her explorations.

She pressed herself to his back and rubbed her aching breasts against him as her touch drifted lower. She felt his sex, hard beneath his britches, and a surge of feminine power went through her. While she wasn't sure of many other things, she was confident of his desire. He wanted her, and that meant so much. It meant everything.

She ignored the small voice whispering that something else was more important.

She unbuttoned his pants and slid her hands inside. Her fingers traveled across his manhood, tracing the hard, hot length before he caught her wrist and drew her around in front of him.

His eyes glittered, reflecting the firelight and proving to her that he did, indeed, want her. Locking his gaze with hers, he drew her closer and moved his hips against hers in a breath-stealing rhythm. He pressed his erection into her and rubbed the tender flesh above her thighs. Her eyes closed and her head fell back and she moaned.

And then he kissed her again, devouring and stroking and drinking from her until she shuddered against him.

She clutched his back, threading her fingers through his hair and holding his mouth to hers, holding him to her as if she could keep him there always. She wanted to keep him there, to feel him buried inside of her, to pull him deeper until there was no possibility that he was a fantasy, but a real man. *Her* man.

Colt eased her arms from his neck and dropped to his knees in front of her. Touching her ankles, he stroked his way up over her legs, underneath her dress, caressing her in a slow, torturous movement that made her want to rip all her clothes off.

But she wanted this to last, to go slow, to prolong the inevitable.

And apparently so did he, because he touched her softly, slowly, working her into a frenzy before he finally pulled her down to the rug and slid off her dress. At last she lay before him wearing nothing but a thin chemise.

He toyed with its ties, but he didn't free her breasts. Instead, he dipped his head and drew one nipple deep into his mouth, suckling her through the fabric, his mouth hot and wet.

Her knees went weak and her stomach hollowed out as she arched against him. Wanting more. Wanting everything.

If only . . .

She ignored the thought. Tonight she was pretending, she was having everything. She would face the truth tomorrow. The leaving. She had to leave.

Tomorrow.

She closed her eyes and reveled in the mind-shattering tingles that mapped their way across her body. He pulled away, but only for a few moments as he shed his clothing. Then he was next to her again, gathering her close with his powerful arms. He pulled off her chemise and drawers. Soon, not a stitch of clothing separated their bodies.

Kissing his way down her abdomen, he seared a path toward the patch of red curls at the juncture of her thighs. Breathlessly, she waited.

And waited.

Her eyes popped open. "What are you doing?"

"Looking at you."

"That's nice and all, but I'd really rather you *do* something." Her gaze locked with his and he must have read her desperate desire, for he smiled.

The expression was slow and steady and sure, and then he dipped his head. When the heat of his mouth touched her, she felt it like a jolt of lightning. Clutching at his well-muscled shoulders, she bucked wildly, opening herself to him, extending a silent invitation she knew he wouldn't resist.

Colt drank in the sweet taste of her, as if he'd never had her before. As if he would never have her again.

I love you.

Her words echoed through his head, sending pleasure through him even more intense than the pleasure he was giving her. He cupped her bottom and pushed his tongue deeper, tasting, feasting on the woman in his arms.

Elizabeth Joanna Carlton. Prim and proper and from the *future?*

As outlandish as it had sounded, Colt knew she had to be telling the truth. He'd noticed too many things about her that didn't add up. The way she'd fallen off the stage straight into his lap that first night. The way she talked and walked and behaved. Horseshoe had attributed her strangeness to the fact that she was a city gal, but Colt had known too many citified women to believe that. He'd known experienced citified women—and it had always seemed Elizabeth wasn't one of them.

Of course, he'd never considered that she'd come from the future.

Not that it mattered. She loved him, and he loved her—and not because of some crazy garter. Although she still hadn't gotten that through her thick head.

Not yet.

Maybe this would help. His hands slid up her leg and he grasped the piece of satin.

She went totally rigid in his embrace, her hands going to his.

"*No.*"

"It's just a garter."

"Leave it on."

"Darlin,' it might make you feel sexier, but it doesn't make you kind or generous or intelligent. It doesn't make your eyes light up when you look at my kid brothers. It doesn't make you the woman I love."

Fear flashed in her eyes, a sight that tightened his chest and made him ache to chase it away.

"I love you," he said again, looking up at her from between her thighs. "*You.* Not the damned garter." Before she had time to respond, he dipped his head again and savored her with his tongue.

He tugged once more at the garter, but despite his declaration, she seemed hell-bent on keeping it on. Fine, he was going to let her.

For now.

He didn't want her hesitant. He wanted her wild and unchecked in his arms, and he wanted her to trust him. Even more, he wanted to chase the fear from her expression, and so he set about doing just that.

He touched her, caressed her, and showed her how much he loved her, using his mouth in a much more persuasive manner than simply forming words. Her frantic cries fueled his own desire and when he knew he'd pushed her to the limit, he withdrew. She was hot, moist, ready for him, and he knew he could hold back no longer. Rising, he pushed her long legs apart and braced himself over her.

"Open your eyes, Peaches." His words were soft, commanding. "Open them." He touched a finger to her long lashes.

Her eyelids fluttered open and their gazes met.

"I want to see you," he whispered, losing himself in the dark depths of her eyes, so clear, so alive, mirroring his own need. "I want to see everything you're feeling."

The passion. The desire. The *love*.

She loved him. He could see it.

In one swift motion, he thrust fully into her.

Colt stilled himself, relishing the hot tightness for a long moment. Only when Elizabeth cupped his face did he open his eyes. He found her staring up at him, frantic with want.

He dipped his head and caught her mouth. She glided her tongue across his parted lips, dipped inside the soft interior of his mouth, bold in her possession. She wanted him, all of him. Body, heart and soul.

Outside, the thunder raged and the rain pounded, but it didn't touch them inside. A low moan rumbled from deep in his throat as she tightened around him, her body a glorious fire that enveloped him, suffused him, until he thought surely he would be consumed. With anxious hands, he eased her thighs up on either side of him and began to move.

He drove into her, his movements swift, powerful, until she begged for release. Every muscle in his body was wound as tight as possible, waiting for the white-hot explosion as he buried himself deep inside of her one last and final time.

Elizabeth cried out as she burst into a thousand pieces. Weightless, she floated in a sky of brilliant, incredible color, so vivid and alive. She drifted like a feather past the vibrant hues and marveled at their beauty, their intensity. Seconds, minutes passed and slowly the colors faded, leaving a deep sense of peace in their wake.

It was unlike anything she'd ever experienced before. Even reading *The Naughty Nine* hadn't prepared her for what she felt now.

True love.

Colt rolled onto his back and pulled her on top of him. He was still inside her as he held and stroked her damp flesh. Closing her eyes, Elizabeth concentrated on his warmth. She'd been so lonely for so long, but the heart that beat against her ear told a story filled with promise. A happily ever after. She listened, letting herself believe in the power of what they had just shared, daring to consider a future with Colt Durango. She had to, for she didn't know if she could face tomorrow without him.

Lizzie Jo. That was what he'd called her. The name echoed through her head, wild and wicked in its own right, reminding her that while he now knew she wasn't Sinful, he still hadn't accepted who she was—not Lizzie Jo, but Elizabeth Joanna Carlton. Much too prim and proper and boring to keep a wild man like Colt Durango interested for long.

He'd wanted her to take off the garter, but he didn't know what he asked. Maybe it *was* the garter stirring his feelings. If she took it off, maybe he wouldn't want her anymore.

Worse than that, if she took it off, she knew she would lose him forever because the garter was her one link to the past. Her link to him.

She couldn't take it off without returning to the present—which meant she would never really know Colt's true feelings.

Ugh. Life truly sucked.

Elizabeth woke to a loud crackle as a half-burned log slipped in the fireplace. She had a fierce ache in her bladder. The punch from the party was finally getting to her.

She reveled in the warmth of Colt's arms for

a few long moments before she finally untangled herself and scooted toward the edge of the bed. The last thing she felt up for was a trip to the outhouse, but nature called.

What's more, she needed a few moments away from Colt. To think and sort through her feelings.

Namely, she loved him and she had no idea what she was going to do about it. She could keep the garter on and stay here, but she would never know if his feelings for her were real, and she wanted them to be. More than she wanted her next breath.

On the other hand, if she took the garter off and went back, she would still never know if his feelings for her were real.

Her options didn't look good.

She reached for her crumpled dress and slipped it over her head. Seconds later, she was creeping through the darkened house. The boys had obviously returned from the house. There was a large cake that she recognized from the cake-auction table sitting, half-eaten, on a small crate. Horseshoe snored soundly in a large, overstuffed chair in the corner of the living room, a cookbook open on his lap.

Elizabeth crept by and slipped out the front door. She drew in a lungful of fresh air laden with rain and her nostrils flared. Still, it wasn't enough to get Colt's scent out of her system. Or the man, himself, out from under her skin.

He was inside her now, and she didn't know what she was going to do—

"Hold it right there." The deep voice came from behind her a split second before a hand clamped around her mouth. It was Burly, and this time he was wearing a thick riding glove.

Oh, no. *Here we go again.*

It was barely sunup when Colt leaned through the dining room doorway and swept a gaze around the room.

"Looking for someone?" Horseshoe sat at the head of the table, his mouth half-full of pancakes.

Colt swept another gaze around before settling his attention on the older man. "What?"

"I asked if you was lookin' for somebody." Horseshoe scowled. "You must be lookin' for someone, and in a damn hurry about it. You didn't even bother to put some decent clothes on, and there's a lady just out there in the kitchen."

"Is it—"

"Lucy Mae." He shoveled in another bite of pancakes and smiled. "Damn, but that little filly can cook."

"Are you saying she makes better pancakes than you?"

"I ain't sayin' no such thing—"

"Eustice? How are they?" The female voice carried from the kitchen.

"The best I ever tasted," he called back. At

Colt's raised eyebrow, he shrugged. "So she can make a damn sight better pancake. Big deal. I still make a better stew. Why, I could definitely show her a thing or two . . ." His words faded as he eyed Colt. "So who you lookin' for?"

"I'm not looking for anyone." Colt leaned against the doorframe and ran a hand through his tangled hair. He wasn't looking, not anymore, because it was pretty obvious she was gone.

"You all right, boy?" Horseshoe cocked one bushy gray eyebrow at him.

"Fine."

Liar. He wasn't fine. He was mad and disappointed and worried . . . Hell's bells, what if she was really gone? Back to her home? Back to the future?

Even as the thought echoed through his head, he marveled at it. The future? Did he really believe she was actually from the future?

He did. While he'd wanted to balk like any normal man at hearing such nonsense, the explanation had made too much sense. She was too different for there to be any other.

But now she was *gone*.

"You need a dose of my all-cure? 'Cause you look this close to passing out."

"I'm fine." He *was* fine. Maybe she was gone. If so, he'd do what he always did. He'd keep going. Working.

Good riddance to her, in fact. Why, she hadn't

even had the decency to wake him up. To say good-bye.

Had he really thought he loved her?

Hell, no. He'd *known* he loved her. He knew he still loved her. And he'd thought she'd loved him.

And he'd obviously been wrong.

Colt walked over and plopped down into a chair directly across from Horseshoe. Leaning forward, he folded his hands and rested his forehead against them.

"So why did you decide to sleep in this morning? Tired from all that dancin' last night?"

"You could say that." They'd danced all right. The oldest dance alive. And then she'd left him. The notion sent a jolt of annoyance through him, followed by anger.

"So what's eatin' you this morning? You seem put out." Horseshoe lifted a huge checkered napkin to wipe the corners of his mouth. Tucking the linen back under his chin, he picked up his fork again and poured a healthy amount of syrup over the last few bites of his pancakes.

"I'm just tired." *Tired of thinking about her.*

"Good, then I guess you ain't too woried 'about losin' your horse."

"My horse?" Colt's full attention riveted on his friend.

"Yeah, your horse. Not your favorite, mind you. Just that one one you rode back from the dance last night. And speaking of the dance, you sure missed all the excitement."

"I was right there for all the excitement." And speaking of excitement, he still hadn't found out what had happened. What had he been thinking? She'd been abducted and he hadn't even asked what had been going on. He'd been too busy touching and kissing and loving her . . .

The thought faded into a sense of deep-seated dread.

"Not your city gal screaming up a storm in the barn. I'm talking the *real* excitement. This other woman showed up—a dancing girl from the looks of her—and nearly broke up the entire place looking for some man. Said she was a witch and nobody was getting out without getting zapped unless they came clean as to where the cowboy was.

"A right pretty little thing she was, too. Had a couple of men volunteer to step in for her cowboy, but she wouldn't have none of it. She was mad. Even poured punch over a few people who tried to calm her down. Including Sheriff McGraw." The old man paused. "Did you know he's allergic to strawberries? Bad, too. One drop of this stuff and his face swelled up like a giant Bing cherry.

"It was a damn pleasant sight, seeing as the bastard cheats at cards and every man for miles around knows it. Why, me and old Slim Canterwall were hootin' and hollerin' so loud that McGraw whips out his gun and threatens to arrest us. Then Sherman steps in and—"

"What about the horse?" Colt cut in. If he

didn't, the old man would ramble on forever.

"Guess you don't want to hear the rest of the story?"

"The horse, Horseshoe. Just tell me about the horse."

"Let's see." The foreman took his time, eating another bite and thinking back, as if he were enjoying making Colt squirm. "He was in the stable when me and the boys came in last night, but he ain't there no more." Horseshoe gave a grin, then. "But you don't really need to worry. I thinks your lady friend took it."

"What?" Colt asked.

"You musta scared Miss City Britches off awful bad," the old man said. "She rode outta here before daybreak, like this ranch was Hell and you was the devil hisself."

Colt's mind was racing. If Elizabeth had taken his horse, it meant that she'd gone someplace in *this* time. Which meant he could still find her and talk some sense into her stubborn head.

"You saw her leave?"

"Yep. From a distance, mind you. Nearly shot her, too."

"You *what*?" A vision of Elizabeth lying dead on the ground flashed in Colt's mind and turned his heart inside out.

"You deaf, Colt? I said I nearly shot her. But you know how bad my sight is and she was a good ways away by the time I spotted her. I thought she was someone else. I mean, I couldn't figure out who it could be. Then I realized. Besides I had a full stomach after Lucy made me a midnight snack. Lucky for you, otherwise, I would have been wide awake and ready for action."

Colt glared at Horseshoe, who howled.

"Damn, boy, if looks could kill, I'd be slumped over this plate of pancakes instead of enjoyin' it." He smacked his lips. "That Lucy rustles up some of the best grub I ever ate. You want some? I can holler out to the kitchen and I'm sure she'll fix you up some. Why, she's so good I might just have to marry her myself. For the food, mind you. Ain't a man in his right mind would pass up daily pancakes like these."

"You've got twisted priorities, Horseshoe, you know that?"

The old man grinned. "And damned proud of it, too. So are you going after her?" Horseshoe asked when Colt pushed away from the table.

"I've got to find my horse."

And his woman. Most of all his woman, because Colt Durango wasn't letting go. He'd let go too many times in the past, cut his losses and moved on. No more.

He was fighting back and holding on this time.

And he would find Elizabeth and make her see that.

Chapter Seventeen

Sadie considered herself many things, but a horse thief wasn't one of them. She'd never stolen anything in her life. She'd conned and bluffed and begged for whatever she wanted, but never had she simply taken without asking.

But a woman had to do what a woman had to do.

She held the reins tighter and urged the animal faster, eager to catch up with the group of men and the woman ahead.

The woman.

She'd had no clue when she'd followed Billy and his brothers from the Cotillion out to the large ranch on the outskirts of town that all this time they had been hot on the trail of her sister's impersonator. She'd followed them with an old horse she'd conned a scared farmer out of who'd feared her finger so badly he'd nearly wet his pants.

A pang of guilt shot through her, but she forced it aside. She'd already paid for it. The animal had been old and slow and she'd lagged behind so far she'd been convinced she was going to lose them.

It had been so loathsomely slow, she hadn't thought twice about ground-tying the animal. Not after all the *giddyup* and *yeehaahh*ing she'd had to do to get it to move in the first place. But the moment she'd slid off the horse's back and turned her attention to Billy and the boys, the animal had perked up and taken off. Probably back to its master.

There'd been no sense crying over a flighty horse, however. She'd been too caught up in watching Billy and his brothers case the ranch house and argue over who was going to stand where—that and who had the biggest pistol.

Men. Always so wrapped up in size. Sadie would have thought that by now that they would have figured out that it wasn't the size of things that mattered, but the effort they put behind them.

Then again, if they'd realized that, there would be a mess of happy women from here to the Rio Grande. And there weren't.

Sadie hadn't a clue at that point who they'd been looking to abduct. Not until she'd peeked past the outhouse and seen the woman from The Red Parlour Room.

The brothers had pounced and taken the woman hostage while Sadie had made a mad scramble to find a horse.

She hadn't had to look past the barn. Standing inside had been many horses, one of them ready to go. Climbing on, she'd headed off after them.

The truth was in sight. This was better than she could have expected. All Sadie had to do was catch up to the woman and find out what she'd done with Sinful, plus she'd be able to avenge herself on Billy for running off.

That had been the only thought on her mind until she'd seen Billy help the tramp up onto his horse. Now they were riding double and Sadie could barely contain the jealousy boiling inside her.

Jealousy?

She forced the thought away and gripped the reins tighter. For crying out loud, she was *not* jealous. She was mad at being duped and lied to and ditched. Jealousy didn't figure in. She hardly knew Billy enough to be jealous. Sure, he was a nice guy on occasion and he treated her like a lady instead of a leper—the way everyone had always treated her when they discovered her powers. Heck, that's why it had been so easy to be a dance-hall girl; she was already on the fringe. But Billy had seemed different. He wasn't afraid of her or judgmental. He was nice.

Her gaze riveted on the two heads up ahead

and she frowned. He was too nice from the looks of things.

She ignored the strange ache in her gut and concentrated on her worry over her twin. While she did have the feeling something was wrong with Sinful—namely that she had disappeared from the face of the earth, Sadie didn't have a terrible feeling about it. Something was happening to her sister. She was obviously caught up in circumstances she didn't understand, but she was alive and unharmed—Sadie felt sure she would have known otherwise—and that meant that there was hope.

Hope for Sinful, and hope for Sadie. She was going to find her twin and get her powers back. She needed Sinful, needed the reassurance and confidence of her twin.

No more settling for throwing punch on stuffy old sheriffs and their deputies. She wanted to chase something.

At the moment, she wanted to zap one nice-as-pie cowboy and the redhead practically sitting on his lap.

In time, she told herself. They couldn't keep riding forever. They were undoubtedly heading back to the abandoned cabin where they'd been holed up the past week while they scoured the countryside to find that Mr. Ripley's precious ring. Surely that was where they would question their captive.

And Sadie was heading back there herself. But she was after something much more important. She wanted her sister back, and at the same time she wanted a little revenge.

After all, Billy was riding *double*, of all the two-timing things. And worse, from the smile on his face whenever he glanced at his brothers, he was obviously enjoying it.

"Would you stop grinning like a cow in a pasture full of daisies?"

"It's been over a day, aren't you over her yet?" Burly asked.

"I told you he was caught up on that woman," Medium muttered. "I told you."

"I ain't exactly caught up." Skinny said. "But I'll be glad to see her again. She's been out here all by herself. I'm concerned."

"And whipped," Medium added. "Ain't you figured out yet that woman ain't worth the trouble?"

"Just cause Edna Louise Meyers dumped you for that cattle rustler doesn't mean all women are bad. You and Edna just wasn't meant for each other. You should look for someone else."

"I got my hands full right here helping out my brothers. I don't put no stinking women ahead of my kin, not like some I know."

"I ain't puttin' her ahead. I'm just worried. We should have left a note or something."

"Whipped," Medium muttered, urging his horse faster.

Faster? Elizabeth thought. Did that mean they were almost there?

The realization sent a spurt of panic through Elizabeth. She had to stall—to buy herself some time to figure out a way out of the danger that lay in wait for her the moment they got her wherever they were headed.

For she knew it would be bad when they did.

The first two times they'd caught up to her, there had been people nearby. But they were taking her someplace isolated now, where they could conduct their business in private. While she knew they weren't going to whack her before they found their ring, she wasn't so sure what would happen when they discovered she didn't have it. Or know where it was.

She began to shiver.

While she wasn't placing bets that Skinny was ruthless—after all, he'd helped her onto the horse and even loosened her bindings just a tad when Burly had nearly cut off the circulation to her hands—she wasn't so sure about the other two. Medium was obviously a woman-hater and Burly. . . . He was a money-lover. He wanted the ring, and he was going to be mighty pissed if he didn't get it.

She had to stall, all right.

"I've got to go to the bathroom."

"We're almost there."

"I've really got to go now."

"She's gotta go," Skinny called to his brother.

"You jes' hold it," Burly snapped. " 'Cause we ain't stoppin'."

"But I can't."

358

"You'll have to."

"No, I don't. I'm warning you. I've gotta go. *Now*."

"Don't go threatening us, missy," Medium said. "We don't take kindly to no women threatening us. You got that?"

"It's not a threat. It's a fact. I either go, or I *go*. Right here, right now."

"Like hell," Skinny muttered as her meaning sank in. He scooted backward as much as possible, putting a few inches of distance between them. "She can't go here. Not with me sittin' behind her!"

"She's bluffing."

"What if she ain't?"

"She is."

"But what if she *ain't*?" He pulled on the reins and slowed the horse. "I ain't findin' out."

"Dammit, Billy," Burly snapped. "We need to move."

"I don't give a flying fig leaf. She ain't goin' on me."

A few seconds later, she found herself hauled off the horse and steered toward a large bush. "Go on and relieve yourself," Skinny told her. *So, Skinny's name was Billy.*

"Go with her," Burly ordered.

A horrified look crossed Skinny's face. "I ain't goin' with her."

"You don't have to watch. Keep your back to her, but stay close."

Skinny shook his head.

"She cain't very well go by herself," Burly said. "She'll run for damn sure."

"Run to where? There ain't nothin' for miles." Where Skinny's remarks usually stirred an argument, he had his brothers on that one.

"Even so, tie your wrist to hers."

"I ain't—"

"We can't screw this up, Billy. We *ain't gonna* screw this up." Burly tossed him a small rope. "Now do it."

"Sorry about this," Skinny said as he slipped the small nooselike knot around her already-bound wrist. He tightened it and slid a matching knot around his own wrist.

But Elizabeth wasn't sorry. The rope worked as a perfect excuse when she took longer than expected. A lot longer.

"What the hell are you doin' over there?" Burly called out.

"You try pulling up your bloomers with one hand! And then I've got all these skirts." Thank God nineteenth-century women hadn't yet discovered spandex or she'd have been in deep, deep trouble.

Even so, she could only postpone for so long, and eventually she found herself back on the horse, gagged this time, riding double with Medium and heading toward a tragic fate.

A full-body search? Or what?

Her gaze flitted around to the open pasture without a soul in sight. No one to hear her cry or scream or beg.

The thought sent panic through her and her mind scrambled for anything else that would buy her some time. Maybe Colt would come. She prayed he would.

But she couldn't wait for a maybe. She had to do something now. To save herself. Just as she'd done last night.

There would be no screaming, thanks to the gag that was now back in place. No kicking, thanks to the ropes tied around her feet. She sat on the side of the saddle, Medium's arms around her waist, the landscape passing before her eyes. Her hope of rescue passing with it.

Her gaze lit on the ground and an idea took root. It was a dangerous idea, but she was fast running out of choices. Besides, stuntwomen did stuff like this all the time. Stop, drop and roll, she told herself.

Okay, so that wasn't a stuntwoman thing. It was a fire thing, but it sounded like good advice for anyone hitting the ground at a frightening pace.

Before she could rethink her decision, she pitched forward, throwing all her weight toward the ground.

Medium's arm anchored her, but she knew by the horse's sudden shift in direction that she was too heavy for him to hold for long.

She'd never thought in her wildest dreams that she'd be so thankful that she'd eaten all those double-orders of chili-cheese fries. But gratitude filled her now, along with desperation as she sent up a silent prayer.

She hung to the side of the saddle as the men cursed and Medium held on to her for dear life. His own life, from the sound of Burly, who threatened and hollered and told him to keep a hold no matter what.

"Dammit!"

"Get her back on the horse."

"She's gonna fall."

The ground loomed closer to her face, passing at a frightening pace, and she instantly regretted her decision. But it wasn't as if she'd had options. And she didn't have any now. She had to get off the horse. She had to get away. However she could.

She squirmed and fought to break Medium's hold, but he was strong, his arm cutting into her waist. The air lodged in her chest and she felt as if she were breaking in two.

She would have never made it as a stunt-woman. She'd never make it now, period. Not when the Three Stooges found out the truth. They would have no reason to keep her alive.

Not to mention, there would likely be a body search beforehand.

No.

But all the protests in the world couldn't help break Medium's hold, and when the horse started to slow and she caught sight of a broken-down shack in her peripheral vision, her hopes plummeted. They were out in the middle of nowhere. There was no one to hear her scream. No one who knew she was even there.

She was completely on her own, and there wasn't a thing she could do. No talking or yelling or begging.

Tears burned her eyes and she did the only thing she could, she cried.

"Now, now, look what you did." Medium's voice grew surprisingly gentle. He'd finally gotten control and as he set her on her feet, he caught sight of her tears. His face went from surprised to apprehensive in the blink of an eye and she got the distinct impression that Edna Louise had likely turned on the waterworks a time or two—and gotten her way. "Now, now, don't go and do that. There ain't no reason for it. Just hand over the ring."

"She cain't hand over anything all trussed up like a pig at a barbecue," Skinny said.

"Just stop that, you hear?" Medium glared at her. "Stop that and I'll loosen the ropes just a little once we get inside, but you have to promise not to—"

"Are you plum crazy?" Burly boomed. "Why, she already bit two hunks out of my hand last night, and my ears ain't stopped ringing from all that yelling. I swear I ain't screwing this up on account of you two! I ain't, I tell ya. I ain't lettin' the Bartlett brothers get what's rightfully mine. We been after her too long to lose out on Ripley's reward." He hefted his rifle and aimed it at his middle-sized brother. "Touch those ropes again and you won't need that crazy old witch zapping you with her finger. I'll take you from a buck to a doe with one shot."

"You wouldn't do no such thing," Medium insisted. Despite his words, he moved his hands away. "We're kin."

"For the time being. But you go defying me and we ain't kin no more. You got that?"

"Tell it to Billy. He's the one who took up with that witch."

The three entered the shack, Elizabeth in tow.

"I ain't takin' up with anyone. 'Sides, she ain't here." Billy glanced around the empty cabin. "Why, she ain't here!" he said, shocked and a little crestfallen.

"Thank the ever-lovin' Lord."

"I wonder where she went. She didn't say anything about takin' off."

"Who cares?"

"What if she figured out what we was up to and left?"

"All the better."

"What if she's gone for good?"

"I should be so lucky."

"What if—"

"What if you stop with all the questions, and get this rope tied nice and tight to the bedframe?" Before his younger brother could reply, Burly tossed a coil of rope at him.

"I cain't believe she took off," Skinny muttered as he went to work.

"What do I do?" Medium asked.

"Put her over in that chair until Billy gets the bed ready," Burly said. "Then we'll take care of business."

"Please don't cry," Medium said as he steered her into a chair. "Please, lady. You shouldn't-a taken the ring."

She shook her head frantically and cried harder.

"Aw, hell," Medium said, "I cain't do this."

"Get out of the way." Burley pushed in front of his brother and gripped Elizabeth's shoulders. The next thing she knew, she was flat on her back on the bed, the three men looming over her.

"One last chance," Burly said as he leaned closer. "You gonna give us the ring?" When she didn't respond, he cursed and then pulled her kerchief gag down enough for her to lick her lips. "You gonna come clean?"

"I don't have the ring," she said, gasping. When he moved to put the gag back on her, she twisted her head to the side. "But I know where it's at."

"And so do we. At least we know what Ripley told us he lost it—and that's where we aim to start."

Rough hands jerked her legs apart and Elizabeth had the sudden urge to laugh. This couldn't be happening to her. First, she'd traveled back in time, met the man of her fantasies, fallen in love, and now she was about to be searched for a ring she'd never seen before, stolen by a woman she'd never even met. It was ludicrous. It was impossible.

It was real and there wasn't a thing she could do about it.

No. The denial rushed through her head and she launched one last struggle. She kicked and squirmed and landed her heel in Burly's mid-section.

He was ready for her, though. He caught her ankle just as she made contact, twisted and flipped her onto her back and then he leaned down.

"Now, let's see about recovering our property."

"Mr. Ripley," Billy said, in a strangled voice.

"I know it's Ripley's. That was just a figure of speech."

"No," Medium said. "It's Mr. Ripley."

"I *know* it's Ripley's. Are you boys deaf? I said it was just a figure of—Mr. Ripley?" Burly blurted out. Elizabeth watched as a man stepped from the doorway into the dim interior of the cabin.

She wasn't sure what she'd expected, but after hearing Burly talk about the "Big Boss," she'd expected someone . . . *big*.

Ripley was barely five feet tall, with a balding head and a thick middle and chubby cheeks. He reminded her of a western version of a Tele-tubby. Three large men followed him in, looking imposing in long black dusters and enough attitude to give any bad guy from *Bonanza* a run for his money.

"What in the hell's going on here?" the man demanded.

"We got her, sir."

"Got who?"

"Sinful Sinclair." Burly motioned to Elizabeth. "Ain't no reason for these boys to be here. Ya hear that, Jack Bartlett?" he asked the tallest of the men in black.

"We'll let Mr. Ripley decide that."

"Ain't nothin' to decide. We finished the job. This here's Sinful and we're about to get his ring back."

Ripley walked over to the bed and peered at Elizabeth over his spectacles. "This is not Sinful." He glared at Burly. "You boys are fired."

"But it *is* her. We picked her up where you said. The Red Parlour Room. She was prancing around on stage. They even introduced her."

"It's *not* her."

"It has to be her."

"It isn't. Come on, boys," he motioned to the Bartlett goons. "It's your turn."

"Looks like you've been replaced," Jack Bartlett told a red-faced Burly.

"Like hell. Mr. Ripley," Burly pleaded, following the man to the door. "Wait up. You gotta give us another chance. We need that money you promised us. I'm buying myself a nice little spread up near Fort Worth. Already put the deposit . . ." The men disappeared outside, leaving

Elizabeth sitting on the bed, relief rushing through her.

"I told you she was telling the truth," Billy said to Medium after they exchanged several bewildered looks.

"Maybe."

"I did."

"Maybe."

"Admit it. Say, 'you said it, Billy. You were right.' "

"Like hell."

"Why can't you just admit it?"

" 'Cause there ain't nothin' to admit."

"Is too."

"Is not."

"Is too."

"Excuse me," Elizabeth choked. "But could you boys please untie me, otherwise I'm liable to hire the Bartlett boys to kick your behinds from here to New Orleans. That or do it myself." They obviously had no fond memories of the "nutcracker" because both men winced at the last statement. A heartbeat later, they rushed forward to work at her ropes.

"Sorry about that," Billy mumbled as he untied her hands and rubbed her chafed wrists. "We didn't mean to hurt you. We just had a job to do."

"Yeah, yeah." With Burly outside and Skinny and Medium acting like typical adolescent siblings, she was beginning to feel a lot less afraid and lot more angry. "Tell it to the judge. I'm pressing charges. You boys are going to be sitting behind bars!"

"Billy Ulysses Redd!" A loud female voice cut off Elizabeth's threat and drew every gaze toward the doorway where a blonde, her hair mussed and face wild, stood with her hands on her hips and a glare in her black eyes. "Get your hands off that woman!"

It was the woman from the Red Parlour Room. The crazy woman with the zapping finger and the knife and . . .

Elizabeth's gaze riveted to the woman's hands. No knife. Relief rushed through her, especially when she saw the woman's gaze fixed on poor Billy.

"Now, honey, it ain't what you think," Skinny started.

"Honey? She ain't your honey," Medium exploded. "She's a crazywoman. What the hell is wrong with you?"

"*You*," the woman hissed, turning her gaze on Medium and pointing her finger. "You hush up right now."

"I cain't believe you're sidin' with her over your kin. We're blood. One for all and all for one. Ain't that what we always promised each other when ma and pa passed away?"

"We promised to stick together. That don't mean never settling down and being happy. You nearly tied the knot with Edna Louise."

"Biggest mistake I ever made. I let her come between me and my brothers."

"Did not. You *wanted* her to come between us. You wanted her, but she didn't want you and now you don't want me to want anyone because nobody wants you and—"

"Plenty of people want me. I just ain't got time for no crazywoman with a crazy finger and a—"

"I'm warning you," the witch woman hissed at Medium. "I've had enough of you."

"Too bad, sister, because I've had enough of you."

"That's it." The woman shoved up her sleeves and pointed her finger. "Rattlesnakes eyes and tail of dog, turn this cowboy from ornery man to fat bullfrog!"

"You're plum loco, woman. Keep that crazy finger to yerself or I'll . . . *Ribbit*." The loud, froglike sound erupted from his throat and he turned a startled gaze on Billy.

"If you're going to act like an old, mean bullfrog and grumble, then you might as well sound like one." She turned back to Billy. "And as for you . . ."

"It worked."

"Don't go trying to weasel your way out of this. You were riding double with this woman and—"

"Sadie, it worked. You zapped him!"

"—I bet you even liked it. I know you liked it. I saw you smiling and . . ." Her voice faded as her gaze shifted back to Medium. He gave a burplike *croak* and astonishment lit her eyes. "I *did* do it."

Billy smiled. "You got your touch back."

"I wasn't even thinking about that. I was just thinking about you and this loosey goosey woman."

"Now wait a second," Elizabeth started, but the woman wasn't listening. Her gaze flew back and forth between Billy and his brother the bullfrog.

"I just thought it and it worked." Pleasure lifted her mouth. "I really did it. All by myself."

Sadie Sinclair stared at the proof of her power and marveled at how easily it had come back to her.

Because it had never really left. She'd just been too filled with doubt, too insecure. But Billy had changed all that. She'd been so overwhelmed at the thought that he'd been touching, connecting, liking, another woman, that she'd forgotten her own insecurities in the blink of an eye. She'd been mad and completely uninhibited, and she'd done it.

"I swear there's nothin' between me and that woman," Billy assured her. Staring deep into his eyes, Sadie believed him. She felt it, the same way she felt her own power. It was there, back inside her. It had been there all the time. Plus, now she had trust in Billy. Trust in herself.

"I lied to you, and I'm sorry. The boys wanted to ditch you and I went along with them. I didn't want to ditch you, but I was afraid. They were my brothers."

"They're still your brothers," Sadie pointed out.

"One of 'em's a brother." He grinned. "The other sounds more like one of those bullfrogs our daddy used to catch out back of our cabin."

"I can zap him back. I *will* zap him back. If you want me to."

"Actually, I kind of like it. He likes to argue too much." That earned him a glare and another loud *ribbit* from Medium. Billy laughed. "You can change him back later, maybe. Now we got some serious talking to do."

"Serious?"

"As in you and me and what we're going to do. This job's over and I think it's time I thought of the future. I don't want to be runnin' with these two for the rest of my life. Maybe it's time I settled down."

"With me?" Pleasure rushed through her, along with hope.

"If you'll have me."

"Of course I'll have you." She rushed toward him and threw her arms around his neck, holding on for dear life.

"But you have to make me a promise." He put her away from him and stared into her eyes. "When you get mad, no pointing at me. I ain't so sure I'd do well as a frog."

"I think you'd make a great frog." At his frown, she smiled. "Not that I'll turn you into one. I love you, Billy." At his skeptical glance, she nodded. "Okay. I don't swear I'll never point, but I'll make sure you're out of my line of fire."

"You've got yourself a deal, little lady."

"I really do love you, Billy."

"And I love you."

And then she kissed him the way she'd been wanting to and he kissed her back, making her feel more special than when she'd turned Sinful from a normal woman into a siren with her finger and a magic garter.

Sinful.

"What did you do with my sister?" she asked, turning to the woman sitting on the bed rubbing her wrists and watching the exchange between her and Billy.

"If I knew, I'd tell you. I don't know what happened to her."

"Is she all right?"

"I don't know."

"Did you hurt her?"

"I don't know."

But Sadie didn't need to ask. If Sinful had been truly hurt, she would have known. She would have felt it. The only thing she felt was her own insecurity because she'd lost her twin and her power, or so she'd thought. She'd just been afraid to stand on her own, afraid to make a life for herself that didn't involve her sister.

Wherever Sinful was, she was okay. Sadie felt it, and while she didn't know, she *knew*. And it was enough to ease her mind.

She turned back to Billy. "There's a preacher back in town."

"A preacher?"

"You do want to marry me, don't you?"

"Are you kiddin'? Lead the way."

Sadie took his hand and held tight. She was going to lead the way, all right. Never again was she going to live in anyone's shadow, in fear or self-doubt. Billy had taught her that, and now she was going to teach him a thing or two. About love and commitment and happily ever after.

Because that's what Sadie Sinclair wanted more than her power. She wanted forever, and she was finally going to have it.

Chapter Eighteen

Elizabeth watched Billy help Sadie onto her horse a while later after Ripley and his men had cleared out. Burly had stomped off along with Medium—Sadie had given him his voice back— both brothers snarling that they were leaving the youngest to fend for himself.

Despite what they'd said, Elizabeth saw them just on the horizon, watching to make sure Billy and Sadie got off okay, and while she couldn't see their faces, she had the distinct impression they were a lot more envious than they let on.

She knew she was.

A bizarre sensation filled her as she watched Billy and Sadie exchange glances. They *were* in love. It was obvious to anyone who looked at them, in the way they looked at each other and smiled and spoke, and it made Elizabeth's heart hurt with an odd bittersweet intensity. Why did it hurt so much, she wondered.

Because she loved Colt Durango.

Because she wanted nothing more than to ride off into the sunset with him.

She climbed up onto the horse Sadie had swiped from Colt and gripped the reins, all the while conscious of the garter that still adorned her thigh.

She wanted to believe Colt, to trust his feelings, but she was afraid, just as afraid as Sadie had been to trust her own feelings when it came to her powers.

But this was different. If Elizabeth acted on her trust, she would lose Colt forever. If she slid off the garter, she would find herself back in the future. Alone. Lonely.

And if she didn't?

She would never know how he truly felt and she would always wonder. Was this true love or simply potent magic?

The question haunted her as she rode with Billy and Sadie back to the Triple-C. Elizabeth's sense of direction wasn't too good—she'd yet to learn the territory, especially on horseback—and Sadie wanted to apologize for stealing Colt's horse.

They were halfway there when a posse headed by Colt, Horseshoe, and a red-faced Sheriff McGraw intercepted them.

"That's her," Horseshoe declared, pointing a

finger at the trio as the men reached them. "That's the horse thief right there."

"It was an accident." Sadie held out her hands to the advancing men, who bypassed her and headed straight for Elizabeth.

"I was just borrowing it for a little while, but I . . ." Her voice faded as she noticed the men closing in on Elizabeth. "What are y'all doing?"

"Nabbing ourselves a horse thief," the sheriff declared.

"That's right. Saw her with my own two eyes." Horseshoe took a bite out of the sandwich in his hands.

"Wait a second." Elizabeth started to say as the sheriff reached for her hands. "I didn't—"

"It was me," Sadie said. "I stole the horse, but I didn't mean to. I mean, I did mean to, but it couldn't be avoided. I couldn't let Billy get away."

"That's right. She stole it in the name of love." Elizabeth dodged one of the sheriff's beefy hands. "Look, my wrists have had it from all this bondage crap. I'm not putting up with another—"

"Leave her be." Colt's voice sounded and she stared past the sheriff to where he'd been watching from the sidelines.

"That's right. It was love that drove me to do it." Sadie wagged her finger at the sheriff, who recognized her from the previous night and was now crossing himself in good Catholic fashion. "And you boys had better understand that, or

377

there just might be trouble." She gave them the eye. "I've got powers, you know."

"We arrest horse thieves around these parts," the sheriff started to say, but Elizabeth noticed that he didn't try to slip the handcuffs on her. Instead, he looked to Colt, who eyed Sadie as if he were sizing up a new horse.

"She didn't mean any harm," Elizabeth blurted. She couldn't believe she was speaking up for the woman who'd threatened her with both curses and knives. But then, she knew what Sadie had been feeling. She'd felt the same when Lucy Mae had shown up and declared herself Colt's fiancée.

Of course, it was obvious, from the expansion of Horseshoe's gut and the look in his eye when he looked at the woman, that he wanted her for himself. He just hadn't realized it yet.

Ugh. Love was everywhere, and she was out in the cold.

She stared up at Colt, wanting to see the warmth in his eyes, the concern for her. Instead, she saw a cold anger that made her blood run cold. Then she realized why he was angry; Sadie had put her in danger, and Colt would have hard time forgiving that. Well, she could make him understand.

"It's your call, Durango," the sheriff said. "You want us to take her in?" He handed the handcuffs to a wide-eyed deputy and motioned the man forward. "I'll have Trevor here seize her."

"I ain't seizing her." He tossed the handcuffs to the guy next to him. "Willard can do it."

"I ain't doin' it." Willard tossed the cuffs to the man next to him. "Let Jackson try."

"I ain't doin' it." Jackson tossed the handcuffs to the next man. "Let Snakebite do it."

"I ain't—"

"Aw, you men hush up," the sheriff grumbled. "Or you're all de-deputized. If Colt here wants her taken in, he can put the cuffs on and I'll take it from there. If not, I got work to do. Heard the Bartlett brothers were in town. They's trouble if I ever saw it."

"Billy here can identify them," Sadie spoke up. "That is, if there's a reward."

"I couldn't," Billy started, but a quick glare and a crook of Sadie's finger and his mouth clamped shut.

"If the reward money's good, Billy just might be able to point them out to you. If you're interested. Of course"—she turned her gaze on Colt—"Billy would be much too distraught to help apprehend dangerous criminals if his sweetie was sitting behind bars because of some misunderstanding."

"I'll let it go," Colt said. "This time."

She smiled and turned back to the sheriff. "Now, back to the reward. How good is it?"

"Good enough."

"Good enough to buy a nice little piece of land just right for a mess of kids and a garden?"

"I s'pose so. For all three Bartlett brothers,

that is. We ain't just interested in one."

"You got yourself a deal." Boots crunched and horses' hooves stomped and the posse turned and headed off after the Bartletts with Billy and Sadie riding along.

Horseshoe took his last bite of sandwich. "Guess I'll be moseying back. It's nearly lunch time."

"You'd better hurry, then. I wouldn't want you to waste away," Colt said.

"Damn straight." The ranch foreman turned his horse around and urged it to a gallop, leaving Colt and Elizabeth in a cloud of dust.

"Come on." He reached down and slapped her horse's rump, starting the animal forward.

"Where are we going?" She gripped the reins and held on.

"Home."

The thought should have sent a thrill through her, but it didn't. Because the Triple-C could never really be her home as long as the garter stood between her and the man she loved.

Take the chance.

The words haunted her all the way back to the ranch, until Colt pulled to a stop outside the ranch house. There, an excited Cain waited to help Colt with the daily chores while Cameron intercepted Elizabeth and gave her the rundown on the previous night. She let herself be led into the kitchen.

". . . And I kissed her," he finished after he'd relayed the entire story of how he'd used her advice until he'd had Caroline melting in his arms. "And what's more, she kissed me back, tongue and all."

"That's a little bit more information than I needed to know, Cameron, but I'm happy for you. So you two are an item now?"

"An item?"

"Courting?"

"Shucks, no."

"What do you mean?"

"I kissed Becky Sue Montgomery."

"What?"

"And then Shirley Fletcher."

"*What*?"

"And then Jada Ann Darlington."

"I thought you wanted to kiss Caroline!"

"I did, but then I figured it was a shame to waste all that tutoring on Caroline when she had the nerve to turn around and talk to Bobby McGregor, so I thought I'd see if it worked on the other girls. And it did." He smiled and stared her squarely in the eye and his ears didn't so much as turn pink, much less red.

It looked as if he'd gotten over his shyness.

"I wanted to kiss Mary Ann Moore, but she was dancing with Frank Jamison the whole night. But tomorrow night . . ."

Oh, no. She'd created a nineteenth-century player.

Elizabeth listened for the rest of the afternoon to Cameron talk about his conquests and soon-to-be conquests, all the while on the lookout for Colt to return from his chores.

It wasn't until much later that night, after everyone had turned in and she was sitting on the front porch staring into the darkness, that Colt finally appeared.

She watched him approach, her heart thundering faster than a stampede of horses. Why had he been avoiding her?

"I've been waiting for you."

He fixed her with an unreadable expression and said flatly. "You left this morning."

"I wasn't going to. I had to go to the bathroom. That's when the Three Stooges jumped me."

"The who?"

"They're a trio of guys from the future. Funny guys. They make television shows."

"These men were dangerous, not funny."

"Not really. One of them even sounded like a frog."

"You could have been killed." He stared down at her for a long moment before hauling her into his arms. "I went crazy when I found you gone. I thought you'd taken my horse and left."

"Do you really think I would have *ridden* back to where I'm from?"

He moved slightly away, and his gaze searched hers. "So you wouldn't have left?"

"Not on your horse." She'd meant the statement to lighten the intensity of the situation, to lessen the feeling coiling around them, but it only made matters worse. He looked at her all the more intently, trying to see inside her.

And as he looked at her, she saw inside him. He was so concerned. So scared.

So much in love.

I wouldn't leave you. The reassurance was there on the tip of her tongue, but she couldn't give it to him. Because she wasn't so sure herself. So she did the only thing she could to ease his mind, or at least distract him.

She kissed him.

"We really need to talk," he said when they finally came up for air.

"I don't want to talk. I need to feel you. Now. Please." The past day had taken its toll and she wanted to be with him again, to be in his arms, to feel him so alive and real inside her. Because he made her feel alive and real, and after being tied up and held at gunpoint, she needed to feel that way again.

She needed him.

And he needed her.

He kissed her this time, sucking every breath from her as he lifted her into his arms and carried her through the house, into his bedroom. *His* bedroom, the way he had the night before.

He pulled her close and moved his hands over her, exploring her skin, leaving no part untouched. Cupping her bottom with his palms, he drew her to him, pressing her firmly against his hardness, leaving no doubt that he did, indeed, need her at that moment.

Want her.

Love her.

This isn't love. It's lust. Fueled by the garter. The voice inside her head seemed to whisper the truth, but there was something different in the way he touched her. There was a sense of desperation she'd never felt before, as if he couldn't pull her close enough, couldn't be enough. As if he wanted to absorb her, to become a part of her, to make her a part of him. To keep her always.

If only.

The thought rolled through her mind, quickly lost in a wave of sensation as he pressed himself against her, grinding himself into the space between her legs. She clutched at his shoulders, holding on as her legs trembled and fire rolled through her.

When he pushed her trousers down past her hips, his bare fingers grazing her flesh, she gasped. He knew just how to touch her, to stroke her, to love her.

He unfastened his own pants and slid them down. His hot shaft sprang up between her thighs and her wanting grew. She locked her hands about his shoulders and pulled him closer as he stroked her back, her buttocks.

"Please," she begged, needing to feel him inside of her.

He grasped her behind and lifted her out of her pants. Easing her legs up on either side of him, he pulled her against him.

The electrifying contact sent shock waves

through Elizabeth. He hadn't entered her, not yet, but she wanted it. More than she'd ever wanted anything before. He rested against her, nestling inside, and she felt the burning of his need flare as hotly as her own.

"Are you ready for me?" He gazed down into her eyes.

When she nodded, he slid her down the length of him, until he'd pressed himself all the way inside. They remained like that, pressed as close as they could be, with him filling her as fully as ever before.

She threw her head back and moaned, he felt so good, so right. Nothing could be so wonderful.

He thrust into her, after a moment, then began a powerful rhythm, his movements urgent and demanding. She writhed with pleasure.

The sensations increased, building within her until she could hold back no longer.

Grasping his shoulders, she dug her nails into the hard muscles there as she cried out. Pure rapture shook her, but she kept moving against him, anxious to draw him with her, to pull him down into the abyss of completion that she had already fallen into.

He plunged into her one final time and she felt him explode, filling her with his hot juices. She clung to his shaking body and buried her head in the curve of his neck. His ragged breathing filled her ears, coupled with her own the only sounds penetrating the sudden quiet that surrounded them.

She clung to him as he carried her toward the bed. He spoke not a word as he eased them down onto the soft mattress. Gathering her closer, he pulled the quilt up over their damp bodies.

She'd meant to distract herself from her thoughts, to distract them both, but as she listened to the furious pounding of his heart and felt her own keeping time, she knew what had just happened only made matters worse.

They'd made love. Fast, furious, sweet love that went beyond the physical and into the emotional.

She knew then as she stared into his eyes that she would rather face a lonely future without Colt Durango than live a lie. She wanted reality, not fantasy.

Just like Sadie, she wanted her own happily ever after.

She couldn't spend the rest of her life with him wondering if the emotion she'd seen so hot and bright in his eyes was meant for her and her alone, or if the garter were feeding it, making him feel things.

"I love you," he murmured.

"Do you?"

"You tell me." He faced her. "Take off the garter."

"What if it takes me back?"

"It won't. I won't let it." He touched one hand,

twined his fingers with hers. "Now take it off."

He hand trembled as she leaned down. She grasped the piece of satin, gave him a last, lingering kiss, then closed her eyes. True love, or nothing. She could accept nothing else.

The tingling started the moment she pushed the satin down. It swept through her body, dropping over her like a veil, but even as the sensation increased, she concentrated on the feel of Colt's hand holding hers, his fingers wrapped tight, anchoring her to him though the future tried to snatch her away.

It didn't.

She discovered that several moments later as she pulled the garter completely free and opened her eyes to find Colt staring down at her. She hadn't gone back. Why not? Was there a magic more powerful than that of the garter?

She looked up into Colt's eyes, their blue depths shining down at her, and she realized he was her anchor now. His love had held her in the past. It had dispelled whatever enchantment had brought her, but left her in the power of something greater.

She knew then as she stared up into his eyes that he loved her as much as she loved him.

"Don't say I told you so."

"I told you so."

"I hate a know-it-all."

"And I hate stubborn, pigheaded women." He glared at her. "You could have done this a damned sight sooner and saved us a lot trouble."

"I was scared."

"You were stubborn."

"Scared and stubborn." He grinned. "But either way, looks like you're marrying me."

"There we go with the know-it-all stuff again."

"You're marrying me and having my babies."

"Maybe." She tried for her best stubborn pout, but it came out a smile. "If you ask me real nice."

"Peaches, I'm not asking. I'm begging. When I hired you for three weeks, I didn't know who you were. Now I know I vastly underpaid and that I want you for longer. Forever. Make my fantasy come true. Marry me and have my babies, and maybe isn't good enough. I want a yes."

"Yes." She touched her lips to his and kissed him, relishing the love that they shared.

A love strong enough to draw her back in time and turn her wildest midnight dreams into a tender, loving reality.

"Yes, yes, *yes!*"

Epilogue

"Are you sure this will work?" Elizabeth stared across the sawbuck table at Sadie, who sat on the opposite side, a saucer of fresh milk in her hands.

"Are you kidding?" The woman gave her a what-kind-of-sloppy-witch-do-you-think-I-am look. "I could do this blindfolded." She stared down at the milk. "Okay, not exactly blindfolded. The whole point of the seeing spell is to *see*."

Which was why Elizabeth had come to Sadie in the first place. She needed to see into the future, to touch base one last and final time and ease the guilt and worry that had plagued her for the past six months since she'd whisked off the garter, declared her love for Colt and walked down the aisle with him in a triple ceremony with Horseshoe and Lucy Mae, and Billy and Sadie.

"I could do it with my hands tied behind my back," Sadie went on, glancing again at the saucer she held. "Okay, make that one hand tied behind my back. The point is, I can do it. I did this to find my sister six months ago, to see if she was all right."

"I don't just want to see into the future. I want to communicate." While Elizabeth was fairly sure her family wasn't losing any sleep over her disappearance, she wasn't so positive about Jenna. The young woman was sure to be wondering and worrying. After all, her boss and friend had up and disappeared.

Elizabeth needed to reassure her that everything was fine, to let her know that she'd found happiness and love and a future.

In the past.

It was crazy, yet if anyone would believe, it was Jenna. That girl had faith in love. She would believe, and understand, and she would explain things to Elizabeth's parents. While they wouldn't be overly concerned and weren't likely to believe, perhaps they deserved an explanation. And a good-bye.

"Trust me," Sadie told her again as she stared into the saucer. "I told you I did this with Sinful. I saw her plain as day." A puzzled look crossed her face. "Thought I couldn't make out what she was up to. But I do know that she's healthy. I'm not sure where she's at, though. I don't think she is, either."

"I know the feeling." If Sadie's description of Sinful's surroundings was any indication, the young woman had landed in the future. From what Elizabeth had discerned, they had somehow, some way, switched places. She'd been sucked back by the garter, while Sinful had gone forward. Since the garter had done well for Elizabeth, she had to assume that it would do the same for Sadie's sister.

"So relax," Sadie went on, "and let me concentrate." She peered closer at the saucer. "I see . . ." She leaned even closer. "I see . . ."

"What? What is it?"

Sadie wrinkled her nose and eyed the saucer. "Dirt."

"You see dirt?"

"Coffee." She shook her head. "Why, I told Billy to make sure he washed these dishes carefully, otherwise I was going to do it myself. 'Course that sent him into a tizzy. No, he says. You take it easy. I'm just pregnant, I told him. It ain't like I'm an invalid."

"He's just concerned." And maybe a little crazed. Elizabeth knew that from her own experience. Since the first moment she'd told Colt they, too, were expecting, he'd been acting like a man possessed. She couldn't even lift a book without him jumping to attention. She'd never been so fussed over in her life.

And she'd never felt more loved.

"Then again," Sadie said, a small smile touching her lips. "He was just trying to be helpful. He really is sweet. And thoughtful. And good looking. More than my wildest fantasies." A dreamy look crept over her expression for several moments before she seemed to shake it away. "Now." She adjusted herself in the seat and held the saucer. "Let's get started."

"Should I chant or hum or something?" Elizabeth asked. "I mean, this is sort of like a séance, right? And they usually make some sort of noise during those things." At least they had in every horror flick she'd ever watched.

"You could hum. 'Old Susannah' would be nice."

"Why 'Old Susannah'? Is there some hidden meaning?"

"I just like it. A good song gets me in the mood."

Elizabeth started to hum as Sadie stared into the saucer. "I see it," she declared after a few choruses. "I mean, I see her. She's wearing . . . good Lord, I don't know what she's wearing, but it's very sparkly and it doesn't cover much."

"That's her," Elizabeth said excitedly. "That's Jenna. Tell her I'm okay."

"Hold your horses. I've got to get her attention first." She closed her eyes. "Jenna, I call you. Hear me. Hear Lizzie Jo—"

"Elizabeth," Elizabeth cut in. "She knows me by Elizabeth." Colt's name for her had caught on over the past few months, particularly with

392

Sadie and Billy, who'd settled down on a neighboring farm to raise babies and tobacco.

"Hear Elizabeth. She needs to talk to you. She needs you to know that she's okay."

"Tell her not to worry about me. That I've met the man of my dreams and she was right. Love does make the world go 'round. And backwards and forwards. And side to side. Love is it. I know that now and I'm okay."

"She knows that."

"She does?"

"Look." Sadie indicated the saucer of milk and Jenna's reflection. The young woman sat behind Elizabeth's desk at It's Only Make Believe, a smile on her face, a book open before her. It was the book on gunslingers that Mr. and Mrs. Laramie had brought her during their first visit when they'd requested the gunslinger–saloon girl fantasy and sent Elizabeth to the decaying Red Parlour Room on her quest for the perfect saloon.

But it wasn't the book that snagged Elizabeth's attention so much as the picture. It was an old black and white of a man and woman and five children.

"That's me and Colt," Elizabeth said as she stared at her own likeness standing next to Colt's. His arm held her tightly to his side, a smile on his face and a look of such love and devotion in his eyes that it took her breath away.

"And your five children," Sadie pointed out,

drawing Elizabeth's attention to the surrounding children. Boys. All five.

"Those are our kids?" She peered closer, eager to make out the caption beneath the picture.

Very few of the Old West's bad boys had a chance to mend their ways before being caught and hanged. Colt Durango was one of the exceptions. He traded in his guns and settled in Texas as a respectable cattle rancher to live out the rest of his days with his wife, Elizabeth, and their five children.

Sadie eyed Elizabeth. "She knows you're okay and she'll tell your folks something to ease their minds."

"Your psychic powers are telling you that?"

"My gut is telling me that. Stop worrying."

"That's easy for you to say. You don't have five children on the way."

"Actually, I hope I have six. I've always wanted a big family."

"Me too." The deep, familiar voice rumbled from the doorway and Elizabeth turned to see Colt. His concerned gaze zeroed in on her. "What's wrong?"

"She's a little shocked."

"Is it the baby?"

"Try babies."

"What are you talking about?"

"It's a long story."

"We've got the time."

They did, Elizabeth realized.

They had the rest of their lives together, filled with love and happiness and five boys that were the spitting image of their father. The future looked very bright, indeed.

And whatever they didn't have, they could fantasize about—and Lord knew it just might come true.

Dear Reader:

I've always wondered what it would be like to actually live out a fantasy. To be bold and daring and fearless, without any thought to the repercussions. For most of us, this in itself is a fantasy. We've got kids and hubbies and mortgage payments and a load of other responsibilities and expectations that keep us from acting on our most secret desires.

But what if we could?

It was this question that sparked the idea for *Midnight Fantasies* and my heroine, Elizabeth Carlton. Elizabeth is like all of us—she works hard, lives up to her responsibilities and fulfills her family's expectations of her. She's everything to everybody, but she longs for more. She yearns for a cowboy to take her away, to bring her deepest, most erotic desires to life, and she finds him in wild and wicked bad boy Colt Durango.

I hope you enjoyed reading *Midnight Fantasies* as much as I enjoyed writing it! I love to hear from readers. You can write to me at P.O. Box 1584, Pasadena, Texas 77501-1584 (please enclose an SASE for a reply and an autographed bookmark), or check me out online at www.kimberlyromance.com.

I wish you many hours of happy reading and lots of sizzling nighttime fantasies!

All my best,
Kimberly Raye

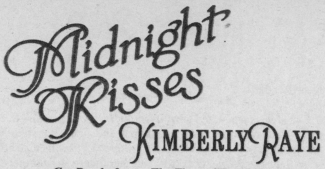

KIMBERLY RAYE
FAITHLESS ANGEL

Faith Jansen has closed the door on life and love. After the death of her young ward, she is determined not to let anyone into her little house again. So when she finds Jesse Savage standing on her stoop, a strange light in his eyes, she turns the lock against him. But Jesse returns to her home each morning, gardening tools in hand. Despite her resolution never to reach out again, she finds herself drawing closer to him. So when she finds herself deep in the desert night with him, the doors of desire are flung open, and the light of something deeper is let loose to flood her heart and lead her to a heaven only two can share.

___52296-9 $5.50 US/$6.50 CAN